SHADOWS
ON SAMHAIN

D1712031

DRUSCILLA FRENCH

ISBN: 1-4196-5446-2
ISBN-13: 9781419654466
Library of Congress Control Number: 2007900171

Visit www.booksurge.com to order additional copies.

PROLOGUE

Maria
October 31

"This kid is old enough to move out." Dr. Whitaker snapped off her white examining gloves and tossed them in the trash. "Your baby's fine, which is more than I can say for his mom. Are you taking vitamins, getting enough sleep, eating?"

Maria Gonzalez-Kincaid was the last patient of the day in the obstetrical clinic. As tired as she was, she wondered if she would be able to care for her little boy once he did make his appearance. For the time being, at least, he was safer in her womb. She sat up and perched at the end of the examining table. Silent tears dripped down her face, splashing on the paper gown. Dr. Whitaker handed her a tissue.

"I'm sorry," said Maria, sniffing and wiping. "Sometimes it's overwhelming." She wrapped her fingers around skinny arms puckered with gooseflesh. "I can't believe

John isn't here. Remember when we came in for the sonogram? He was jumping up and down, pointing and yelling, 'Look!' Like a little kid. The photo's still on the refrigerator where he put it." Her voice dropped to a barely audible whisper. "I don't think I'm going to be able to handle this alone." She mopped her face again and climbed down, using the step stool. "I'm sorry I'm such a basket case. There was an ugly scene in your parking lot before I came in. It has me completely unnerved."

"*My* parking lot! What happened?" The doctor's voice hinted at alarm.

Maria wadded the paper dress and tossed it on the examination table. Naked, she stood caressing her extended abdomen, the skin so taut her navel turned inside out. The basketball belly seemed to be stuck on to emaciated arms and legs like an olive on a toothpick. She reached for her underwear, droopy and gray.

"Have you ever heard of a group called 'The Whites'?" Maria watched the doctor's face warily.

"A bit, maybe. Aren't they Neo-Nazis or something like that?"

"I don't know whether they are Nazis, but they *are* white supremacists. They've been harassing me." She swallowed hard, fighting down another round of tears. "Did you watch the news after John was killed?"

"Yes. I thought the media kind of milked it. 'Heroic firefighter dies fighting forest blaze. Leaves behind a beautiful wife and an unborn child.' Did that bother you?"

"Naw. It was a nice story. They asked me for interview, but I tried to get out of it. I don't want to be on TV, especially not in my condition. It scared me, but they were very persistent. Finally I decided it was a way to honor John, so I agreed." She shivered, partially from cold, but also from fear. "Big mistake." She pulled on navy blue maternity pants and a white knit shirt.

"Why? What happened?" The doctor leaned against the examining table, arms folded across her white lab coat.

Maria's lusterless brown eyes were ringed with dark circles of fatigue. Reluctant to answer and trying to conceal the trembling of her hands, she clipped her black hair into a twist on the back of her head. Her suit jacket hung on a coat hanger on the back of the door. Slowly, she removed it, gave it a shake and struggled into the sleeves. When she finally thought she could speak, she found the words still stuck in her throat. Only the tears would flow freely. Buttoning the smock, her hand once again caressed the belly that cradled her child. She felt him move—in response to her caress, she hoped.

"This White family, as they call themselves, is opposed to relationships between what they call 'whites' and any other kind of people. They've been after me since that interview. They call me, hang around my house, and generally hassle me whenever they can. They leave messages on my home phone. Ugly ones. They pop up beside me in the store and whisper hateful things. I see them parked across the street, leaning up against their cars, watching. At first I didn't pay much attention. I've been so preoccupied with everything—the funeral, the baby, trying to figure out how in the world I'm going to pay for it all. John left twenty-five thousand in life insurance. That isn't a whole lot. Life insurance wasn't really one of our priorities. We never even thought about it. We wouldn't have had any if it hadn't been paid for by the fire department."

"Wait, go back. I don't understand," said Dr. Whitaker. "John is gone and you're a single mother. I would think they'd direct their attention to someone else at this point."

"They're rabid on the subject of race. They think of themselves as pure. Pure what, I don't know."

"That's nuts. There is no such thing as a pure race. Where do you start—fish, reptiles, apes? Besides, *your* marriage is none of their business." Dr. Whitaker slapped her stethoscope down on the counter in an act of dismissal.

"Oh, it's their business, all right. Their primary business. They have a website where they post venomous discussions, some about John and me. They called him a traitor to his race. They even put our pictures up on their site. There's one of me—pregnant with a big red target superimposed around my belly. I don't know how they got the photo. They must have taken it themselves, because I don't recognize it."

Dr. Whitaker's mouth tightened into a thin line. "So, what happened in my parking lot?"

"When I drove in a Silverado pickup pulled up beside me. Three guys got out and leaned against the truck, watching me struggle to get my belly out from behind the wheel. They found it very funny. They made sure that I heard them yukking it up before they started talking about me. Not *to* me, but *about* me." Maria's shoulders began to shake. She turned her face to the wall, leaning into her arms. It embarrassed her to keep losing control of herself and she fought back the tears.

The doctor's eyes glittered with fury. "What did they say?"

"They said..." Maria paused, then whispered, "that I should abort my baby." For several moments the two women stared at each other in silence. Then Maria seemed to find her composure. After she picked up her purse and buttoned her jacket, she was dry-eyed, the sorrow in her eyes replaced with anger. "They called my baby a 'Mud Child.' I lost my temper and let them have it. I told them exactly what kind of low-life, no account, trashy scum buckets I think they are. First in English and then in Spanish." Her voice shifted from defiant to fearful. "That probably wasn't a very smart thing to do."

"I'm calling the police."

"It won't do any good. They're probably gone and I've already talked to the police. Repeatedly. There's not anything I can do about it."

"There must be something."

Maria gave her a little smile, by way of an answer.

It was twilight when she left the medical building. Streetlights cast spindly tree shadows across the white stripes of the parking slots. Dark shrubbery edged either side of the asphalt. The pickup was gone, her car was the only vehicle in sight. Dr. Whitaker must park somewhere else, she thought, perhaps around back.

It surprised her, but she felt better. Telling her story to a sympathetic human being had helped. She felt so alone these days. Well, she was alone. After the baby is born, she thought, we'll move. An accountant can always find a job, particularly a bilingual one. We'll disappear. Those redneck assholes will find some other target for their hatred but we're going back to Mexico City where I have relatives and friends. I can get some help with *Juanito*—from my mother, my aunts, my cousins. My family can provide all the *machismo* he needs. When Juanito is an adolescent, I'll need some help. How can I teach him what he'll need to know about being a boy, becoming a man? I'll ask my brothers, and some of my crazy cousins. Well, maybe not the really wild ones. This boy is going to be *bueno*, like his father. Not *loco*, like some I could name. He'll be happy and funny, like his Daddy. Not serious all the time—like his uptight mother. The more she thought about it, the more she liked the idea. *Maria y pequeño Juanito viven en*

Ciudad de México. Son muy felices. Absently, she dug in her purse for keys. In her mind, she watched a small brown boy run toward her in the bright sunshine, red shirt and blue shorts, brown eyes sparkling, arms held out to her. She could almost hear him laugh, almost feel his weight as he jumped into her arms.

A hand came around her from behind and gripped the wrist holding keys. She felt his calluses on her skin, the bristle of wiry hair. His big gold ring had an unusual symbol on it, a † combined with a 1. The other hand crept around her belly, switchblade open and pointing toward Juanito. The white pickup pulled into the parking lot. Two men in white ski masks were in the front seat.

"I'll be doing the driving," he said. He clicked the unlock button on the key. "Just slide on in, Greasaria," he whispered.

CHAPTER 1

Cate
Samhain, exactly a year later

"Knock his teeth in."

"Grandma, you are vicious!" Chrys said. She wore an apron that was too large for her, the bib coming up to her chin. She straddled a stool at Cate's kitchen island, which was covered with newspaper and stringy pumpkin innards.

"You took an *oath*. Harm to none." Her twin brother, PZ, bounced up and down, testing the latest in basketball footwear. Too hyper to take a seat, he practiced his air dribbling, whirling away from an attempt to steal the make-believe ball. He turned; he shot from the outside. The crowd was hushed in anticipation. Swish. Two points. The buzzer sounded and the game was over. Victory by one point. PZ soared into the air to high five his imaginary teammates, knocking over a stool.

"I think it's okay to turn grandchildren into toads," said Cate. "Now watch. Stick the corn skewer into the little pieces we've cut between the teeth and push toward the *inside* of the pumpkin." She matched her actions to her words. "It's much harder to pull his teeth out than to gently knock the unwanted bits into the cavity."

"I think I better do it. PZ will ruin it for sure. He has absolutely no patience," said Chrys. She took the small knife from her grandmother and carefully inserted it where the face was drawn.

"You cut the holes. I'll punch his lights out," said her brother, PZ. He gave his sister a sock in the arm, which she ignored.

Chrys climbed higher, kneeling on her stool to carve a pumpkin that was easily two feet wide. The room was crammed with autumn produce. Baskets of apples and pears were stacked on the floor, beside cardboard boxes of Indian corn. A variety of funky squash covered the counters—turban, spaghetti, butternut, acorn. The largest pumpkins, gleaming bright orange, were lined up on the kitchen table awaiting transformation into illuminated lanterns. A wicker basket held miniatures, little white and bisque colored pumpkins were jumbled in with twisted, bumpy gourds of yellow, green, tangerine and beige.

"Do not cut into any of my blue pumpkins. Well, actually they are Redlands Trailblazer squash, but they look like pumpkins," said Cate. "Don't touch the white ones either. I'm going to use them on the tables."

"A big blue scowly face at the front door would be awesome," said PZ "We can get a rope and make it look like he strangled to death. Maybe use some marbles for popping out eyeballs and a long licorice tongue." He stuck his tongue out and bugged his eyes.

"I *said* leave them alone. I like your face like that. Makes a nice change." Cate picked up a sponge and began pushing pumpkin guts into the sink. She reached for the disposal switch.

"Noooooo!" yelled PZ. "I'm saving that stuff."

"For what?" said Cate, her hand poised in midair. "You want to roast the seeds?"

PZ rocked from side to side, the only reason being the expenditure of energy. "See, last year Brad had this totally awesome pumpkin with a great big mouth. He took his little brother's training potty and made it look like the Jack-o-lantern was ralphing this stuff into it. It was so cool."

"Gross," said Chrys.

"We could have ours barfing all down the front steps." He leapt in the air, crossed his legs, landed and whirled to one side, executing a hip hop move he had seen on television.

"In this case," said Cate, "I believe I concur with your sister." She switched the disposal and fed debris down the sink. "Pumpkin upchuck is not consistent with the ambiance I am trying to create."

"Bummer," said PZ "Then I'm outta here." He grabbed his jacket from the back of a kitchen chair and pulled a Denver Broncos baseball cap from the pocket, which he put on backwards. In that careless way that ten-year-old males often make their exits, he left. The kitchen door slammed behind him.

His mother Mattie wandered into the room in time to watch the door shudder. She stood motionless for a moment, blinking like an underground animal emerging into daylight. She wore an oversized T-shirt—"March for Women's Lives," and rumpled pajama pants. Auburn hair sprang away from her head, a tangle of serpentine curlicues writhing in all directions. She stumbled to a cabinet, took out a cup, and made a squinting search of the countertops littered with plant material. Propping one foot on her leg and furrowing her brow, she tried to recall what she was searching for.

Cate had her back to her daughter, too engrossed in her task to acknowledge her arrival. She was drawing gnarled trees on a large white pumpkin with a black grease pencil. "You'll have to make it yourself," she said. "I don't drink it anymore."

Mattie stood clutching the cup, frozen in puzzlement, eyes wandering from apples to corn to gourds.

"In the cabinet, under the windows," said Cate, without a glance in Mattie's direction. Cate wore her hair in a single braid down her back. What had been a dark chestnut was now liberally sprinkled with grey. When strands of it escaped and fell in her eyes, she wiped them with the back of her hand and blew a puff of air out the side of her mouth.

Mattie nodded, slowly comprehending. From the cabinet, she extracted the coffee maker, and set about the task of brewing.

"How are you going to do it, Grandma?" asked Chrys. "If you cut out all that, won't it collapse?"

"You're right. But I'm not going to cut through it. I will scrape off the outside layers until the flesh is thin enough to be translucent. I'll work in the spaces between the trees. The trunks and limbs will appear as dark silhouettes," said Cate.

"Fabulous! Like, maybe a sunset or sunrise in the forest," said Chrys.

"Or a bonfire," said Cate.

Chrys pushed aside the unfinished jack-o-lantern and went to get a white pumpkin, matching the one her grandmother was sculpting in size and shape. "Can I use this one? I think I'll do one with leaves all over it, like they're falling from the trees."

"That'll look really good," said Cate. "If you like you can trace them. There are some oak leaves on the back porch that I bought. They're pickled, or something. They feel weird, but are good colors and look nice. Take several so you have a variety of shapes."

"Okay, and I'll go get some aspen leaves to use with them. I'm going to make the light shine through the leaves though, instead of around them like your trees."

"Brilliant," said Cate. She drew in quick, deft strokes, the outline of the spooky limbs emerging.

Chrys got her jacket and followed her brother out the back door. She did not, however, allow it to slam.

Mattie stood mutely watching the liquid gurgle down through coffee grounds. She inhaled deeply, making a sound as the air went through her nose. "Smelling is the best part," she mumbled.

"Coffee never tastes as good as it smells."

"Nothing could." Mattie put her hand on the half-filled pot and said, "No dribbling." She pulled the glass container out, midstream. One rebellious drop hit the warming plate as she poured her cup full. "Hmph," she said. "Impudence." She replaced the pot and moved to the frig for cream.

Cate's old house had been remodeled many times in its long lifetime. "Las Sombras," as it was called, sat on the north side of a mountain covered with pines and a few aspen. It was off the beaten path, but only about forty-five minutes from Denver. Herds of elk and deer visited her meadow at dawn and twilight. Smaller animals such as little brown rabbits, black squirrels with pointy ears, red-tailed hawks, grey coyotes, rainbow trout, and the occasional black bear either visited or made their home in her domain. The only mortal danger to them was from each other. She permitted no human predators.

Cate had been living at Las Sombras most of her life—since her early twenties. Her own addition to the rambling dwelling was a single large room, built about five years ago. At one end, the fireplace dominated, flanked by windows. At the other end, equipment for serious cooks and food consumers took up half the area. A wall of glass provided a spectacular view of the Rockies, suitable for contemplation while stirring and spooning. It was a grand space—casual and comfortable, equally conducive to work or relaxation.

"Build us a fire, Mattie," said Cate.

Mattie grinned at her mother. "You ask a lot of a girl who just got out of bed." She reached for a remote control and pointed it toward the stone fireplace. The ceramic logs burst into flame.

"I knew you could handle it," said Cate, holding up orange palms. "My hands have pumpkin goo all over them."

"Fire. Gift of the gods." Mattie sat at the table with her bare feet wrapped around the chair legs, watching the mountains, drinking coffee. Cate worked on her pumpkin, carving around the tree branches, absorbed in her task. An easy silence hung between them.

Mattie rested her cheek on a fist, closed her eyes and gave a sigh, long and expressive. "I am so tired, Mom. I think I could sleep for a week."

"You would miss the party," said Cate.

"Maybe you should cast some sort of rejuvenation spell, because I really don't want to miss it."

Cate laid down her scalpel, rinsed her hands, and came up behind her daughter. Wrapping her arms around her thin shoulders, she said, "I don't know any rejuvenation spells. Try a big breakfast, an hour soaking in the bath and a day with people who love you. The twins will be glad to get reacquainted with you."

"I've been working 24/7 for almost a year. It's a wonder they survive with such a crummy mother."

"It *is* a wonder. The wonder is called Luna. They not only survive, they thrive. She keeps them on schedule and full of *frijoles*."

"And their wonderful grandmother gives them everything they want and teaches them stuff they'd never learn in school."

"We take good care of them," said Cate. "But we can't replace their mother. We're all glad this ordeal is over."

"No one is as glad as I am."

For the past year Mattie had been waging a legal battle against a supremacist organization calling themselves the "White Family." Mattie had been representing Maria Gonzalez-Kincaid, a young woman whose husband John Kincaid was a firefighter who lost his life in a devastating wildfire. The heart-twisting story of his pregnant widow had appealed to the media. Maria was featured in both the *Denver Post* and the local news broadcast. It was not her suffering that attracted the attention of the Whites, however, but the fact she had been born in Mexico and her husband had an Anglo surname. They spewed vitriolic hatred from their websites, with online tirades. Some of their members made suggestions regarding justifiable punishment for offending Hispanics who dared to marry and have children with Caucasians. Fury fueled frenzy. Members of the organization began to stalk Maria. She bore it with dignity, ignoring the harassment. However, one evening, following a visit to her obstetrician, she was snatched from the parking lot, blindfolded and beaten. She went into labor, but her little boy was already dead.

Maria had been unable to identify the masked assailants. She did, however, provide the information that they each wore a large gold ring with a distinctive symbol, a † combined with a 1. Her identification of the ring provided proof that the assailants were part of the "White Family," whose Cross and One had symbolized the organization for over a century. Along with evidence of their online malevolence, this identification allowed Mattie to institute a civil case against the organization's leaders. Maria was awarded the compound that had served as their headquarters for decades. Whitewater Ranch consisted of more than a hundred acres, along with a house and several outbuildings.

"Is Maria coming tonight?" Cate stood back to admire her handiwork.

"No. She left for Mexico. She's afraid those assholes will come after her again."

"I think you can safely assume they will if given the chance."

"They won't get the chance. No one knows where she is except me. She wants me to sell the ranch and send her the proceeds. I haven't decided exactly how to go about it yet. If they find out that the property is on the market, they'll try to get it back. For all I know, they can raise the cash easily. I'm going to handle the sale privately."

"I'm sorry we won't get to see her tonight. I've grown quite fond of Maria. A party might have been good for her."

"She got a kick out of your invitation. A 'Come as You Are Party' where the guests come as who they really are. I suggested she come as a feminine version of Zorro. Zorra? It was the first time I've ever seen her laugh. But then she said she planned on spending All Soul's Day praying for John and Juanito. It stopped being funny then. I doubt that she'll ever get over this." Mattie breathed in the coffee aroma emanating from her cup before taking a big swig. "Dr. Whitaker doesn't think there will be any more children. Maria said that there will never be another John, so it doesn't matter. The whole thing still makes me so angry I could spit. One of these days I am going to find out who did this to her and make sure they all get *exactly* what they deserve." Mattie's eye glowed with zeal. Her hair seemed to radiate a kind of static indignation, standing away from her head in wiry coils.

"All right, Mattie. We'll put our wits together and see what we can do, but we've all been focused on it for a long time. Today, can we just enjoy Samhain and the party? Why don't you help with the decorating?"

"Mother, you know I'm hopeless at that sort of thing. You and Chrys are the Martha Stewarts of the Wiccan World."

"All right. Go get in the hot tub then. Make up your own rejuvenation spell and emerge reborn. Take three candles with you and a slice of zucchini bread with cream cheese. Sure fire remedy. When you get dressed, you can whisk together the 'eye of newt and toe of frog, wool of bat and tongue of dog'."

"I can handle that," said Mattie. Pointing one finger skyward, she assumed the pose of an evangelical preacher. "I say unto you, my brethren—rejuvenation, regeneration and lustration!!" She began to hum "I'm Gonna Wash That Man Right Outta My Hair," as she sauntered out of the room.

PZ came banging back inside, bringing cold air and dogs with him. "Come on, Belle. Come on, girl. Here, Booker. You too."

Two medium sized brown mutts of indeterminate lineage, raced in, ran between his legs, jumped on his chest, leaving muddy paw prints on his jacket and jeans.

"Get down," he ordered. They dropped to the floor momentarily, but quickly resumed their assault. Both dogs had come from the Animal Rescue League, where Cate volunteered weekly and served as chair of the board of directors. One of the temporary residents of the shelter had whelped. Cate found homes for most of the puppies, but ended up taking two of them home with her. Booker, the male, liked to point at things, would eat anything but smoked oysters, and loved foraging in the trash. Belle, his little sister, was more polite about her eating habits. Both would beg at the table and jump up on anyone. They befriended strangers, friend or foe, welcoming them on to the property and into the house.

"Where's Candle?" asked Cate.

The third and most recent arrival was a small caramel colored puppy, afraid of her own shadow. Chrys found her one day when she was riding her bike. The terrified puppy cowering by the side of the road was obviously abandoned. Chrys stuffed her in her coat pocket and brought her home to Cate. Together they fed her, petted her, and found her a warm spot by the fireplace.

For weeks the twins argued about her name and tried to teach her something, anything. They had instructed her on shaking, sitting, staying, rolling over—all without luck. She was entranced with Booker and Belle, and followed them everywhere. Finally, in frustration after hours of failure at fetch, PZ told his sister, "You know, she's not the brightest bulb on the strand."

Chrys gathered the puppy into her arms and they nuzzled one another. "Then we will call her 'Candle'," she had said.

"PZ, I asked you where Candle is," repeated Cate.

"She's right here," he said, unzipping his jacket. The puppy wriggled her head out, a pink tongue hanging happily out the side of her mouth. PZ set her down on the floor, where she promptly squatted to pee. PZ, pretending not to notice, ambled toward the back door.

"PZ! Clean that up." Cate's voice was firm, but without anger. She nodded toward the yellow puddle.

"Were you, like, just gonna leave dog pee on the floor?" Chrys added. "Gross."

"What?" said PZ, feigning ignorance. "What?"

Cate didn't bother to answer, but Chrys snatched a paper towel, stomped over to the offending puddle, and pointed downward with a dramatic flourish. Candle bolted underneath the sofa.

"Oh, I didn't see that," said PZ. He took the paper towel, mopped up the pool of puppy urine, and handed it back to his sister. "Thanks," he said, turning away to hide his smile.

"PZ, you're impossible."

CHAPTER 2

Artemis
The same afternoon of October 31

The invitation to Cate's party lay on Artemis's dresser. Glued to heavy black cardboard was a small mirror with an elaborate silver frame drawn around it. Line drawings of fantastical creatures, real and imagined, peered around the edges. "Come As You Really Are," it read. On the inside, in small silver lettering, it read:

Join us at twilight on All Hallow's Eve
When the veil is the thinnest and
the spirits do weave.
For Evening Communion with
the Quick and the Dead
Where much is revealed and all will be fed.
Precognitions & Prognostications
Consumption of Tasty Morsels
Shadows on Samhain
BYOA—Bring your own ancestors

When Artemis had opened the envelope, a cascade of tiny silver moons and stars fluttered to the floor. This annoyed her greatly. The little sparkles were difficult to capture and kept flashing themselves for days—in the carpet, under the sofa cushions, stuck to the bottom of shoes. She wondered how in the world the damn things became so widely dispersed. That the enclosures had been the work of her niece and nephew, she had no doubt. The twins had been living with Cate for almost a year while their mother waged war against the Whites. Their grandmother put them to work as often as possible in an effort to keep them out of trouble. When asked to help with the party, Chrys and PZ had thrown themselves into preparations, entranced with their grown-up roles as co-hosts. Cate's celebration at Samhain had become a family tradition originating from before Artemis and her twin, Atticus were born. Cate believed that that thirty-first of October was an extraordinary birthday and every year she celebrated her own maturation by outdoing herself from the year before. She started scheming and planning shortly after the vernal equinox. Artemis generally avoided parties, but she looked forward to this one. She thought about the wonderful food, the extravagant decorations, and the eclectic guest list. "A" (as she was referred to by family) wasn't much of a mixer. She'd probably spend most of her time in the kitchen, or perhaps engaged in a one-on-one discussion of politics or philosophy. Her cousin Mattie would be gorgeous, she imagined, the center of attention following her highly publicized legal victory. Her twin brother Atticus, dressed in the latest from GQ, would pontificate on a variety of subjects of little interest to anyone other than himself. (Poor Atticus. He seems to think that blathering on endears him to the ladies. The poor girls are bored to tears.) Cate will be totally in her element, glowing with benevolence, the gracious hostess moving from one group of chattering guests to another. People will be all over the house eating and drinking, dancing and enjoying themselves. Luna's Tarot readings, per usual, will prophesy great things in the year to come.

For Wiccans, the thirty-first of October is like New Year's Eve—the last of the old, the first of the new. In pagan traditions, beginning at sunset, the veil grows thin between the world of the living and the world of the dead. It is possible to communicate with those who no longer dwell among us, to honor and acknowledge their gifts to the living. It's a time for foretelling and fortune-telling, petitioning the gods for abundance and prosperity in the days to come. Samhain (pronounced Sä win) is the third and final celebration of harvest. It is a time of gratitude, of preserving fruits and vegetables for the long winter ahead, of looking forward to a new and divine cycle of life. On that day, Cate's little kingdom overflows with a spirit of abundance and thankfulness. Artemis was willing to venture out of her solitude in order to participate in this wonderful communion of souls.

A's dress was very short, a silver mini from the Sixties she had found at a consignment shop when she was in graduate school. She wore silver stockings and sandals to match. She stood before the full-length mirror, brushing her hair back. Her forehead was too high, her chin too sharp for her to be considered a beauty in the conventional sense. Nevertheless, wherever she went, she drew attention and, usually, a momentary pause in the conversation. She had a premature streak of grey at the brow that added interest to the dark brown bob. She detested hair in her face, so she used a silver clasp to keep it back. She also wore a silver necklace, a thin chain with a sliver of a moon attached. Her nails were short, unpolished and her hands were ringless.

She looked at her reflection. A memory sparked of a younger self in this very dress at a long ago party, in the arms of a handsome young medical student, whose name had vanished with the years. They had danced to exhaustion on a hot summer night, listening to Sixties oldies and partying with other students in a lush Southern garden belonging to her friend Caroline. Caro was celebrating her completion of medical school, and the bestowing of an inheritance that included the garden, a house on Franklin Street in Chapel

Hill, and enough money to do as she pleased. What she pleased was to provide pediatric care for the poor in the easternmost part of the state. For one night, however, Caroline was Queen of the Ball. Flowers floated in the pool. Glowing lanterns hung in the trees. They ate seviche and gazpacho, drank gallons of sangria. In the early dawn, when most of the guests had left, Artemis and her date had gone skinny-dipping amongst the blossoms. They swam in the warm water, watching the stars disappear and the sunrise into a cloudless summer sky. She had wished on a morning star and, to a large extent, her wish had come true. She hoped his had as well.

Caroline still owned the house and occasionally stayed there when she was in town for some reason. The many bedrooms were occupied by female graduate students living rent-free. Caro called it her "scholarship program." Artemis often thought of those wonderful Carolina springs as she suffered through a snowy March in Colorado. She could *not* remember that boy's name.

However, she certainly could remember his eyes, and his mouth. Definitely his mouth.

"Ah, my little nymphs," she said, turning from the mirror and looking into the three sets of dark eyes that were glued to her. "I hate to leave you alone tonight. You guard the house from all the goblins and ghouls that are about." The three greyhounds sat motionless, with that kind of suspension of movement that dogs have when they know they are going to be asked to do something they do not wish to do. Perhaps she would change her mind and stay, or at least forget about them and leave them to roam the house. Against all odds, they entertained the hope that their mistress was going to get back in her bed and let them snuggle next to her. Perhaps she'd invite a few of their favorite people over to join the curl up and snooze.

"I know you don't want me to go. But I won't be too late. I'm not much of a party girl." Like an orchestrated chorus line, the three hounds averted their eyes and laid their heads on their paws in despair, abandoning all hope.

"In the kitchen. Come on." Artemis snapped her fingers and pointed in the direction she wanted them to go.

The dogs remained motionless. Artemis crossed to the door of her bedroom.

"Moon Doggie! Lightning! Streak! Come." They rose and walked out in dignified silence—obedience under protest.

Artemis owned three female greyhounds, all adopted from the Greyhound Rescue League. The oldest, Moon Doggie, was black with the beginnings of grey at her muzzle. After a distinguished career as a runner, she had come to live with Artemis. Silver Streak was referred to as "blue," meaning she was grey in color. She was the middle sister—quiet, affectionate, restrained. Gris Lightning, the puppy, was white. She had been rejected by her breeder as a less than perfect specimen. Artemis had rescued her hours before the scheduled execution. Lightning repaid this kindness by being the most boisterous of the bunch and the most likely to run away if given the opportunity. She was not above foraging in the pantry for food, digging in the garbage can, or climbing on cabinets to devour unattended plates. Despite A's efforts to train her, she greeted all arrivals with front paws on their chest. All three were as graceful as ballerinas and adored by their mistress.

Artemis locked the door of her little house in the Highlands area of Denver, an old section of town that was originally Italian. Ethnically mixed, it had a large Latino population. Young professionals, newlyweds and small families were attracted to the area because of its proximity to downtown and the friendliness of the neighborhood. The houses were small by contemporary standards, but most had a nice size yard with mature trees. It was a neighborly neighborhood. People walked to restaurants and stores, sat on front porches in the afternoon, recognized each other's dogs and children and would return an escapee when one was encountered. Lightning was an acquaintance of most of A's neighbors for that very reason. Fortunately, Lightning surrendered easily and didn't mind being returned to her owner after a freedom spree.

Artemis had mixed emotions about her house. After graduate school, she had improved her living arrangements as her level of affluence permitted. For Artemis, privacy was always the goal. At first she had been delighted with her own bedroom in a shared house. When a lucrative consulting contract provided the opportunity, she moved to a one-bedroom apartment. She discovered that apartment living was not to her liking. She was distracted by the presence of strangers, above and below, of unseen children in distress, and unwelcome cooking odors. The absence of a yard deprived her of the joy of gardening and private moments in nature. When she fell in love with Moon Doggie, she had a good reason to move. She'd been saving for a down payment, and she found a small house where she and Moon lived together. She planted the yard with tulips, which never bloomed because the squirrels ate the bulbs, and daffodils, which they left alone. She built a fence and finished the basement as an office. She planted shrubbery and encouraged the grass when there was enough water in Denver's reservoirs. The house was now crowded with three dogs and she was feeling claustrophobic. She needed a better place to write the book she had contracted for, to file the endless papers generated by her consulting business, to house her growing library. The dogs needed to run, but were cramped in the little postage stamp backyard, which they used as a toilet. For a woman who liked to go barefoot, this was a problem. Artemis longed for solitude, for remoteness, for isolation, mountain views and wide-open skies. The more she thought about it, the more she knew she wanted to live like Cate, among the wildlife, in the woods. She could probably afford it, but she hadn't the time for a real estate search. The idea of tromping around, invading other people's closets and basements with a talkative real estate lady in high heels and a suit, made her shudder.

Artemis's last book had sold well, an analysis of corporate ethics. *Pursuit of Integrity* examined the evolution of the American business culture in the twentieth century. She outlined the process by which a set of assumptions is created and adopted. The book included a discussion of corporate practices which are blatantly inappropriate, yet have come to be seen as acceptable. According to the author, such practices produced damaging economic repercussions in the last part of the twentieth century and into the twenty-first.

Artemis defined herself as a cultural mythologist. Trained as a psychologist, she became interested in the psyche of the collective. In her discipline, the term "mythology" refers to a set of assumptions or beliefs held by a group of people. Some of these beliefs are conscious. Others are not. As a consultant, Artemis worked with corporations to identify and evaluate their own mythologies. Careful examination and observation allowed her to assist an organization in articulating the specifics of their mythology—how it was created, what the effects are and how it can be modified.

Artemis's remoteness was a significant contributor to her prominence in her field.

She was able to make non-judgmental observations from a place of detachment. She could identify crippling, unconscious assumptions. Her ability to do this earned her a global reputation, an auspicious clientele, and a fat portfolio.

It is time, she thought. Time to be moving. Some land, enough to maintain privacy, give the dogs running room, and enjoy Colorado's glorious beauty. She wanted to look at water, a lake or a stream, with mountains. She wanted to watch the wildlife. The house must have enough room for work, dogs, paintings, books. Maybe a guesthouse, close enough to walk, but far away enough to be unseen. She could imagine it, but she didn't want to search for it. It'll come, she thought. I just need to be clear what I am looking for.

In Colorado's October the landscape was a sultry dying color, the juice draining out along with the freshness of summer. In the aspen trees, the departure of chlorophyll left behind tissue paper wafers in school bus yellow, their color repeated in the stripes meandering down the middle of twisting asphalt roads. The hinged leaves shimmered, only slightly more exuberantly dancing than the children who came running off the bus, clutching bits of construction paper, still wet with tempera paint and sticky white glue. She was too far away to actually catch the aroma, but a memory came back to her, of afterschool sweat mingled with freshly sharpened #2 pencils, a new box of crayons, and that peculiar non-sticking glue that comes out of a pot and smells like something you are supposed to eat, but don't want to.

She headed west in heavy traffic. She could see the mountains in the distance, through the grey brown smog hovering over Denver. She climbed and climbed, leaving the dusty city behind for the crisp freshness of higher altitude. I'm moving to higher ground, she thought.

It was only then that Artemis remembered. She was so surprised she spoke out loud. "Today is our birthday!" She wondered if her mother ever thought about the Halloween in 1971 when she gave birth to twins. By Christmas, Leigh had given the infants to her sister Cate and disappeared.

CHAPTER 3

Atticus
The same afternoon

Atticus flipped his cell phone open and said, "Golden." His blonde hair, unfashionably long, whipped around his face. It was a bit chilly to have his top down, but November would bring snow, putting an end to open chariots. This was his final race with the sun until next year. He listened to the voice that came through the phone.

"No, that's not how I usually answer the phone.... I knew it was you. I know what you are going to ask. Hold on." He punched the dial on the CD, to stop the billow of Mozart.

"Probably more logic than clairvoyance, Cate. I'm in Golden. Isn't that what you were going to ask? I assume that there is something you need. Ice? Wine?" The golden

Porsche streaked along the interstate, threading between SUVs like a firefly in the woods.

"Oh, Cate. No. I don't think....Call Artemis. She won't mind." He paused to listen, then sighed. "Okay, okay. Where does she work?" Resigned, he snapped the phone shut and tossed it on the console.

The sun was a tangerine ball ablaze behind a panorama of lavender mountains. The last rays glinted on the bronze mirror of his sunglasses. He crested the hill and sped down to the exit. Whipping into a parking place, he jumped out and strode into McDonald's. Tall, muscular, and amazingly handsome, Atticus drew attention wherever he went. A bedraggled mother sat waiting for two six-year-olds to eat their Happy Meals. She wiped catsup off her arm and looked at Atticus with the same fascination that she had for her soap operas. At a long table of teenagers, the girls giggled and the boys slouched lower in their seats, glowering. Atticus removed his glasses and leaned over the counter, impatiently looking behind the cash registers, beyond the stainless steel burger chutes, around the fryers.

"I'm looking for Flora," he said, tapping his foot. A young woman in uniform scowled at him, disappointed.

"Flora's on break." She indicated a general direction with her head. Atticus turned, scanning the tables. He spotted another uniformed girl, sitting alone, sipping a drink. She was absorbed in a calculus book.

"Flora!" He strode to her table, towering over her. She looked up and grinned at him. She was clean and shiny, with skin the color of caramels and eyes like amber beads.

"Hey, Uncle At. Have a seat."

"No, I'm in a hurry. Cate sent me to check on you."

"Why? I'm fine. Maybe feeling a bit sorry for myself because I have to work until nine." She closed the book, one finger keeping her place.

"Cate and Luna wanted me to stop and make sure you're coming to the party. They aren't sure what time you get off."

"Oh, I'll be there. Just tell Mama I'm going home to change first." She indicated her outfit with a wave of her hand. "No way am I showing up in this uniform. I don't want anyone to think this is who I *really* am! Where's your costume?"

Atticus stared down at his expensive slacks and cashmere sweater. "This is my costume." His flat tone gave no clue as to whether he was attempting humor.

"Oh. Well, I'm coming as Cinder Ella. The Latina version of Cinderella. Don't you think that's pretty funny?"

"I guess," he said, absently. "Is your car running okay?"

"Punkin is all ready to go to the ball. I just had it serviced." Abandoning her book, she jumped up and gave him an affectionate hug, which he received rather stiffly before making a swift exit. As he backed out, he could see her big smile through the window. She waved and went back to work.

As she came back to the counter, the girl at the cash register grabbed Flora's arm with both hands, tugging rhythmically. "Ohmygod! Ohmygod! Is that *really* your uncle?" she whispered.

"Gosh, Rosa, didn't you notice the family resemblance?" Flora's eyes twinkled, amused at the confusion on Rosa's face. "That's Atticus. My mom works with Cate, his mom. Well, sort of. He's a bit of a stuffed shirt. PZ and Chrys call him Uncle At, so I do too—just to tease him. He's not really the nickname type, if you know what I mean."

The girl rolled her eyes upward and rocked her head as an indication that she thought Uncle At was luscious. Sighing, she turned her attention to the bubbling french fries.

In a booth across the room sat four men, smoking and watching. They had been attempting to eavesdrop, but only caught snatches of the conversation between Atticus and Flora. Their eyes followed Atticus out the door and into his Porsche. They observed Flora and Rosa ogling and giggling. Three of the men turned their attention to the oldest, a white-haired man who was slowly shaking his head in disapproval. Each clutched a paper cup of coffee. On every ring finger there was an untanned band where a ring had been removed.

"You would think their men could control them, wouldn't you, Whitey?" With a puppy-like appeal for approval, Buzz addressed the older man, who only shook his head wordlessly.

"Hell, Buzz. Their men ain't around. They *send* that jail bait over here to catch some poor sumbitch gringo and ride the gravy train for the rest of her life." Hank wore a greasy John Deere gimmecap, which he did not bother to remove while eating. His Adam's apple bobbed up and down as he spoke.

A third man, in a red plaid shirt and jeans, chimed in. "Yeah, and when their women are knocked up and about to pop, they send them running across the river so their bambinos can become American citizens and get welfare." He nodded in the direction of Flora. "You suppose that little Señorita has one in the oven yet?"

"Hell, Ace. If she don't, she will soon, the way she was kissing up to him. Poor guy probably thinks he just getting free pepper pussy. He don't know he's being set up," said Hank.

The white-haired man looked up. In a soft, low voice, he said, "Buzz?"

"Yes, sir," said Buzz, snapping to attention, delighted to be singled out.

"Go and see if you can figure out which car might be hers. Bound to be a piece of junk. Probably with Meskin shit stuck all over it. They love them stickers 'n' crap like 'at." He leaned back in his chair, stretched out his legs and admired his elaborately tooled white cowboy boots. His Stetson was parked on an empty chair beside him.

Buzz leapt to his feet. The old man sat placidly looking out the window, apparently considering matters of great consequence. He ignored Ace and Hank, whose eyes never left him, least a twitch of a jaw muscle require interpretation. After a few moments, Buzz came hopping back in, bursting with news. He leaned over to whisper.

"Didn't you hear her say something about a pumpkin? Didnja? Huh?"

The old man gave a slight tilt of his head. The other two followed his lead with vigorous affirmation.

"Well." Buzz paused for effect. "Out back, there's an area for employee parking. There's an orange Honda, with the back window covered in flowers. Guess what the license plates says!"

"What?" asked Hank.

"P U N K I N. That's what."

Whitey smiled, slowly putting on his hat. "Good job, son." He ambled toward the door and his white Cadillac.

"Buzz," said Ace. When he stood, he towered over the other two. "How many cars are in the employee's lot?"

"Two," Buzz said, suddenly in a hurry to button his jacket.

"You are one hell of a detective, son."

CHAPTER 4

Artemis

Artemis enjoyed the drive to Cate's house. By avoiding the interstate, she could give herself time to adjust her mood. The twisting road required a low speed, which made her impatient at first, but forced a discipline on her that felt good. She calmed her mind as she watched her headlights illuminating the narrow canyon with its blasted rocks, a roaring stream and dark mansions. These were grand old houses, built to provide refuge from sweltering summer temperatures before the advent of air-conditioning. Many were imitative of Swiss chalets, made of dark wood and native rock. Small windows had leaded panes and green shutters with stylized cutouts of pine trees. Huge evergreens overhung the stone steps, outdoor fireplaces and painted benches. She could almost smell the gin and roasting meat, see the faces of the children back from their mountain hikes clutching bouquets of wildflowers, hear the rattle of the rickety bridges over the creek as visitors arrived for the weekend. She drove vigilantly, watching for deer and elk that were not watching for her. Eventually she reached a state of pleasure on the lonely road, savoring a few last moments of isolation before joining her noisy family.

Atticus, on the other hand, loved speed. He concentrated on the Porsche's purring, enjoying her performance as she handled the curves, hugging the road. He pushed her speedometer, skillfully maneuvering the well-engineered machine. Why had Cate sent him to check on Flora, he wondered. She'd been adamant, a state not generally associated with his laid back aunt. The only parent he had ever had, her mothering had been unobtrusive. Mattie, Artemis and he joked that she controlled them with her mind. It might be so. It seemed to him that she had let them all three learn about life through experience, generally giving advice only when asked. However, when a young one under her protection, animal or human, was in danger she could be a real she-wolf. She didn't interfere often, but when she did, the aggressor was going down in flames.

Luna worked for Cate since before Mattie's twins were born. Flora, Luna's only child, had grown up as a part their family. Now she was in high school and had been working at McDonald's for three years. It was uncharacteristic for Cate to be overprotective, particularly of Flora, a girl who seemed to have her act together. If Flora could become the class valedictorian, which she very likely would do, she could probably get herself to a party after work unassisted. Atticus scowled, thinking how much he had hated walking into that fast food restaurant. It was undignified.

At the light, he got off the parkway and turned on to a dark mountain road. He decided he had better slow down—if he hit a deer, it would wreck his car. Perhaps Cate is having one of her premonitions, he thought, or a vision of some sort. Atticus was ambivalent about Cate's wizardry. On the one hand, he felt that her over-protectiveness was surely foolish.

On the other hand..., she was never wrong. He hated to admit it, but the data was indisputable. There was a lot about Cate he preferred not to know. As a child, he had absented himself when witchcraft was brewing. Nonetheless, when their mother had abandoned them, Care had taken him and Artemis as her own. He felt a fierce loyalty toward her and he would do whatever she asked, even go to McDonald's. If her reasons involved precognition, he preferred not to know.

Atticus had his own prophetic moments, a fact that he hated to admit to himself. There was the time he had sold all his tech stocks when it looked like the top was nowhere in sight. Six months later, he bought many of them back, at a quarter of the price. It certainly wasn't intuition; rather a kind of hunch based on sound reasoning. Sometimes the brain worked that way—calculating unconsciously, so that the "answers" that occurred to him seemed to just pop in out of nowhere.

At the stop sign, his sister's silver Audi shot out in front of him. With a burst of speed, he attempted to pass her. Artemis sped up. He drew beside her, on the wrong side of the road. They both flew along, eyes glued to the road. As they approached Cate's unpaved driveway, Atticus left the road and managed to squeeze past her, trailing a cloud of dust. Simultaneously, they slid to a stop near Cate's barn. Dozens of cars, parked higgledy-piggledy, were in the pasture, along the road, beside the house. Glowing jack-o'-lanterns lined the front porch steps, a bouquet of illuminated grins in the late afternoon twilight. Small white lights winked like fairies in the evergreens surrounding the house and trailing off into the pines on the mountainside. An enormous pinecone wreath hung on the door, laced with fresh chrysanthemums, marigolds, and greenery.

Artemis climbed out and slammed her car door. "You ass. Making me eat your dust all the way up the drive."

"Better you than I," said Atticus, laughing. "My top's down. You had it figured for the other way around."

"You're exactly right." She leaned against his car door, arms crossed.

"You could have waited until my dust settled. Wouldn't have taken too long. Five or ten minutes." He laid his arm across the passenger seat, grinning.

"Not likely, Bro." Artemis opened the car door for him. "Oh, Atticus. A cashmere sweater? What kind of costume is *this*?"

"The real me costume. You, however, seem to have enough glitter for us both."

"Well, you look very analytical and prosperous. Speaking of which, how are things in the world of Sun Systems?"

"Calming down, I think. The techno-coaster ride seems to be leveling out. We're precariously perched on a narrow ledge rather than plummeting through thin air. At least that's what I told them in my speech this afternoon."

"Hence the Geek look."

"I guess. Besides, I've outgrown the Helios costume that Cate made for me when I was in the school play."

"More than twenty years ago." Artemis shivered and wrapped her arms around herself. "It gets cold once the sun goes down. Let's go inside and...."

"Mingle," they said in unison, frowning. Artemis bumped his arm with her shoulder, with the kind of intimacy that is shared by two who began life in the same womb. Just as quickly, they bounced apart and faced the festive house with identical grim expressions.

"Happy birthday, Sis," said Atticus.

"Oh, yeah," she replied.

CHAPTER 5

Leigh
San Francisco in the early Seventies

"Come on, wild thing," muttered Zeke, under his breath as he sat watching a whirling girl with very long hair and a very short skirt. Strobe lights flashed; a smoke machine emitted a foggy vapor. Red, blue, green and yellow lights pulsated with the rhythm of the blasting music.

Leigh was dressed in swirling colors, lime green, day-glo orange, hot pink. The tangerine toenails on her bare feet glowed strangely in the black light. She danced alone, lost in the rhythm and the buzz of some tablet given to her by a passing stranger in a blue top hat and rainbow suspenders. Her pelvis rocked. Blonde hair flew in wide arcs around her head and her hands flailed the air.

Zeke Swan sat grinning like a wolf considering Red Riding Hood, his teeth an eerie blue glow in the dark. He set his Scotch down on the table, where three other middle-aged businessmen sat visually groping the writhing beauties on the dance floor. Bankers at a convention in San Francisco, they had slipped away after "cocktails followed by dinner" to prowl the clubs of the Haight. Ties and wedding rings stuffed in coat pockets, their dark suits still stuck out in the blur of psychedelic colors. Some of the kids thought they might be narcs, but others knew that narcs always tried to fit in. Most of the girls assumed they were dorky businessmen away from home, hoping to get lucky.

Leigh didn't give a shit who they were. She was absorbed in the sensations of her own body—the thump of drums in her brain, the ripple of her spine as she writhed, the arousal in her pelvis. Eyes closed, she felt Zeke's presence as he began to move in sync with her. His hands touched her ribcage, a conspicuous white band of untanned flesh on his left ring finger. She noticed, but didn't care. Instead, she moved her body toward his as his hands pulled her forward. Their hips rocked together, and she smiled when she felt his erection.

Nine months later, October 31

Leigh didn't think she could walk without bursting. Her belly bulged like an overstuffed duffel bag.

"Fucking bitch," she muttered. She was referring to Hedda, wife of Zeke. When she discovered her pregnancy, Leigh had tracked him down in Kansas City and the sleazy bastard had simply turned her over to his wife. Leigh thought the wife might freak out, threaten divorce or be jealous. Goddess knows, Leigh didn't *want* the jerk. All she wanted was some bread to get by on until the two little muffins were ready to come out of the oven. She hoped he might give her a big wad of cash to disappear. Instead he'd thrown her to the Lioness.

Too late for an abortion, Hedda had whined. Leigh didn't want an abortion. She just wanted cash, but it looked like that wasn't going to happen. Hedda made all the arrangements. Adoption would be arranged. Hedda would provide medical care until delivery. After that, Leigh was expected to vanish, go back to whatever.

Hedda and Zeke owned a house on Virgin Gorda, isolated, on the beach. She would have plenty of privacy and could rest, Hedda explained. Leigh didn't give a fuck about privacy, but the twin thing was proving to be more difficult than she thought. As big as a house, she didn't feel like doing anything but lying around and eating. Fine with her if the old bag paid for everything up until the big day. Then she'd collect her babies and vanish. It sounded like a good plan to Leigh. Free food, free house, time on the beach, and a doctor to deliver the munchkins. Then bye-bye Mr. and Mrs. Tight Ass. Fuck you very much, you power tripping Establishment Pigs.

It was mid-morning when she stepped off the back of the yacht. ("Belongs to some very dear friends of ours. The crew will take you right to our dock. Very discreet, you know.") Leigh was thinking about Cate's birthday party. This was the third year in a row she'd missed her sister's birthday and she was bummed. Cate threw the most amazing Halloween parties. People dressed in fantastic costumes, more bizarre than their usual street apparel. There would be tables of food, more than even the Mary Jane crowd could devour. Candles, incense, mirrors, beads, and loud, loud music. Totally groovy. Next year she'd get there for sure, maybe go as a swan. God, this year she could've gone as a planet.

"I'm Dr. Smith. I will be attending your delivery," said the creepy geezer who stood on the dock, reeking of booze and old sweat. The hair on the back of her neck stood up, her internal alarm bells clanging away. Leigh stared at him, but didn't say a word. She followed him to a rusty open-air jeep and managed to climb in. He threw her suitcase in the back and planted his droopy butt in the driver's seat.

"Ready, young lady?" he asked, giving her a limp smile that revealed brown, crooked teeth. The hand on the ignition trembled as he inserted the key. He backed out, mounting the curb, then bouncing off. She groaned.

What in the name of the Great Mother am I going to do, she wondered. They took off down a bumpy gravel road and she felt some unpleasant stirrings in her pelvic area, but didn't give it much thought. She was too busy trying not to fall out of the jeep.

By sunset, she was in hard labor. Writhing on one of the twin beds in the guest room, she vomited down the side, staining a silk dust ruffle and pale yellow carpeting. Early on, she had called out to him, but he had ignored her. He was in the living room, watching television and pounding down the vodka and orange juice. The contractions took her into a dark place of pain and she forgot about him.

At midnight, when he came in to check on her, she was in the process of delivering the first infant. She screamed with pain, begging for help.

"Well. Um. Actually," he said. "I don't know anything about babies." His eyes were wide. He stood with his back to the wall, as far away from her as he could get.

"What the ever loving fuck do you mean?" screamed Leigh. Her hair was matted. The skin under her eyes had gone dark like a fresh peach slice, cut and left on the kitchen counter. The sexy vibrancy that usually resonated from her like a high-pitched dog whistle had disappeared. She was a stinking mound of female flesh in excruciating agony. She had shoved the sheets to the foot of the bed, a wet tangle of cotton, soaked in urine, amniotic fluid and blood. She lay on the bare mattress.

"This isn't at all what I expected," he said, as if that explained something.

Leigh let out a yell that rattled the windows. The old man hurried to close the blinds.

"Look," he said. "I'm not really a doctor. *She* paid me to pretend, just to get you here."

A baby girl finally slipped out on to the bed.

"Help me here," whispered Leigh, her eyes closed.

"I thought it would be like puppies, you know? My dog had puppies. She didn't need any help, so I figured you'd be okay all by yourself. Are you sure you're doing it right?"

"You have to cut the cord." Leigh's voice was barely audible.

"Not me. I'm not touching it." He shook his greasy head, put both hands behind his back.

"Well, I'm not chewing it in half like your dog. Get me something. Bring me a knife."

He disappeared and returned with a large butcher knife. Leigh snatched it from his hand and cut the child free.

"Go find a doctor. A *real* doctor. There's another baby coming and I need some help."

"No, Missy. I'm under strict order not to let anyone know you're here."

"Then what are you here for? To murder me?"

"Just the babies," he muttered.

"What!" she bellowed.

"The babies. They are supposed to 'disappear'."

"Please get me a doctor," she pleaded, opening her eyes to give him what she hoped was an appealing look into the irresistible pools of blues. He took a step backward. The expression on her face immediately transformed from seduction to ferocity. "If you touch either one of these babies you are going to bleed to death." She wielded the butcher knife at him.

He stared at her for a full minute, debating his options. Finally, he backed out of the room. She heard the front door close and the jeep start up. She didn't hold out much hope for his return.

Leigh managed to wrap the child in a pillowcase. The infant seemed okay, if squalling was any indication. The second child just didn't come and didn't come. The baby girl cried and cried. Leigh thrashed about in pain and eventually lost consciousness.

Las Sombras
Three weeks later

"Hello, Cate?" The back door opened to the big old house that Cate called "Las Sombras." Leigh came walking into the kitchen, gaunt and shabby. She had her hands tucked into her armpits, her shoulders hunched. She wore a long, black poncho that hid her belly. "I'm here, sis. Can you believe it?"

Cate stood at the sink, surrounded by food and bubbling pots—the quintessential "Earth Mother," dressed in a brown and green caftan and sturdy sandals. Her hair was in a thick braid down her back, mahogany-colored. She turned to see who had entered, and blinked with surprise. "Leigh! What on earth? How are you? What brings you to Colorado?"

"I knew you'd be fixing a big Thanksgiving dinner and I felt like being with some family." Leigh's long legs went for miles beyond the hem of her denim skirt, and her gleaming yellow hair stopped just before her knees. After giving her older sister a hug, she pulled the poncho over her head, shaking her hair free from the garment. Leigh didn't quite have her sparkle back, but she exuded sex appeal like a lily gives off scent.

"Whoa. Get a load of those boobs. What did you do to yourself in California? Jeez, they're the size of cantaloupes."

"Well, that's what I came here to tell you. I have a little—well, *big*—surprise." She ran out the door and returned with a baby stroller.

"A baby?" Cate stared at her. "A baby!"

"Ba BIES, actually."

Peering into the carriage, Cate saw two sleeping infants, entwined like yin and yang. "They're yours?"

"Yeah. A fucking miracle, let me tell you. I damn near died. Last winter I shacked up with this banker asshole and the next thing I know I'm not having periods. So I go dig his sorry ass out of his office in Kansas City and ...."

"Kansas City? What were you doing in Kansas City?"

"I told you. Looking for Mr. Ohbabyfuckmebaby. I wanted to tell him that *baby* was coming."

"Wait. Wait." Cate held up one finger. Leigh gave her an impatient look that said, I thought we were talking about *me*. Three seconds ticked past before a cry came from a monitor sitting on the counter. "Mattie's waking up. Let me go get her and you can tell me the whole story."

"Mattie? Who's Mattie?"

"My daughter, Leigh."

"Jeezuz, Cate. You had a baby and you didn't even tell me?" Leigh frowned, putting her hands on her hips.

"Tell you how? Where?"

"Yeah, okay. Whatever." She shrugged dismissively.

"She's two." Cate left the room and returned with a sleepy Mattie riding on her hip. The child curled into her mother, who took a seat at the table. "Sit down and start at the beginning."

Leigh went through the whole story, from her weekend with Zeke, to the plans made by Hedda, through the fake doctor and the nightmare delivery.

"So, she just screamed and screamed and screamed, and finally this woman on the beach heard her. By that time I had left this world, you know?"

"Comatose? White light? What?" Cate absently rocked her baby, her attention on her sister.

"No, no. Just passed out. But the other little bugger was stuck. Going nowhere. I woulda died if Diana hadn't made so much racket. That's why I named her Diana. She 'stayed by me,' like the song. If she'd croaked or something, we would've all been goners. Her brother too."

"What did you name *him*?"

"Atticus. Do you remember? That's my favorite movie! I named him after Gregory Peck's character 'cause he's so smart and good-looking. I mean, this kid's daddy is a three-piece suit. I couldn't see naming him 'Helios' or 'Rainbow Sky.' I figured if I named him Zeke, after his Dad, Mrs. Banshee of the Western World would track him down and murder him herself. So, Cate. Meet Atticus and Diana. They were born on your birthday, so they're bound to have the Sight. Well, he would've been born on Samhain, except he got stuck. I don't actually know when he saw the light of day. I'm not sure I was there at the time."

"Do they have birth certificates?"

"Naw. Why? So he can be drafted one day?"

Cate pulled the baby carriage over. She and Mattie stared down at the two infants. Diana opened her eyes and stared into Cate's, with the recognition and knowing of one very old soul meeting another. Her brother sucked her thumb.

✵ ✵ ✵

The three children shared a room in Cate's mountain house. Leigh stayed for weeks, growing stronger and healthier. She laid off the alcohol and drugs, ate Cate's wholesome cooking, went for solitary walks on wintry roads. She seemed to have no interest in her twins, however. Gradually, Cate assumed the care of all three of them, while Leigh grew increasingly restless.

On the morning of the Winter Solstice, Leigh sat down at Cate's kitchen table. " Time for a change. The days are going to be getting longer; we're moving toward the light."

Cate was fixing bottles of formula, her back to her sister. Without asking, she knew what was coming.

"You know, Cate...."

"I know, Leigh."

"I can't take care of them, you know. I considered aborting them."

"Why didn't you?"

"I don't think they're really mine any-way. I think they're really *yours*. I was just the channel, or something." Her voice trailed off. She fiddled with the long fringe on her suede jacket, twisted her freshly washed mane into a knot on top of her head. "Think of them as a kind of birthday present."

Cate's eyes were full of fury when she turned to meet her sister's eyes. "Let me get this straight. It's a division of labor. You do the fucking around and I do the childcare. Is that how it is going to be?"

Leigh was momentarily frozen—then gave a small shrug. "I can't keep them. I guess I just assumed you would want them." She stared down at her long legs, momentarily thinking that she was glad to have her own slender ankles back after the pregnancy. "I thought the bastard's wife would pay me off to give them to her. Instead, she tried to kill them. What else can I do, but leave them with you?"

"As long as you understand," said Cate. "They *are* mine. From now on. No changing your mind. Ever."

"No problem." Relief was evident in Leigh's voice. Releasing her hair and giving it a flounce, she stood up and pulled a suitcase from behind the door. "This guy I know is picking me up. Well, actually he's outside. So, I'm gonna.... You know. I'll try to send some bread, if I ever get any." She giggled.

"No. Don't send money," said Cate. "Please take care of yourself. I love you, but don't bring me any more 'presents.' Get on the pill."

With a final flick of her hair, Leigh was gone. Cate heard an engine start, then grow fainter as the car went down her dirt road. The house was silent.

Cate lit the large candle that sat on her kitchen table. She sat down and stared into the flame. "Thank you, Mother," she prayed silently, "for these wonderful children. I gratefully accept this miracle. Grant me the wisdom and strength to be a good mother to them. May their destinies be fulfilled and their lives be lived in service to the highest good. So mote it be." She started to stand, then sat down abruptly. "Oh, and Mother? I'm changing her name to Artemis, if that's okay with you." The flame flickered and a small swirl of smoke flashed upward, which Cate took as a sign that her prayer had been heard, her request granted.

CHAPTER 6

The Whites
The evening of Samhain

"I and the Father are One!"

Male voices rattled the timbers in the tiny frame church, sounding more like stadium cheer than a religious affirmation. Cobwebs hung from the ceiling and a hole the size of a dinner plate obliterated the dove that had once been descending in the stained glass window. The front three rows of pews were filled with men sitting thigh to thigh, jammed together, eyes upon the dusty pulpit, their breath coming out in silvery puffs. Fat candles burned in the window, on the floor and on the altars. They were ordinary men, primarily working class, wearing the kind of clothing available at any Walmart or Sears—jeans, plaid shirts over thermal underwear, cowboy shirts with pearl snaps. Some held hats in their laps, baseball caps or cowboy hats. However, sprinkled among them were a few peacocks, resplendent in Skinhead attire—eagles and swastikas, crosses and serpents twining around muscled arms, shaved heads, safety pins and studs through pierced body parts. In the front pew there were several men in business suits and overcoats. All were, without exception, Caucasian.

At the front of the church, on a platform elevated by four steps, was a row of folding chairs, occupied by three men. One wore a grimy white ski jacket over white pants and running shoes. The second was unusually tall, wearing a somewhat yellowed white choir robe that just covered the knees of his jeans. His boots were elaborately stitched in a cowboy design, black with white flames and a gold cross. The oldest, clearly the leader, pushed back a shock of white hair and stood to approach the pulpit. Slowly, he removed a white knitted scarf and a white cashmere overcoat. He was dressed in a suit of white wool, obviously homemade. He wore a starched white shirt and a white tie, also made by his wife and embroidered with the symbol of a cross superimposed on a 1. His white boots made a clomping sound as he crossed the wooden platform. He sighed loudly, moving slowly and deliberately. His hands gripped the edges of the pulpit. On his left ring finger, where there might have been a wedding band, he wore a heavy gold ring of a size generally associated with Super Bowl champions. Diamonds glinted in the candlelight, encrusted in the same symbol as appeared on his tie.

The room was silent. The speaker tightened his grip, making his knuckles lighten. He looked at his meager audience with a glare intended to intimidate with its intensity. "My brothers," he said in a low but powerful voice. "We have been robbed by a pair of whores." He punched at the last three words with a pointed finger. "We have lost a battle in the holy war to save our race, but we are far from surrendering. Our birthright has been violated, once again. Land, created by the Almighty Father, handed down to me by my fathers and grandfathers, land that was placed in trust for my sons and grandsons, has been *stolen*." His voice rose in intensity and volume. "Stolen from me by a foreigner, a trespasser, one among many who have overrun this country, and she did it with the assistance of Satan's very own concubine, a hellcat witch chosen to do his evil work. This witch was set upon robbing *us* of our rights and *me* of my inheritance. My land, seized by an illegal government, has been handed over to a filthy, dirty immigrant, a Meskin whore who came to this country for the sole purpose of stealing from us and polluting our holy race through fornication. Well, my brothers, the profane product of that union is, Thanks be to God, NO MORE. That child will not contaminate this country of ours. This woman has been stopped by God from bringing an abomination to life, from spreading polluted blood for generations to come."

The veins were standing out on his forehead, pulsing as he grew more furious. He flailed at the air, shouting, "It is Our Father who has destroyed this child, as a sign to us of His undying allegiance, and it is Our Father who will return us to the land that is rightfully ours. Our Father, the Lord of the

Universe, is all powerful. Om nip o tent. He isn't going to stand for our being swindled by a couple of prostitutes from Hell. Our God is a wrathful God, a jealous God, a vengeful God. He will show us the way to reclaim not only our home, but our beloved country."

As he raised his fist into the air, the candlelight glittered on the diamonds in his ring. "Let us affirm."

"I and the Father are One." The tiny flames trembled with the force of their breath, the stomping of their feet. They sang, "Onward Christian soldiers, marching as to war...."

CHAPTER 7

Las Sombras
The evening of Samhain

"Uncle At! Aunt A!"

The front door flew open and the wreath shuddered precariously. A slim girl stood silhouetted in the doorway, her blonde hair hanging down her back. She struggled to hold aloft a wooden sword painted gold while, in the other hand, she balanced a pair of wavering scales. Her toga hung to the floor, tied with a cord that encircled her waist and crossed her chest. She gained control and posed, still as a statue.

"Ah, Justice," said Artemis. "A wonderful costume, Chrys."

The girl grinned and relaxed her arms. "Themis, actually. I just couldn't see spending the evening in a blindfold. But, you are exactly right. Don't you think it's an appropriate attire for the daughter of the world's greatest attorney?"

"I wasn't aware that designation had been officially conferred upon her," commented Atticus wryly.

"Well, practically. She's been getting great press for weeks." Chrys stepped out on to the wide old-fashioned porch, threw down her props and opened her arms to embrace them. "Uncle At! That's the worst costume in the world. What are you dressed as? The Chic Geek?"

"Exactly." He turned slowly, and struck a model's pose, hands in his pockets, shoulders thrown back, gaze directed outward, offering his handsome profile.

"Humph." She threw her arms around him in a hug, which he returned stiffly, if not unwillingly. She sprang away and pointed to the glowing pumpkins on the steps. "How do you like my 'illuminart'? That's what I decided to call it. I didn't think 'jack-o'-art' had the proper ring, do you? Grandma did the ones with the trees. I did the leaves. Like them?"

The pumpkins were clustered in groups of threes, candlelight glowing through the flesh where it had been scraped to a mere membrane. Long strands of ivy trailed between and around the porch railings.

"They are incredible," said A, stepping forward to embrace the girl. "How in the world did you make them?"

"Magic," said Chrys. "…and extraordinary talent."

"Did PZ help?" asked A.

"Are you kidding? You should've heard *his* idea for the front porch."

"I'm sure he'll give them to us in detail," said Atticus. "You didn't let him carve any of them?"

"Nope. Not a one. Besides, he spent all afternoon working on his costume. It's pretty cool."

The front door opened again and a giant horse's head peered around it. Prancing out on to the porch was a white horse, rearing up on his back legs, hoofs flailing the air. On his back, white wings jutted from his shoulders.

"Holy cow!" said Artemis.

"Horse, actually," corrected Atticus.

PZ whinnied, galloping down the steps and around the front yard.

"He's like, totally crazy," said Chrys. "Ignore him. Mom said to watch for the two of you. She won't be surprised that Uncle At is such a stick in the mud. But look at you, Aunt A! You're stunning as the Goddess of the Moon. It's perfect."

"I really should have brought my hounds." Artemis gave her niece's shoulder a squeeze, an unusual display of affection for her.

"The Greek and the Geek." Atticus put his arm under his sister's elbow to escort her inside. "Let's go find Mattie the Magnificent. We can bask in her reflected glory."

Thick garlands of ivy, flowers, autumn leaves and dried foliage draped the front hall. Apples and pears anchored swags over the doors, down the staircase and across the ceiling. To the right the dining room table was overloaded with food and decorations. Cate's blue and white pumpkins shone with the images of wood nymphs and fairies. The largest, in the center, bore the dual faces of the horned god and the goddess Copia.

Artemis stood by the table, her mouth watering as she considered the display of food. Green, yellow and red apples, purple grapes, mixed squashes and gourds, pears of amber and deep claret, mahogany pecans, pomegranates cut in half to display glistening ruby fruit, almonds in their shells, miniature pumpkins—all tumbled out of a giant horn made of straw and down the center of the table. Three-tiered candelabras stood on the table and the sideboard, glowing with tapers in colors ranging from pale yellow to sepia and grass green. There were bowls of salads and fruits, a crock of steaming pumpkin soup atop a small flame to keep it warm. Cheeses and cold meats were heaped with garnishes of berries to tempt the appetite. A ham anchored one end of the feast and a roast beef the other. Baskets of muffins, rolls, crackers, and breads appeared between the overflowing trays. The sideboard was laden with pies, tarts, cakes, cookies, chocolates and fruit.

Artemis picked up a miniature cheesecake and popped it into her mouth. The velvety white sweetness melted on her tongue. She considered what to pick next, but Atticus grabbed her arm and steered her away from the food.

"Let's go find Mattie," he said, "before you jump into the food."

Costumed celebrants crowded around the table. Chrys disappeared down the hall, speaking to a unicorn, sidling past a somewhat aged Dorothy and her dog Toto. An old man with long grey hair stood leaning against the door to the library. He wore a full-length brown robe, a pointed hat with golden stars and a moon on it, small round spectacles and an owl affixed to his shoulder. As they walked by, he nodded to Atticus.

"Who's Merlin when he's not mentoring Arthur?" asked Artemis.

"Vice President, Research and Development."

"Of course."

"And Cate's current flame, or so I hear."

"Really! Well good for her." The smile on Artemis's face contrasted with Atticus's frown of disapproval.

"You girls know no boundaries," he said.

His sister shrugged, a "get over it" gesture. "We recognize only one boundary, and that one wouldn't keep Cate from loving whomever she chooses."

"Harm to none," recited Atticus, grimacing.

"Good boy. Go to the head of the class," she said. He tilted his head and rolled his eyes upward by way of response.

Two boys came bouncing up—Michael Jordan and Tiger Woods, in miniature. "Ya seen PZ?"

"Last I saw him he was galloping in the front yard."

"Thanks," they muttered and bolted for the door.

Cate's large room was the center of activity. In two simmering iron cauldrons on the stove, spicy cider sent a delicious odor into the air. One was labeled "Leaded," the other "Unleaded." Similar vessels, on the island and the deck, held iced drinks. Bottles of red wine had been uncorked. Two huge arrangements of flowers, primarily the "pickled" autumn leaves and yellow marigolds, filled large floor urns. The music was blasting Fleetwood Mac. A couple dozen dancers, in pairs and singles, created a dance floor in front of the fireplace. A gay couple, dressed as Sonny and Cher of the Sixties, were enjoying themselves in their own personal revival of the Pony, the Mashed Potato, the Cool Jerk and the Swim.

Luna was setting up a small table covered in a black cloth for her Tarot readings. Dressed as an upper class matron of the 1900s, her gown had a low neckline, elaborate sleeves, a skirt that went to the floor, trimmed in lace and silk roses. The matching hat had a wide brim featuring a huge ostrich feather and more artificial flowers. Wherever her flesh was showing, she had covered herself in black body paint and drawn the stark white bones of a skeleton. It made her look very strange indeed.

"*La Catrina. Buenas noches. Usted luce encantadora esta noche,*" said Artemis.

"*Usted está hermosa esta noche. Mattie y Cate han estado esperando su llegada y la del Sr. Atticus.*"

"You know how weak my Spanish is, Luna," said Artemis. "I understood you up to this point, but perhaps we should switch to English before I get lost."

"All right, Señorita Artemis. I see that both of you have come as yourselves this evening. You are very much the maiden goddess, but your costume is incomplete without your hounds."

"Just what I told Chrys. The nymphs were quite annoyed at being left behind. I'll bring them out for a romp when there isn't as much going on. My little backyard hasn't nearly enough space for them. They love to run."

"Such is their nature, I think," said Luna. "They are very civilized ladies, particularly in comparison to Cate's menagerie. Candle still pees in the house, which I am not enamored of. I locked her in the bathroom for the night. I'll have enough mess to clean up in the morning."

"What about Belle and Book? Did you lock them up too?"

"No, they're wandering around, begging for tidbits and hoovering unattended plates."

"Another reason for leaving mine at home. I don't want them to learn bad manners," laughed Artemis.

Luna turned her attention to Artemis's twin. "Señor Atticus. How nice to see you this evening. Did you stop by and see my Flora?"

"Actually, I did. But I don't understand why you and Cate are so concerned. She was on break, studying calculus. That girl knows where she is going. Industrious, studious and smart as a whip. She doesn't need supervision."

Luna's dark eyes momentarily lost focus. The tiniest glitter of a tear appeared. "I don't know myself, exactly. Cate and I have been feeling uneasy all afternoon. Something is wrong. I wanted to make sure that Flora's safe." She shook off a shudder. "Probably just the ancestors rattling my cage. I appreciate your taking the time to check on her."

"No problem," he said. "I was happy to do it." A small lie, he thought. He wasn't exactly *happy* to do it, but then, it wasn't a big deal. As he thought about it, the stop at McDonald's had given him a vague sense of discomfort, as well. Maybe it was just the nagging sense that Cate was dragging him into something he'd rather not become involved with. He gave an involuntary shake. "Where's the Perry Masonette?"

"On the deck. *Probrecita!* This trial really took it out of her. I'm surprised that she wanted to come tonight. I figured she might stay in her room with a book, or even go back to her house in Denver. It would be impossible to rest here with all this going on, but I suppose she wanted to stay with her kids. Go on out and find her. She's been anxious to see you both."

"Thanks, Luna," said Artemis. "I'll be back for my annual reading, so get the cards warmed up."

Atticus opened one of the French doors to a wide deck. Mattie stood alone, her head thrown back, looking at the moon. A wisp of grey clouds streaked the starry night. Mattie wore the same costume every year—a full-length black velvet cape lined in copper silk that matched her hair. The large hood draped down her back with the lining catching the moonlight. As she turned to face them, a topaz pin glittered at her throat where it held the cape together. Tied in her abundant curls were hundreds of pieces of curling ribbons, gold, silver, black and copper. The ribbons seemed to writhe in the wind, a halo of moonlit and wriggling color. A gust of wind made the cape billow around her body, encased in a long black dress.

"It's not over," she said.

Artemis marveled at how Mattie's eyes gleamed. They could be sapphire blue or deep indigo, depending upon her mood. Tonight they were a glittering steel grey.

"What do you mean?" said Atticus, with a jocularity that rang flat. "Of course it's not over. I would say that your career is about to take off. This press has been great. Let me congratulate you, although I'm sure...." His voice trailed off. His two sisters were staring at him in stony silence. He crossed his arms and said, "Stop it, you two."

"Atticus, why the pretense? You have greater powers of precognition than either of us. Why do you deny your gift? I'm really sick of it." There was ice in Artemis's voice, but it was Mattie's silent stare that froze the blood in his veins.

"You know I consider that kind of thing very unreliable," he said, gruffly. "I admit I have vague premonitions occasionally, but I make it a policy never to act upon them until I have a solid indication of validity. You conjure up 'visions' and go into high gear. Ready, fire, aim. That's the pair of you. I don't get 'visions' and I sure as hell don't want any."

"What have you been getting?" asked Mattie.

Atticus stared at her defiantly, declining to answer.

"I asked you a question," persisted Mattie.

He balked a bit longer. Finally he said, "Nothing I care to articulate."

"But something." Mattie turned to Artemis. "And you, Aretmis? What have you been getting?"

Artemis wanted badly to be able to give her something reassuring, but she couldn't. "Not much'" she said. "Only a vague sense of urgency. Oh, and a recurring image. It keeps popping into my head. The letter omega, in silver, kind of wavering or flowing. I have no idea what it means."

"I rest my case," said Atticus. He walked across the deck and sat down in a chaise lounge, after checking to make sure it was clean.

"I'm the attorney here," said Mattie, "and I'm far from being able to rest." She turned, leaning upon the railing to face the moon once more. Artemis came to stand be-side her. "I need your help. Both of you. I am so tired, I can barely function. It's the kind of tired that will take weeks to get over. But something is haunting me—in my dreams, in my meditations, popping into my head while I'm in the shower. It's not an image. It's more like something screaming from far away, warning me of something very dangerous. Sometimes I seem to hear my name. Do you remember that tone of voice Cate used when we were children, just before you were going to put your hand on a hot pan, or run the car into a pole? That voice that is so screechy scary that you *have* to pay attention to it? Well, that's what I'm hearing, kind of."

"Is it Cate's voice?" said Atticus. He rose, adjusted the crease on his trousers and came to stand on the other side of her.

"No. It's not a voice I recognize, but it is so insistent that I dare not ignore it." She turned to Atticus and he put his hand on her shoulder, then withdrew it. "I'm feeling very vulnerable, like I haven't much strength left to fight. I'm not *sure* that I'm the one at risk. It could be my kids or someone else in the family. It could be all of us, but whatever it is, and whatever it's after, I can't take it on alone. Not right now. Will you help me?"

"Of course," they said together. Artemis wondered if either of them could really be of any help.

The door opened. Luna's weird skeletal face and plumed hat stuck out into the night. "Cate's getting ready for the welcome. We're waiting on you."

Arm in arm, the three of them followed her inside. Cate stood on a bench in front of the fireplace. She wore a long silver dress, tight sleeves with a gossamer cape of pewter. Her ruby studded athame hung on a silver chain around her waist. Dark hair sprinkled with grey hung down her back in the ripples that loosened braids leave behind. Around her neck hung a silver pentacle, set with smaller rubies. Red stones also gleamed in her ears and on her fingers. She raised her hands and the crowd began to shush itself. She nodded to PZ, who turned off the sound system. For a moment, her eyes fell on Artemis, Mattie and Atticus, still entwined, standing just inside the French doors. She gave them a big smile that faltered a bit when she realized that the twins seemed to be holding Mattie up. She tilted her head, drew down her eyebrows in a silent question. Artemis raised her palm, gave a slight nod in a reassuring gesture, telling Cate to go ahead.

"Welcome, my friends. On behalf of our family, I extend hospitality and affection to all of you. Thank you for choosing to share this very special evening with us. Some of you have, for decades, made a tradition of attending my parties on All Hallow's Eve. Some of you are new to our annual gathering. Old friends or new, it is our fervent hope that you will find here, not only a celebration, but also a renewed sense of purpose in your own life. In Celtic mythology, Samhain is the time of No Time, a momentary pause between what has been and what is to come. It begins at sunset on the last day of October, for November is the first month of the Celtic year. It is a time for acknowledging the abundance of the fruits of our labors, for recognizing both the gifts and wounds of our life experiences, for contemplation of the wisdom and curses inherited from our ancestors, for releasing that which impedes us, and for imagining that which might come to be. On this night may we be renewed in power, absolved of past mistakes and old resentments, enlightened, inspired, reborn. Samhain is the space between conclusions and beginnings."

Chrys came to stand beside her grandmother, carrying two baskets full of small bouquets—yew branches and yellow marigolds tied with silver ribbon. The girl read from a card she pulled out of one of the baskets. "A sprig of yew is often distributed to each celebrant at Samhain. It is a symbol of our ability to commune with those who have gone before, a recognition of our need for renewal and connection to the qualities of release and timelessness. The marigold, or *cempasuchil*, was considered by the Aztecs to symbolize death. Used in celebration of the Day of the Dead, its bright color and strong fragrance mark a path for the spirits to return to the underworld after their visit to this earthly plane. Please accept these as a gift from your hosts and assign to them whatever meaning seems appropriate to you."

Cate spoke up. "Should you desire to avail yourself of this opportunity to commune with the world of the unseen, Luna will be giving readings in the Tarot and I will be scrying in the library. If you prefer to forego communion with the spirit world, we invite you to continue your revels, and perhaps commune with spirits of a more Bacchanalian nature."

The crowd rippled with mild laughter. She lifted a glass of wine in a gesture toward her guests. "A toast to those gone before and to those yet to arrive. To honor the former and serve the latter, in such a manner, may we live our lives. As we wish, so mote it be. Blessings on us all."

CHAPTER 8

The Whites
On the mountaintop

"This through countless ages, Men and angels sing. Onward Christian soldiers, marching as to war. With the cross of Jesus, going on before. Amen."

The man in white once again lifted his left hand, turning his palm toward himself so that his ring faced his audience. The last note of the hymn died away. The leader stood motionless in the silence until a restlessness began to grow in the room. Still, he paused, eyes lifted heavenward.

"Amen. And So It Is. Behold," he boomed, thrusting his ring forward. "The symbol of ALL that is right and holy. Behold the symbol of God's will for his chosen people. By this sign have we known each other. By this sign have we acknowledged that we are ONE with the Father. We read in Genesis

1: 26 and 27, 'Then God said, "Let us make MAN in our image, after our likeness; and let them have dominion over the fish of the sea, and over the birds of the air, and over the cattle, and over all the earth, and over every creeping thing that creeps over the earth. So God created MAN in his own image, in the image of God he created HIM.'

A meager chorus of "amens" echoed in the little church. Whitey was getting a second wind. "With this sacred sign have we borne witness to the truth, that Man and Man alone was created in the image of the Father and he shall have DOMINION OVER 'every living thing that moveth upon the earth.' This is the symbol by which we have recognized those with whom we share this birthright, the right of dominion over." He thrust his ring finger forward, then touched his tie. "I have proudly displayed this symbol for all my life. The blankets my mother wrapped me in bore this sign. This ring belonged to my grandfather. It was given to me on my twenty-first birthday, a symbol of my inheritance and the reins of authority that go along with it."

Whitey choked on the emotions that rose within. "This tie was embroidered by my loving wife, in recognition of her obedience to the will of the Father and her subservience to her husband, His representative on earth. Indeed, this is a symbol of her *gratitude* for God's gift to her of a strong father and a wise husband to guide her all the days of her life. 'For man did not come from woman; no, woman came from man; and man was not created for the sake of woman, but woman was created for the sake of man,' as God tells us plainly in First Corinthians 11:8-9. Yet, I tell you my brothers, that this very sign has been seized upon by the forces of evil, by Satan's whores who have twisted its meaning and profaned its power. These women are an abomination in the eyes of the Lord and must be destroyed. He tells us in First Timothy, 2: 11-12, 'Let a woman learn in silence with all submissiveness. I permit no woman to teach or to have authority over men; she is to keep silent.' This lawyer woman is, by her own admission, a witch. She has presumed to have authority over men and is an abomination in the sight of God. I have no doubt that on this very night, she and those like her engage in a frenzied celebration of evil, calling forth the spirits of the dead, copulating with the powers of darkness, communing with the demonic realm. This woman has raised herself above her natural place in the Divine Order. She represents corruption, unjust laws that have been forced upon us by an illegal government. She has championed the powers of darkness and stolen not only our property, but also the symbol of all that we hold to be holy. Therefore, my brothers, it is with great sadness that I tell you that we must conceal this symbol, least Satan and his witches use it to further harm us. Your Leadership Council has already stopped wearing our Power of God rings outside our sacred sanctum. It tears my heart out, but I must ask you to remove anything bearing the symbol of the Cross and One when you are outside these meetings. Place them in a safe place, for the day will come when you will wear them proudly once more. Now that means old Ace here is gonna have to give up his new boots, just as he got them broke in good. It means I have to save the tie made by my beloved wife for the sanctity of our gatherings. It means that Brother Buzz will be putting his Granddaddy's ring in a drawer. You young bucks who have tattoos—if you will recall, I told you not to get them. Now you are going to have to wear a shirt, *with* sleeves, like it or not. If I catch you walking around showing the Cross and One, I personally will see to your thrashing. Every time you show this symbol, you are lending power to the enemy. But I know and you know, that in the end, we shall prevail over the Lord of Darkness and his witch whores. 'For sin shall not have dominion over you: for ye are not under the law, but under grace.' Romans 6:14. One fine day, we shall reclaim what is ours. On that day the Cross and One shall proudly wave again and be a symbol to everyone who shares our proud heritage that the White Man has reassumed his proper place of dominion over all. We shall crush our enemies and burn the witches that have DARED to defy us."

The old man's face was as red as a slab of beef. His white hair was disheveled, his tie askew from repeated pointing and waving it as a prop. His wrath had him staggering, but he still had one last Biblical blast in him. "'I am the way, and the truth, and the life; no one comes to the Father but by ME.'"

CHAPTER 9

Las Sombras
The Samhain Party

Cate's arms enveloped all three of them in a big bear hug. She smiled when she felt both Atticus and Artemis flinch. For all of their lives she had been hugging and kissing them, and they had been resisting. She knew they didn't actually mind; they just weren't able to respond with enthusiasm. Cate believed in being overtly affectionate and she wasn't about to let the twins' introverted nature stop her from giving them their share. Unloved kids grow up to be mean adults, of that she was sure. No child of hers would ever suffer that fate. Mattie, on the other hand, was all passion. She could be an avenging fury or an enthusiastic supporter. As a child she had been as prone to bursts of affection as she was as a mother. Mattie was dramatic, like a heroine in a romance novel. She "sailed in," "stormed out," "smoldered with passion," "seethed with anger," and "loved with abandon." Most of the time, that is. Tonight she seemed to be "swooning."

"My dears. I can't begin to tell you how delighted I am to see you together. It seems like forever since we have all four been in the same room," said Cate, kissing their cheeks in turn.

"It was Summer Solstice," said Artemis.

"Yes, but Atticus only made a cameo, and Mattie was so preoccupied, she might as well have not come," said Cate. "Tonight I hope you all will relax and enjoy yourselves. There is plenty to eat and drink, some interesting new faces and some old friends you haven't seen in a while."

"We don't feel much like socializing," said Atticus. "Artemis and I are our usual antisocial selves. Mattie's half-dead, and spooked, to boot."

Cate looked in her daughter's eyes, questioning.

Mattie shot Atticus a killer look. "I'm fine, Mom, but I could use some food. Did you two catch a glance at that dining room?"

"You've surpassed yourself, Cate. The food looks fantastic. The front porch is beyond belief," said A. "The flowers, the candles, everything looks wonderful."

"It's Chrys. She's a huge help. Much more than any of you ever were. Aren't her translucent autumn leaves great! Her 'illuminart,' she calls it. Okay, go fix a plate and get a drink. But when you get through, come see me in the library. There's something I need to talk with you about." Cate turned away and began mingling with her guests. She moved from one person to another, touching them lightly, commenting on costumes, inquiring about relatives, exclaiming over recent events or accomplishments in her friends' lives.

When she was out of earshot, Mattie's smile disappeared like smoke in at high wind. "Damn you, Atticus! What are you thinking?" Mattie's mouth was tight, her eyes, lasers. "If I'd wanted to discuss this with Mom, I would have."

"She knows already," said Atticus and Artemis in tandem. "Luna, too."

"Knows what? We don't even know what there is to know. Just some voice, an image. Who has any idea what it means?" Mattie's hands were fists, her shoulders hunched. She pulled her cape tightly around herself.

"We do know enough not to ignore it," said Artemis.

"What did Cate tell you?" asked Mattie.

"Nothing, except that she called Atticus in the car and asked him to check on Flora—which was a bit off the wall. 'Totally random,' as PZ would say."

"It was the first thing Luna asked when I got here," said Atticus. "I told her Flora was fine and would be here around nine-thirty or ten. When I asked why they were concerned, she said that she and Cate had been feeling uneasy." Atticus paused, wrinkled his brow in a faraway look. "I have too, I guess. Uneasy is about the closest I can come to a description."

"Well, you're going to have to do a lot better than that," said Mattie, her cape swirling about her as she stormed and paced. "And I have to talk with Cate. I only hesitate because I've been leaning on her for so long. She's had the twins to take care of while I've been obsessed with Maria and those assholes that attacked her." She stopped abruptly. "Cate loves this time of the year. She's never happier than when she is getting ready for her party. I don't want to ruin it."

Just then, Rhett Butler and Scarlett O'Hara pushed forward to engulf Mattie. "You *darling* thing!" cooed Scarlett. "I just can't imagine how brave and strong you must be to take on those *wicked* men! Why, Joseph and I have just been *devouring* the Post, reading all about that poor, poor little Mexican girl and the *horrible* things those men did to her! Why, it's just about the worst thing I *ever* heard." The woman had both hands on Mattie's shoulders and was clinging to her. "I told Joseph that I couldn't even *imagine*. I mean, aren't you just scared to *death*! Aren't you just *terrified* that they will come *after you*?"

Atticus attempted to thrust himself between the two women. "Mattie, you're needed in the dining room."

Mattie recoiled slightly, as Scarlett re-asserted herself by grabbing her more tightly. "I'm sorry. You probably don't remember me," she cooed. "I'm a dear friend of your Mama's. We met at the animal shelter one afternoon. Savannah *Frampton* Worthington. This is my husband, Joseph Wyman Worthington, the third." She turned her attention on Atticus. "I *don't* believe we've met," she said haughtily.

Mattie twisted away, trying to slide her arms free. Closing her cape around herself, she took a step backward. "Yes, of course. Cate has spoken of you," she said. "These are my cousins, Artemis and Atticus. Savannah and Joseph moved here from Charleston about a year ago. Savannah volunteers with Cate at the animal shelter."

"Oh, my *God*. Of course." Savannah beamed at them. "I had no idea that's who these two *gorgeous* people are. Why Cate talks about y'all all the *time*. You both must be *so proud* of your cousin. But then, she's really like a *sister*, isn't she? I mean, you *grew up together,* and all." She paused, not because she had run out of things to say, but because she had to breathe.

Artemis jumped in. "I think Chrys is looking for you, Mattie."

"Of course," said Mattie. "I'll be right there. Nice to see you, Savannah. And to meet you, Joseph." His eyes were cold and he didn't speak, but he gripped her hand with both of his own. For a moment he held her hand, just a bit too tightly. Then she snatched back her arm and turned to leave, linking up with Atticus. Neither of the twins made any polite gesture of leave-taking. Savannah's green velvet dress did not look a bit like it had once been draperies, but Joseph's expression was identical to the look on Clark Gable's face when he told Vivien Leigh that frankly, he didn't give a damn.

"He squeezed the hell out of me," whispered Mattie, shaking her wrist to relieve the pain. "He's creepy."

"His energy is really off," said Artemis. "And what Magnolia blossom did she crawl out from under? She actually *speaks* in *italics*. Why did Cate invite her?"

"Because Cate invites everyone," said Mattie. "You know that."

"Cate is *inclusive*," said Atticus. "There are *significant* drawbacks to that *policy*."

"Not as many as there are to being exclusive. And stop talking in italics," said Artemis. "Immediately."

"*Certainly, dahlin',*" mimicked Atticus.

In the dining room, they mounded their plates with food. Additional plates were required when they discovered a counter of Mexican food in the kitchen, courtesy of Luna. Atticus and Artemis found two chairs in a corner of the crowded room, but Mattie was waylaid by congratulatory friends.

The party was rocking. A line of guests waited for Luna to read the cards. PZ cavorted, in what might have either been a dance or a gallop. What he lacked in grace he made up for in exuberance. Atticus and Artemis entertained themselves by trying to guess costumes and the reason for choosing them. A full component of Oz characters accompanied Dorothy and Toto—the Tin Man, the Scarecrow, the Cowardly Lion, and a man wrapped in a shower curtain with a sign that said, "Pay no attention to the man behind the curtain." Artemis's favorite was Glinda the Goodwitch, in a billow of a pink dress. There were, in fact, lots of witches of a wholesome nature— Sabrina, Samantha, Tabitha, Clara, Aunt Jet and Aunt Frances, Sally and Gillian Owens.

By the time Mattie rejoined her cousins, she had managed to eat a chicken enchilada and drink a glass of wine. Somewhat revived, her color was improved and she seemed to be enjoying the deluge of praise coming her way. Atticus gave her his chair and she sat down, draping her cape around the back of the straight chair. Her cheeks were flushed and there was a sparkle in her eye that hadn't been there an hour ago.

"I actually feel a lot better. I don't think I had anything all day but coffee. Perhaps I've just been imagining things."

"Perhaps. But not likely," said Artemis. "It's easy to feel safe and secure in the house you grew up in, surrounded by people who love and admire you, but let's not make the mistake of ignoring the warnings. Wonder if that's why Cate wants to see us."

"I don't think Joseph Worthington is an admirer," said Mattie.

"Then screw him," said Artemis.

"No thanks. I'll leave that to *Savannah*."

Cate was in the library surrounded by several prepubescent girls. There was a ballerina, a Snow White, a generic Queen/Princess and a Jennifer Lopez. One girl was decked out to resemble a rock star, but Artemis was insufficiently current on the music scene to make an identification. The leader of the pack wore a blue gingham dress with a white pinafore, black patent shoes and white tights, golden ringlets. Her identity was established by the fact that she carried three teddy bears—small, medium and large. A shallow copper bowl sat on the desk. A pair of single candlesticks provided the only light in the room. The girls intently focused on the surface of the water in the bowl.

"Mom! Grandma is teaching us how to scry. It's totally awesome." Chrys's eyes, reflecting the flames, were glowing with excitement. Shadows of the girls' heads were projected on a dark green wall behind them.

"I don't see a damn thing," said the girl in blue gingham. She put her hands on her hips and tossed her head.

"Shh," said Cate. "It's important that you not speak. Just watch the surface of the water. Use a kind of soft focus, like you're day-dreaming. See if something occurs to you."

"This is stupid," said the contentious child. "I'm going to go get another brownie. Are you guys coming with me?" The other girls nodded, a couple of them reluctantly. Without so much as a thank you, they bolted from the room, leaving Chrys behind with a stricken look on her face. Mattie took her in her arms, resting her chin on the girl's head.

"Oh, sweetie. Sometimes it's really hard being different. Isn't it?" The tears in the girl's eyes overflowed and landed with a plop on her costume. "It doesn't help a bit for me to tell you that girls your age can be unspeakably cruel, but that we grow out of it, generally."

"No," said Chrys, wiping her face with her tunic. "It doesn't help a bit."

"It didn't help me either, when Cate said the same thing to me at your age." Mattie looked over at her mother, who smiled at her. "What might help is for you to go catch up with them and act like it doesn't make a bit of difference to you. Go get some ice cream and a cookie. Go annoy PZ and his friends. Bob for apples or dance till you're all sweaty."

"But Mom, scrying is really important." Chrys frowned, her eyes taking on the intensity of her mother's.

"But Chrys, not everyone wants to do it. It takes a willing heart and a suspension of disbelief. Primarily, it takes patience, which is not something most kids have, particularly at a party. Maybe it frightens your friends, or maybe they have been told that such things are evil. You know that it works best when you're alone, or with a few very experienced companions. It's not really a game."

"It's my fault," said Cate. "I knew they weren't in the right frame of mind for it, but I thought I might be able to teach them something. When Chrys asked me, I said yes, because I love her so much." She held out her arms and Chrys went willingly. "I can prophesy something, however."

"What's that?" asked Chrys, sniffing.

"That you will outgrow worrying about whether they approve or disapprove. You are a young woman with many gifts and you will learn how to use them responsibly," Cate said. Chrys looked over at her mother.

"Doesn't help a bit, does it?" said Mattie. Chrys grinned and shook her head. "But she's right. Some time I will tell you about this ninny that made my life hell in the fifth grade."

"What happened?" said Chrys.

"She got pregnant in high school. I went to law school. I couldn't care less what she thinks about me now."

"Law school is a very long way off, Mom."

"I know. So, go find your friends and enjoy yourself. Don't talk about scrying. Get Luna to give them all Tarot readings. Tell her you want Goldilocks to think she's going to end up married to a plumber, living in a trailer."

"Luna wouldn't do that! She can't make the cards do what she wants."

"Luna can interpret them anyway she wishes. She would turn her into an earthworm if she knew the girl hurt your feelings," said Mattie. "Look at it this way. If Little Miss Know It All doesn't believe in any of this, she won't be bothered. If she does, maybe she'll decide to be really careful about the boys she dates when she gets older. Either way, I can't see that it would harm her."

"Neither can I," said Chrys. "Thanks, Mom." She ran out of the room, closing the door behind herself.

"Being a mother is much harder than being a lawyer," said Mattie, with a sigh. " I don't think I do a very good job of it."

"Oh, I don't know about that. I think you're pretty good at both," said Artemis, emerging from the dark corner where she had been standing. "Cut yourself some slack. You have a long way to go before you're through. You'll do a better job if you don't beat yourself up every time you can't make something upsetting disappear with a whisk of your magic wand."

"I wish it really did work that way," said Mattie.

"No you don't," said Cate. "Think of the horrendous mistakes we could make if we had that kind of power."

"You're right," said Mattie. "I make enough mistakes without a magic wand."

From the corner of the room, Atticus had been watching them. He dragged chairs to the desk for himself and his sisters. "What have you been conjuring up, Cate?" he said. "What's going on?"

Cate stared into the shallow pool reflecting the candlelight. "Well, this afternoon, while I was working on my table decorations, I kept getting the sensation that someone or something was sending very ugly energy.

It just crept up my spine, like a cold chill. It doesn't seem to be directed at me personally, but it does have something to do with our family. I went upstairs and meditated for about a half hour. All I could pick up was the image of several men in white robes, KKK outfits, attacking a girl. She was dark, but not necessarily African American. Could be a Latin American, I suppose."

"That sounds like Maria. Perhaps you were getting the past, not the future," said Mattie. "They didn't wear robes when they attacked her, but I don't know what they do in private. Thank the Goddess."

"Maybe. It could have been decades ago. They were very active in Colorado, particularly in the Twenties. The governor was a member, as well as the mayor of Denver. The Klan was part of a very powerful political machine." Cate rubbed her hands up and down her arms, as if she were chilled. "I have a sense of an impending threat. I'm feeling it, in my belly and on my skin. Images from the past feel different to me, detached or more ethereal. They usually appear as visions. It could be a spirit trying to contact me, but I don't believe that any Klan types would get through. I'm not exactly a sympathetic receiver. However, it might be a reference to the Whites. I wouldn't be surprised if there's a historical connection. Do you think it's a warning?"

"Could be they're still after Maria, but I doubt they would pursue her to Mexico. They won't find her if they do," said Mattie.

"Did you see a face?" asked Atticus.

"No. I went to find Luna and asked her if she was experiencing anything. She said she would ask the cards. 'Is someone we know or love being threatened?' was her question. The card she drew was the Empress."

"So?" said Atticus. "What does that mean? I can't remember any of that tarot stuff."

"She got white as chalk. That card is Flora's card. It often comes up to symbolize Flora. The Empress is the Mother Nature type, very earthy, generous and nurturing."

"Which sounds more like you, Cate, than Flora," said Artemis.

"Well, you're kind, my dear. Those are also attributes that Luna has. Flora picked the card herself as a symbol of the woman she wants to become. She has the Empress on her bulletin board as a kind of talisman. Flora drew a copy of the card on a big piece of paper and converses with the image. Luna was very upset about that card turning up as the answer to her question. That's when I called you and asked you to check on her."

"And she's fine," he said, with a tone of finality.

"Then where is she?" asked A. "Shouldn't she be here by now? I haven't seen her."

Atticus consulted his watch. "It's just a little after nine. I assume she's gone home to get into her costume," said Atticus. "Don't work yourselves into a needless state of hysteria."

"You wouldn't know hysteria if she got into bed with you," snapped A.

Atticus gave her a disdainful look. "When a *hystéra* is in my bed, I definitely know what to do with it."

"Very amusing, Atticus. I am so impressed that you studied Greek. Perhaps you should have spent more time on abnormal psych," was Artemis's cool reply.

Cate, accustomed to their bickering, ignored the twins. Her eyes were pinned on her daughter. Mattie met them without flinching. "What did Atticus mean when he said you were spooked?"

"I suppose 'spooked' is as good a word as any. I've been uneasy, as if some predator were stalking me, us, somebody. Like you, I don't have anything specific. I don't want to worry you, so I waited for the congeniality twins to show up so I could dump it on them."

"Well, I didn't want to worry you, either, my dear, so I said nothing. You need to rest."

Atticus snorted. "You two are straight out of an O'Henry Christmas story. What we have is zilch. Mattie's hearing voices. Luna's turning up cards. Artemis is seeing the Greek alphabet. Cate has chills up her spine and is envisioning the KKK in pursuit of pretty Señoritas. None of it makes any sense."

"It may not make any sense," said Artemis. "But it isn't 'zilch.' In fact, there's a lot going on. And you," she made a face at him, "are incapable of 'articulating.' Just what *are* you capable of? Calculating? Tabulating? Fornicating?"

"All of those and more."

"Cut it out, you two," said Cate. "What's he talking about, A? Greek letters?"

Artemis repeated their conversation on the deck and her own recurring vision of a watery omega. Cate put her chin in her hand, gazing out in to space as she thought. "You're the most visual, Artemis. Why don't you try scrying?"

Artemis shot her brother a look that warned him against ridicule before she leaned down, put her face very near the copper bowl and squinted.

"Wait a moment, A," said Cate, taking the hands of Mattie and Atticus. "You two grab hold of Artemis. Now get still and centered." They sat holding hands, motionless for almost a minute. "Great Mother," said Cate. "We invite you to be present with us this night. Surround us with your light, protect us with your love, and guide us to whatever may serve the highest good. So mote it be."

Artemis watched the flames flicker on the surface of the water. She let her eyes lose focus; the muscles in her body relax. Gently she let go of the other's hands and placed them on the table, palm upward. Mattie reached behind A's back, caught the hand of Atticus closing the protective circle. Artemis withdrew into herself, detached, separate. Her eyes slowly closed, her head nodded. No one moved for several minutes.

She opened eyes that were clear and alert. Perspiration stood out on her forehead. "I still don't know what it means. It was very dreamlike. I first saw the silver omega flickering on the water. When I closed my eyes, I got the image of pumpkins, glowing from within. They got brighter and brighter until I was surrounded with a searing white light. It wasn't pleasant, either. It was white hot, sizzling. I did see an *ofrenda*, an altar with lots and lots of flowers, candles, a kneeling woman with dark black hair and a circling *angelito*. At first it seemed part of the little altar, but then it grew and grew and burst into flames. The white-hot sensation came over me. It was so uncomfortable that I returned."

The women each looked off in the distance, considering possible interpretations and connections. The candles burned steadily, casting shadows on the bookcases and walls. Atticus gave a jerk of impatience, let go of the hands and got to his feet, breaking the contemplative mood."

"All that and you got Chrys's illuminart and Maria's dead baby. I can't see how that helps us," he jeered. Cate reached for the two women and together they formed a ring around him. "Oh, no," he said. "I don't want to get any more involved with this. This is fruitless."

"Ah," said Mattie, furrowing her brow and casting her fiery eyes upward. "I'm going to make a prognostication. You and Goldilocks are going to live together in a double wide and have a lot of very blonde, very dumb babies. That is, if you don't have to spend the rest of your life as a toad...living in a gutter...in very dirty city...in a third world country."

"Or perhaps you'll grow warts all over, which will certainly have a deleterious effect on your sex life. Not to mention the hair on your back," said Artemis.

"You two think that's funny. What's funny is that a grown, sane man, with a Ph.D. in Economics and a Master's in Business, would try to foretell the future by looking at candlelight reflected in water."

"Atticus. I would appreciate it if you would try," said Cate, in a soft calm voice.

He looked at her, then down at the table. Without a word, he seated himself where Artemis had been. "I can't imagine what good this will do. But if it's what you want, Cate, I'll give it a shot."

He sat straighter than Artemis, his eyes on the pool. His focus was sharp, his gaze unblinking. It seemed like a half hour, but was actually closer to a quarter, before his eyes closed. Still they sat, patiently waiting for his return. He was motionless for another fifteen or twenty minutes. When his eyes opened, he looked directly into each of the women's.

"At first I only saw a single shaft of light. Tall, phallic, and glowing. White hot, just as Artemis described it. Then the shaft sort of sprouted wings, or a crosspiece. It became a simple Latin cross, but the top had a bit of a flag on it. Like a serif, or something. That's when I closed my eyes. I can't seem to remember everything that happened after that. But it ended with a circle. From the circle emerged the face of Flora, Luna, and then another woman, who was also a Latina, but I don't recognize her. Perhaps it was Mattie's Maria. I've never met her, so I wouldn't know. Then it turned back into a circle, kind of red orange, and became a pumumm," he stammered.

"A what?" asked Artemis. "Became a pummum? What are you talking about?"

Atticus was quiet for a moment, stalling. "...A pumpkin. Okay?" Artemis hooted with laughter. "But not carved. Just a simple pumpkin." His back was ramrod straight, his eyes forward, arms folded. "Both phenomena are easily explained. Are you familiar with the Ganzfeld Phenomena? Discovered in the Thirties, significant research was conducted at Duke University in conjunction with the work of Dr. J.B. Rhine. Later, in the late Eighties, Ray Hyman and Charles Honorton conducted more rigorous experiments...."

The three women had dropped hands, abandoned him to his rambling, and reformed a tight group on the other side of the desk. They conferred in low voices, ignoring Atticus's attempt to enlighten them regarding scientific experimental research on the nature of psi.

"Why do we keep getting pumpkins, do you think?" asked Artemis. "Does it have to do with this party? With Samhain? Or is it just because we've been looking at them all day?"

Mattie became very still. She met her mother's eyes. "Does it point to Chrys?"

"Maybe," said Cate. "But it could point to any number of things. It could point to me. Or, as Artemis said, it could just indicate that whatever's happening, it's occurring tonight."

"That's why all this is useless," said Atticus. "We are unable to ascertain an interpretation with any reliability. There is no reference book, no code to break. It makes me crazy. Always has."

Mattie took a pencil from the desk drawer and a sheet of paper. "Atticus, the cross with a serif. Did it look like this?" She drew the sign of the Cross and One.

Atticus's frame was taut with tension, his eyes troubled, as he stared at her drawing. "Yes," he answered, unhappily.

He made his way past the women, fleeing emotions that threatened his composure. As he opened the door, a shaft of light lay across his face and the floor of the dark room. "I admit," he said, "that when such madness comes upon us, it is inevitably the harbinger of something of importance. Nevertheless, there is no basis for action here. I just don't want to...." He stammered in frustration, closing the door as he left.

"Poor Atticus," said Cate.

"I told you it wasn't over," said Mattie.

Cate took a deep breath and stood up. "Here's what I think we should do. We'll wait until after twelve. By then most people will have left, or at least I hope so." Memories of parties gone by filled Cate's mind. "I'm too old for these midnight revels. When I was young we would stay up until dawn, dancing, working with the Ouija board, drinking and stuffing ourselves. There were always some doing drugs, but I find that drugs impair my abilities. Then there were the years in a coven. Very intense, but not much fun. I like it now, a mixed crowd, including kids, who go home early and don't engage in anything illegal. Druggies are nerve-racking. So are drunks." She looked up at the two young women who were watching her. "I'm sorry. I got sidetracked. When things have calmed down, the three of us will try again and see what we get. Can you stay the night, A?"

"I have to go home to the nymphs."

"Maybe Atticus can stop by and let them out," said Mattie.

"Actually, he probably won't mind. He takes them home with him occasionally," said Artemis. "He likes to brag that he brought home three girls."

Mattie and Artemis laughed together. Atticus fancied himself a real lover, and his good looks were invariably attractive to women. His proclivity for tedious discourse, however, usually resulted in women wandering off. Mattie had tried to talk to him about it, to suggest more effective ways of connecting with the opposite sex, but he remained puzzled. It seemed to him that a deep discussion of physics made for good foreplay. Artemis, not one for intimacy herself, simply suggested that he refrain from talking. When Atticus *was* successful, the encounter was usually the result of following her advice. Such couplings were always transitory, which suited him fine.

"Well, then. We'll spend some time together tomorrow morning," said Cate. "I think we can figure something out. Right now we are being rude to our guests. Shall we join the party?

CHAPTER 10

The Whites
On the mountaintop

At the end of a rutted dirt road, the abandoned frame church stood. Peeling white paint reflected the moonlight. A few crooked, broken slabs of marble indicated an old graveyard. The steeple still stood tall with a cross pointing toward the heavens. A big black hole in the stained glass window bore witness to the malice of teenagers unable to resist the impulse to destroy that which is unguarded. Weeds grew through the remaining bits of fence, around the headstones, over the stepping stones that once led the faithful to the entrance. The doors opened. A large man with a full head of snowy hair, dressed in his peculiar white overcoat, stepped out of the dark building onto the wooden landing. As he pulled the doors together the old hinges moaned. Placing his hat on the railing, he reached down for a heavy steel chain coiled at his feet. He threaded it through the door handles and secured the ends with a big padlock. He paused for a look at the moon before putting on his Stetson. Rickety steps groaned under his weight as he descended.

The air was still dusty from the departure of cars and trucks. Only three vehicles remained. Whitey's El Dorado sat right up front, next to the disintegrating steps. A rusty pickup was parked in the deep shadows. Fifty feet away, Ace leaned against his Silverado, one elaborately booted foot on the ground and the other resting on a tire.

"You done a good job tonight, Brother White. That was down right inspirational." Ace took a final drag off his Camel. With a mighty flick, he sent showering sparks into the night air as the cigarette sailed into the darkness.

The old man frowned. "You start a fire and we won't have a damn place to meet. Now go stomp out 'at butt."

Ace flushed with anger, only partially concealed by the darkness. Nevertheless, he obeyed, following the glow that lay about ten feet ahead on the drive. "Gravel don't burn, you old fool," he muttered.

"There ain't but one way for us to get my ranch back," said Whitey. "Stand together. That means following orders. It also means doing *exactly* what I say and *nothing* more. You catch my drift, son?"

Ace whirled around and stalked over until he was right in Whitey's face. "Listen," he said. "You've got Commander General confused with King." His eyes glittered and he spoke in a soft, surly voice. "I live as I see fit. I don't plan on taking orders from you about every damn thing I do. Particularly when it comes to women...*or* boots."

Whitey didn't flinch. He stared, unblinking, at the younger man, until Ace finally backed down. "We can't afford that kind of an attitude. I need you to find out about that bitch lawyer. You come round the house tomorrow, 'bout nine."

Ace's boots made a crunching sound as he stalked back to his truck. Ignoring Whitey, he lit another cigarette, climbed into the driver's seat, started the engine and rolled up his window. "I think," he whispered to himself, "that I'll go carve me some pumpkins."

Buzz came around the corner from behind the church. He watched the boiling dust as Ace gunned it down the road, churning dirt, fishtailing around the curve before he disappeared.

Whitey shook his head slowly. "What you still doing here, son?" he asked Buzz.

Buzz straightened like a private coming to attention before his sergeant, stopping just short of a salute. "Just taking a piss in the woods, sir. I hope that's okay. I mean, it wasn't anywhere near the church or anything."

"A course that's okay, son. Why would I care if you take a leak?" Whitey started toward his car. Buzz beat him to the door and attempted to open it for him, but it was locked.

"Hold on a second." Whitey pointed the key lock and opened it electronically. The headlights flashed and a small beep,

beep came from the horn. "You don't leave your truck unlocked, do you boy? You might get in one night and find an unwanted surprise. Never forget," he paused for emphasis, "we're at *war*." He gave the last word the kind of verbal spin he liked to use in the pulpit.

The old man waited for Buzz to open the door, and he made a ceremony of getting in. He pressed the button and the seat slid back as far as it would go. He raised the steering wheel to be out of his way. He lowered his bulky butt on to the leather, readjusted the steering wheel, and pressed the memory button. He rose higher as the seat came forward and up, making him appear taller. He removed his hat, set it on the passenger seat and closed the door with a thunk. Buzz stood erect and motionless. With a quiet swish the window came down.

"Buzz?"

"Sir?"

"I want you to find out where that girl lives," said Whitey.

"What girl, sir?"

"That Meskin we saw kissing up to that pretty boy in the Porsche."

"Yes, sir. And then what?"

"Nothing, for the time being. Just keep an eye on her. Find out what you can. Should be easy enough."

"Yes, sir."

"And don't discuss this with Ace, or Hank, or anyone else. You hear?"

"Yes, sir."

The Caddie's window slid shut, the headlights a beam of dust floating in the autumn air. She rolled slowly away, a big white land yacht majestically cruising out of the harbor. As the taillights disappeared, Buzz seemed to deflate. He slouched toward his rusty Ford pickup. Pausing, he turned his face upward to the moon—jaw dropped open, Adam's apple bobbing. His old sheepskin coat had sleeves that were too short and a smear of axle grease on the back. He fumbled with the buttonholes before he remembered that the buttons were missing. Still, he gawked at the moon, delaying the moment when he would get back in his truck and go home to an empty double wide and late night television. He listened. A pair of coyotes barked at each other across the meadow, intent on flushing out rabbits and field mice. A bird screeched, maybe an owl. Wind. The valley stretched out before him, empty. The church was deserted, dark, and empty. The churchyard where men had smoked and talked, planned and boasted only an hour or so before, was completely empty.

He tried hard, he thought. Well, he would try harder. He would earn their respect. Whitey would come to recognize his natural leadership qualities, give him greater responsibilities. Maybe even come to see him as a surrogate son. With enough discipline and hard work he would rise like cream to the top. One day, he thought, *I'll* be Commander General. I'll have a wife that makes me clothes and fixes my dinner. I'll be the best, he vowed. I'll make them all proud, make them all see. I'll find a way, by God.

The cloud flowing across the moon darkened the landscape. He turned full circle, watching the open field, staring into the darkness of the evergreens on the mountains. It was still so very empty.

"It isn't right," he said. The only ears that vibrated were his own.

CHAPTER 11

Las Sombras
The Samhain Party

Artemis wondered how people managed to converse with strangers. The very idea of it made her cringe. It was even hard for her to talk with her clients, a difficulty she overcame by focusing entirely on the task and ignoring her discomfort. She preferred working at her desk, occasionally walking with her dogs, hanging out with family and a few close friends. Occasionally she liked intellectual conversation, engaging, penetrating discussions with multiple points of view and intricate arguments. Social chatter and gossip bored her. Why in the world would she care about a facelift or the cost of someone's clothes? She wasn't interested in the sexual adventures of humans. Politics was about as exciting as watching paint dry. The motivations of the participants were so blatantly transparent.

Ostentatious displays of power and attempts to establish prestige, she found exceedingly tedious. However, the topic of conversation that irritated her the most, almost to the point of madness, was weather. She detested inane remarks about levels of precipitation, changes in temperature and the movements of fronts. Weather was to be savored, appreciated, honored—the biting cold and blinding white of snow, the dazzling sparkle of sunlight on a running stream, the smells and sounds of a soft summer rain, the tingling excitement of an oncoming storm. Somehow, to Artemis, the scientific dissection of nature's vagaries seemed obscene. Atticus, who found meteorology intriguing, delighted in annoying his sister with a lengthy discourse regarding the movements of fronts and barometric pressure.

Artemis had her back to the wall, observing the roomful of laughing, dancing, chattering people. They seemed to be enjoying themselves. With an almost clinical detachment, she wondered why she always felt isolated, even in the house where she had spent her childhood. She knew that there were interesting guests, some of whom she had known all her life. She should make an effort to mingle, but she was too edgy. She could avoid entanglement by moving around the room in a manner that seemed to indicate she was on an important mission. She put an intentioned look on her face that deterred all but the most gregarious. She checked the food in the dining room and on the Mexican buffet. She removed empty wine bottles and opened new ones. She collected cups, plates, and wadded napkins. She discarded trash and loaded dishwashers. Finally she barricaded herself behind the kitchen counter, holding vigil over the steaming brew that did not need the stirring she gave it. She amused herself with observation.

Dorothy danced with the Man Behind the Curtain, while Rhett and Scarlett did the Carolina Shuffle to Motown moldies. At the kitchen table, PZ was mesmerizing the girls with his magic tricks. His cronies bounced up and down beside the table, insisting that he do it again, do it again, so they could figure it out. Chrys was enjoying herself, the scrying debacle forgotten. Atticus, leaning up against the refrigerator, was quizzing Merlin regarding the health and welfare of the telecommunications industry. The Tin Man eavesdropped, perhaps hoping to pick up stock tips. Mattie seemed to have disappeared, but Cate was conversing with several young women of the Wiccan persuasion.

Although she had promised to stay, she longed to go home. Atticus was too involved with his wizardly friend to talk with her now. She considered slipping upstairs, finding a book and waiting for the festivities to wind down. Was it too early to disappear? Mattie had a better excuse than she did, and Cate would certainly be miffed if they both vanished. She checked her watch and realized that it was almost eleven. She hadn't seen Flora, but perhaps the girl had arrived unnoticed. Artemis made her way toward Luna, who was putting away her cards.

"No, no. I'm tired. I can't read cards anymore," Luna said to the protesting couple who were appealing to her for a reading. "It's time to quit. I want to get a cup of coffee and a couple pralines, if any are left."

"I'll make it worth your while," said Rhett. He pulled a money clip from his pocket, peeled off two fifty dollar bills and tossed them on the table. "Maybe this will change your mind about folding up your tent, little lady."

Luna continued to pack the cards in their box. When she looked up at him, her eyes were deliberately blank, her face a mask. "Señor," she said in a chilly voice. "This is a party, not a business venture. I mean no offense to your wife, but I must rest now."

"*Jo-oh-ey*," whined Savannah Frampton Worthington, giving her husband's name an extra syllable. "*Please* make her read my cards again. I *hate* the last one she did for me. She said I might have some *marital* difficulties. Make her do it over." Savannah, swaying under the influence of bourbon and water, steadied herself by grabbing her husband's sleeve.

"You heard the lady. I'm sure Ms. Cate wouldn't mind if you made just a bit on the side tonight." He leaned his red face into Luna's and, in a stage whisper, said, "Look, whatever she's paying you for tonight, I'll double it. Just tell my wife what she wants to hear, so we can go home."

Luna raised her eyes to Savannah. She pulled one card from the pack, took a look at it and put it back in the deck. "The card says she will get everything she deserves in romance. Tonight will find her in the arms of her perfect mate." Luna picked up the two bills and tucked them in beside the man's pocket handkerchief. *"Buenas noches, Señor."*

Luna turned her back on the pair. Stowing her cards into her skirt pocket, made her way to Artemis. "Will you join me for coffee and dessert?"

They watched Savannah stomp away, followed by her angry husband. Artemis asked," What card did you pull?"

"The three of swords," said Luna.

Artemis conjured an image of the card in her mind—three swords thrust through a large red heart. Above a stormy cloud dumps rain on the situation. It isn't a card that predicts good fortune.

Together, they laughed and Luna said, "I'm too whipped to do a reading for you. Can we put it off?"

"Sure. I don't feel like it myself right now. I'm staying the night. There will be plenty of time." As the two walked toward the dining room, Artemis deliberately tried to keep her voice light. "Where's Flora? I wanted to see her costume."

Luna's face clouded. "I've been so busy, I forgot to worry about her. Surely she's here somewhere, but I'm surprised she hasn't come to speak to me. She might have noticed how swamped I've been all night. Perhaps she's just waiting for me to quit reading."

They made the circuit of the downstairs rooms, checked the powder room and the deck. Neither PZ nor Chrys had seen the girl. The dining room was virtually deserted. Luna's face became increasingly tense and Artemis's, grave.

"Let's go upstairs," said Luna. "I'm going to call her cell."

They climbed the stairs, hand in hand, entered Cate's bedroom and sat down on her King size bed. Luna dialed the phone and listened to it ring and ring.

"*Hola*! You've reached the cell phone of Flora but she's out living her life. So leave her a message and she'll get right back to you. I promise!"

Luna wrapped her arms around herself, smearing body makeup on her dress. "I knew it when the Empress came up. I knew it this afternoon. Why didn't I go get her? When will I learn?" Tears made tracks through her bizarre make-up.

"Wait, wait," Artemis said. "We don't know a thing yet. Just because she didn't answer her cell doesn't mean anything. Try calling her work."

"I don't know the number for McDonald's. I doubt they are listed. Why would they be? I never heard of anyone calling a fast food restaurant. I always call her on her cell. Why would I know the number for McDonald's? They probably don't even have a phone." She rattled off this stream of consciousness, primarily to herself. Pulling a tissue from a box next to the bed, she began to dab at her wet eyes with trembling hands. The tissue shredded, came away black and greasy, dropping little white flecks on the bedspread.

"Go in Cate's bathroom and take that makeup off. I'm going to go look for Flora in the car. You're overreacting." Artemis's voice was calm. "She's probably with some of her friends. It's Halloween, after all. She could have gotten diverted to any number of places. Perhaps another party, or we could have just missed her. She might have had a flat. There are lots of possibilities. It's not that late."

Luna, shook her head, but did as she was directed. Artemis heard the water running in the bathroom and an occasional sob. Artemis got very still, her eyes losing focus. She stood there until the nervous mother came out.

"Call your house. Maybe she's too tired to come to a party."

"You obviously don't have a teenager," sniffed Luna. "They would stay out all night and sleep all day if they had their way. She's not too tired. She's never too tired. Something has happened."

"Maybe. Probably, something has happened, but it isn't necessarily disastrous. In fact...." She started to say that it didn't *feel* like it was disastrous, but she wasn't sure and she didn't want to give Luna a false sense of security. Atticus was right about one thing. She could sure use a decoder ring.

✯ ✯ ✯

"It's not supposed to be closed, is it?" asked Artemis, staring at the dark interior of the McDonald's.

"How the hell should I know?" growled Atticus. "I am not in the habit of frequenting this establishment. In fact, at Cate's insistence, I made my maiden voyage into the bowels of a fast food chain. I had not anticipated a return. I am not familiar with their hours of operation."

Artemis gazed into her dashboard, her hands still griping the wheel. Moonlight filled her lap, sparking light flecks on her dress and the sheer silver stockings on her thighs.

"She got off at nine. It's highly unlikely that she'd still be here. This is, like so many of your adventures, a fruitless endeavor."

"Try around back," she said.

"Try what around back?"

Keeping her head steady, she rolled her eyes sideways at him, a kind of warning in body language. He gave a long sigh and opened the car door. The interior lights slowly came up from dark to bright, revealing the anxiety in her eyes. Her jaw jutted forward in a tight clench. Atticus closed the door and the interior faded to black.

The parking lot was strewn with debris, paper cups, smashed plastic lids, cigarette butts, and crumpled sacks. Styrofoam containers in an ugly yellow color showed tire tracks. Atticus stooped to pick up various pieces of garbage, holding them between his fingers disdainfully, away from his body to prevent smears on his clothing. He deposited them in the garbage receptacle, withdrew a handkerchief from the pocket of his pleated trousers and gingerly wiped his fingers. He considered refolding the small square with his initials on it, but upon reconsideration, he thrust it into the trash as well.

Artemis watched with irritated impatience. She pounded the steering wheel. "Go *on*!" she said to the empty car. "Gods! This is no time to adopt a parking lot."

He disappeared behind the building and was back in seconds. Walking straight to the car, he climbed in. His jaw was set in the same rigid clamp as her own.

"Her car's still here."

✵ ✵ ✵

"When did the police ever help a witch?"

"Probably never, Cate," said Atticus. "But if Flora is missing, we're going to have to call them eventually."

"I don't plan on calling the police. If you want to, that's up to you."

The house had that look of devastation that follows a party. Dirty glasses and plates were stacked on every flat surface. A heady aroma hung in the air, stale food and old alcohol, extinguished candles, wilting marigolds and human sweat. The furniture pushed back against the walls gave the room an inhospitable, disorganized look like a consignment store on the wrong side of town. The tinge of dawn was just over the edge of the horizon, turning the sky from black to navy. Glitter and sequins, trapped in the rug, caught the lamplight, and a forlorn piece of pink feather boa wafted across the hardwood. A black satin mask, the eyeholes dark and abandoned, hung on a straight-backed chair. Cate was lying down, staring out at a solitary morning star. Luna huddled at the opposite end of the sofa, her arms wrapped around her body and her bare feet drawn up under the hem of the antiquated dress she still wore. One of Cate's feet was tucked into Luna's ribs where she was holding on to it, tightly.

Mattie paced the floor, enumerating possibilities on her fingers. "She's not at home. Her car is at McDonald's, so it isn't some kind of breakdown. None of her friends know where she is. She's not answering her cell. What else is there? "

"The other possibilities are grim," said Cate.

"I still think she's all right," said Artemis.

"Then why hasn't she called?" said Mattie.

Atticus stood up, as if coming to some decision. "I'm going to go let Artemis's dogs out. They must be desperate by now."

"Pissed is the word, I believe." Artemis gave him a small smile. "I would really appreciate that. There's food in the pantry. Give them all a hug for me and tell them I'll be back soon."

"There's a limit to my generosity. I'll let them out and feed them." He was anxious to leave. Inaction made him antsy. He preferred problems that he could rectify. At the front door, he turned and spoke. "If she's not back by this evening, someone will have to call the police. I'll check in later." He left.

There was nothing new to say to break the silence. Mattie walked to the counter and brought out the coffee machine.

"Does anyone still drink this poison besides me?" she asked. A chorus of "I will" came back at her. Even Cate wanted a cup. Mattie watched the pot fill, fixed the cups to suit and distributed them. She had no need to inquire about cream and sugar. These were the women she loved the most in the world. She knew their preferences. Luna clutched hers to her chest with both hands, warming herself in its heat. Artemis took a gulp that would do credit to a drunk, while Cate sipped hers, savoring a rare indulgence. Mattie and A both went back for refills.

The phone rang. They stared at each other, paralyzed with anticipation. On the fourth ring, Luna picked up carefully and brought the portable phone to her ear.

"Hello?" she said, her voice a tentative whisper.

A torrent of angry Spanish flowed first from the caller, then from both sides simultaneously. Luna waved her free hand, rolling her eyes at Cate and pointing into the receiver.

"Speak English, Luna." Cate sat up, put her feet on the floor, and watched intently. Artemis and Mattie had their eyes glued to the woman as well.

"*Cállese un minuto.*" Luna held the phone away from her ear, shaking it angrily. "It's Flora. She's upset because I've been out all night."

Luna's face clouded when Mattie and Artemis grabbed each other in a torrent of relieved laughter. Cate smiled beatifically and leaned back against the sofa cushions. Luna continued with her tirade against her daughter.

"I'm going to bed," said Mattie and Artemis, in unison. Cate got up from the sofa, wrapped her arms around the still scolding Luna and gave her a hug before ambling off to bed herself.

CHAPTER 12

Buzz
The next day

The trailer was immaculate. Buzz tightened the green army blanket on his bunk and folded it into the wall. He picked a piece of lint off the worn brown sofa, straightened the two green and brown plaid cushions that anchored each end. Above the couch was his "Wall of Distinction," a rippling brown pressboard panel holding every honor and medal he had ever received. There were fourteen years of recognition for perfect attendance at the Alpine Meadow Baptist Church Sunday School and a Vacation Bible School Certificate of Merit for Most Verses Memorized. There was a Science Fair award, second place, and a Math Wizards certificate of recognition. He had been a member of the Beta Club and the Future Farmers of America. He had his SAT scores posted, ranking him in the eighty-ninth percentile. He had been an Eagle Scout. His high school diploma hung there in a frame from Walmart, as well as a whole row of marksmanship awards. The summer he was fifteen, he had been to Junior Astronaut Camp in Houston and a plastic plaque indicated that he had completed the program successfully. He had also distinguished himself in computer classes. There were no photos—not even of himself.

He sprayed aerosol furniture polish on the coffee table, a hard-used Early American piece that came from his father's den. The smell of lemon oil immediately asserted itself over the lingering odor of his breakfast—bacon, toast, and eggs fried in the grease. The dishes were washed and drying in the rack. Surveying the tiny space, he took pride in its order.

He dropped to the floor and began his daily set of two hundred push-ups. Afterwards he would work with the weights that gave his back and shoulders definition. A five mile jog would strengthen his legs. He wore an elastic brace to keep his knee in alignment—the knee that kept him out of the Marines. He had wanted to be a Marine more than anything. He watched the ads on television. He knew they were "looking for a few good men." Every time he saw the ads he knew that they were talking to men like himself. He dreamed of wearing the uniform, of having other men salute him. He wanted to climb up through the ranks until he reached the top, where everyone had to recognize his brilliance, his wisdom, his strength. He would be one of "The Few. The Proud. The Marines." He would bow to no man.

It had all come crashing down, his dream blown to bits by a bruiser named Manuel Ortez, who tackled him in football practice, fracturing his femur and destroying his knee. The Chinese surgeon obviously hadn't any idea what he had been doing.

He had thought that it was all over, that he would spend the rest of his life working on his Daddy's pissant ranch and struggling to make the payments on this crappy doublewide, but he'd been wrong. Just like Whitey said. God always finds a way for the righteous to prevail. Sure enough, he had found the place where he could make a difference, where he could distinguish himself, rise through the ranks and be a credit not only to himself, but also to his country, his God, and his race. He had found his calling with the Whites and he intended to dedicate his life to the cause.

He knew he was really strong—stronger than he'd ever been, even when he'd been in high school. He was up every morning doing his workout, running his miles, then showered and ready for work by eight o'clock. Every weekend, and on the summer evenings when it stayed light, he practiced his marksmanship out in the back ten acres of his Daddy's property. He knew his guns, all right. He read all the magazines and never missed a gun show. He felt like he could handle any weapon, even the bow and arrow he used to hunt deer. He was proficient. He liked the sound of that word. Proficient.

His Granddaddy left him his weapon collection. He'd had a virtual arsenal, and Buzz kept them all clean, oiled and cared for.

They were in a metal building out back that didn't look like much but was actually well protected. There would be a lethal surprise for any sumbitch who tried to break in. A man had a right to protect himself and what was his.

He remembered his first gun. He'd been twelve years old when Granddaddy gave him a twenty-two for his birthday. They went out and shot birds. Granddaddy taught him to clean the gun and put it safely away. He learned how to pick the feathers off the birds and they had them for dinner with mashed potatoes and a birthday cake from the Safeway. Buzz knew that this was the day he had become a man. Granddaddy had been gone for nearly fifteen years now, but he would be proud of Buzz, he imagined. He wished Granddaddy could see how Whitey relied on him, counted on him to do the things those other two lunkheads were too stupid to handle. Hank and Ace were mean as snakes and dumb as rocks. Ace was insolent to boot.

Buzz finished his sit-ups, push-ups and weight work. His mind was working as hard as his body by the time he swung out the door of the trailer and started running down the road. There really isn't that much competition, he thought. He'd already risen in the ranks, passed most of the men his own age. As for those young bucks, they were fools. They had no discipline. Tattoos and safety pins. Safety pins! What was that? Safety pins were for diapers. They rode bikes or cruised in souped up trucks, chasing pussy and drinking beer. They didn't have the right stuff and never would. His mind flashed on the faces of the skinheads in the group—bald heads, leathers, heavy boots and pierced parts. Skewered weenies. He grinned to himself. All an act. Costumes designed to intimidate. He didn't have to fool anybody into being afraid of him. He was the real thing. A lean, mean fighting machine. His feet hit a rhythm. He breath was even and steady. He was in fine shape.

He got to thinking about Whitey and the girl they had seen, the one he was supposed to check out. It shouldn't be too hard. She was just a kid. He could easily find out who owned that car, the one with the silly plates. She looked like she might be young enough to still be in school. Maybe, with a little bit of time at the computer, he could scrounge up the information tonight. That would impress Whitey, all right. But it would have to wait until he got out of work. Right now, he'd have to finish his last mile and get ready for work. He was supposed to be at the tire store by eight-thirty.

CHAPTER 13

Las Sombras
The day after the party

It was mid-afternoon before Artemis
and Mattie came foggily into the kitchen.
Artemis wore boxers and a sweatshirt under
an old bathrobe left behind by an unremem-
bered male. Mattie's hair was a mess, still
tangled with last night's curling ribbons. She
had a vintage University of Texas sweatshirt
pulled over her pajama bottoms. They sat
down at the kitchen table and stared absently at Cate, striding around the kitchen talking on the phone. She looked fresh and well
rested, her hair tightly braided in a coil down
her back, a linen shirt tucked into clean jeans
with a leather belt and a silver buckle. The
room was miraculously clean, the furnishings
returned to their usual positions. Two dishwashers made soft surging noises. The floors
had been mopped and the countertops wiped

down. Everything was gleaming and orderly. All seemed to be right with the world. Cate put the phone back in its recharging cradle and gave the two young women a wide smile. They both frowned at her, squinting.

"Who was that?" asked Artemis.

"When did you do all this?" said Mattie, at the same time.

Cate patted them both on the shoulder. "That was Luna. I gave her the day off. She's home with Flora, who still has her butt in the frying pan. When did I clean up? Well, it's almost four o'clock. I've had all day."

"Mom, I thought that old crones slowed down a bit. Did you get any sleep?" said Mattie.

"I don't need to 'slow down,' thank you. I slept about four hours. I'll catch up by going to bed early tonight. It bothers me to have the house in a mess. Would the two of you like anything to eat?"

" Coffee," they said in unison.

"You should both give it up. Fix it yourself, then, if you insist on drinking it."

Mattie had to go into the cabinet once again, for Cate had cleaned the machine and tidied it away. Mattie ground the coffee and started a new pot, creating a fragrance that permeated the kitchen. Per usual, she stationed herself in front of it, watching with urgent impatience.

"Did you never hear about the proverbial watched pot?" said Artemis.

"Would you like to make it?" replied Mattie.

"Absolutely not. You are mistress of the cauldron. I bow to your expertise." Artemis pulled out a chair for Cate. "Come sit down and tell us what happened last night. I was too tired to stay up and hear the story. Oh, by the way, I called Atticus and told him Flora was safe before I went to bed."

"I know," said Cate. "He told me when I called him myself."

"Which is why I didn't call. I knew you two would do it," said Mattie, bringing two mugs to the table and sitting down. "Where are my kids?"

"Shut up. I'm trying to find out what happened to Flora," said A.

"You're welcome very much," said Mattie, gesturing at the mug in A's hands.

"The kids are at school. There's a Halloween carnival all day. Both of them are on the organizing committee. Then tonight there are hayrides, a bonfire and an astronomy lesson, followed by hot dogs and somemores. They won't be home until ten or so. You can pick them up yourself," said Cate.

"Sounds good and pagan to me," said Mattie.

"And so it is. But don't broadcast it, or we'll have an issue with the fundamentalists."

"Would you please tell me what happened last night?" pleaded Artemis.

"I have to know where my children are," snapped Mattie. "If you had any kids of your own, you would understand."

Artemis answered with a long-suffering sigh. "Okay. Now that we know where PZ and Chrys are, can we...?"

"It seems," said Cate, "that about the time Flora was supposed to get off, Rosa got very sick."

"Who's Rosa?" asked Artemis.

"She works at McDonald's, with Flora," said Mattie.

"Rosa was in the restroom, doubled over with pain. Flora decided that she needed to go to the emergency room, so she closed the restaurant and took her."

"But why was her car still in the parking lot?" said A.

"She took Rosa's old station wagon. There's more room and Rosa could lie down."

"Why didn't she call? Why didn't she answer when we called her?" asked Mattie.

"She said she did call. I guess there was too much partying going on. I didn't hear the phone ring. It would have been better if she'd left a message, but she didn't. And she left her cell in her backpack in her own car. By the time she got to the hospital, she forgot about trying to contact us."

"What happened to the sick girl?" said Artemis.

"It's a good thing that Flora took her. It seems that the child had peritonitis and needed emergency surgery. By the time Rosa's parents arrived and the surgery was over, Flora started trying to get a ride. When she got back to her car, there was some problem with it. She didn't get home until nearly dawn and discovered that her mother wasn't in the house. That's when she called here."

"Sounds like she acted very responsibly and maturely. Why is Luna still so pissed at her?" asked A.

"Because she scared her to death," said Mattie. "The fear that your children are dead or badly hurt is the most frightened you can ever be. Much worse than thinking you're going to die yourself. When you find out they are safe, you're relieved for about a half second. Then you are furious with them for putting you through such agony. That lasts a lot longer."

"Oh," said Artemis. "Illogical, at best. But understandable, I suppose." She got up and went to the refrigerator, pondering the interior jammed with leftovers. She got out guacamole and salsa, a slice of cheesecake and a Diet Coke. She pulled a bag of tortilla chips off the top of the frig and sat back down. Mattie and Cate just watched her. "Don't start," she said. "I like this stuff for breakfast."

"I didn't say a word," said Cate. "You've been eating salsa and chips for breakfast your whole life. I've always felt that this business about certain times to eat certain things is a bunch of bullshit. Eat what you like, when you like, is my approach."

Artemis took a bite of cheesecake and licked the spoon. "Ummm," she said. "Is this the last piece of this, or is there more?"

"There's a whole one in the other refrigerator. But you have to leave some for Flora. Pumpkin cheesecake is her favorite and she didn't get any last night. When Luna lets her out of purgatory, she'll come over for her slice." Cate stood and started for the door. "I'm going out and clean up the yard a bit. I'll bet there's some garbage left out there. I'll see you two later."

Artemis was shoveling in the chips and salsa between bites of cheesecake.

"How do you eat all that stuff and still stay so thin?" said Mattie.

"Running, hiking, biking, skiing, snowboarding, swimming. I love them all."

"I don't have time. I have too much to do to spend hours riding a bike or climbing a mountain. Two kids. A year's back up of work because I've spent so much time on Maria's case and ignored everything else. My house needs painting. My yard is a mess. I haven't bought any new clothes since I can't remember and I desperately need a haircut. I planned on being through with this case before school started. Now it's November. My kids are still living with Cate and going to school up here. I don't even know their teachers. Every time I bring up their moving back to town they throw a fit. My life is a mess. I sure don't have time to learn to snowboard." Mattie put her head in her hands and made a gesture of pulling her hair out.

"I'd say your head needs raking at the moment. You still have about a jillion of those little ribbons in your hair. You asked how I stay thin. I told you. If you don't have time, it's because of the choices you've made. Balance, my dear cousin. The Greeks were right. Balance is the key." Artemis set her coffee cup aside, took a gulp of Diet Coke and another bite of the cheesecake.

"*Diet* Coke? Why bother if you're going to eat all that sugar?" said Mattie.

"Balance," said Artemis.

"Ridiculous," said Mattie, pulling bits of ribbon from her hair.

"Oh, I kind of like them. They're very witchy. A bit theatrical, but I wouldn't call them ridiculous."

"I didn't mean that these were ridiculous," she said, holding up a bit of copper curling ribbon. "I meant that your logic is delusional."

"I know what you meant. I was just trying to ignite your candle. Lighten up. Cate's right. You eat what you like and I'll eat what I like. Live and let live. Okay, Cuz?"

"In that case, I think I'll fix myself a bagel."

"Bring me some ice cream, okay?" Artemis had finished the cheesecake and was picking up the last graham cracker crumbs from her plate with a sticky finger. She licked them off.

Mattie laughed as she opened the freezer, taking out a bag of frozen bagels and a half-gallon of vanilla ice cream. She handed the carton to Artemis before putting her bagel in the toaster.

"Can I ask you something, A?"

"Sure. What?"

"Do you think that yesterday's premonitions were about Flora?"

Artemis paused with her spoon halfway to her mouth, then set it back down. "Not really. Well, maybe part of it, but not all."

"They seemed very ominous, and it turned out to be nothing," said Mattie. "I felt a sense of relief last night, but there's still this nagging sense of danger."

The two looked at each other, silently pondering the situation. When the toaster popped up, they both jumped.

"I have to think about this for a bit. I'm going to put on some clothes and go for a walk before I go back down the hill. Would you like to come with me? You can get back on your treadmill life tomorrow. Come on, go with me and maybe something will come to us." Artemis collected her dishes and headed toward the sink. "Both dishwashers are still running. Guess that means I have to leave them in the sink."

"Cate hates dishes in the sink. Wash them and put them away. You're lucky she didn't catch you eating ice cream right out of the carton." Mattie went to the toaster and buttered her bagel. "Just let me eat this and I'll go with you."

The weather had turned cold and a stainless steel sky threatened snow. Standing on the front steps, they fished gloves and knitted hats out of the pockets in their ski jackets. Artemis was absent-mindedly zipping up, when Mattie thrust out a hand to stop her from tripping over a large object at the bottom of the steps.

"What's that?" said A. Mattie was laughing, which irritated Artemis. "Vandalism?"

"Well," said Mattie. "Sort of." A crudely carved jack-o-lantern sat on the step, with Xs for eyes and pumpkin guts spewing from a wide frown. "It's PZ's idea of illuminart. He wanted to make one like this yesterday, but Cate wouldn't let him. So, he's presented her with it this morning. She undoubtedly has seen it, but is waiting to make a big deal of it when he gets back. It'll spoil his fun if we just clean it up."

Artemis grinned at her, shaking her head. "Your kids are the only ones that ever make me wish I had some. Can I buy a time share?"

"Sure. You get college and graduate school."

"I think I should be able to pick my times," said Artemis.

"Why? I can't."

"But you're the one that brought them into this world. They're your responsibility."

"Cate didn't get to pick her times with you and Atticus."

"Good point. Okay, I'll take college and grad school. But I want something before then too."

"You're probably safe with PZ. I doubt that he'll make it to graduate school."

"He may be too much of a genius," said Artemis.

"Or a delinquent. Hard to tell at this point."

The two women laughed at their own bantering. Having grown up together, they related to each other as siblings—part rivalry, part affection, part resentment. They loved each other unconditionally and annoyed each other immensely.

"Mother of Gods, it's gotten cold out here." Mattie's breath blew out like smoke from an unfiltered Camel. "It will be a lot colder when the sun goes down. Feels like a front is coming through."

Artemis gave her an aggravated look. "Don't you know how I feel about weather reports?"

"Sure I do. I just don't care."

The glory of the aspens had passed much earlier in the autumn. In time for Samhain, the aspen lose their gold and silver shimmer and become stark tree skeletons, casting long afternoon shadows across the withered grasses and parched dirt. Fat pinecones lay on the ground, the promise of possible future pines tucked inside. The vegetation was a monotone of wheat color, contrasting with the dark evergreens. The river made soothing sounds, splashing over rocks, creating tiny waterfalls. They stared into the stream, trying to catch a glimpse of the trout that so resemble the rocky bed they become nearly invisible when motionless.

Artemis picked up a pebble and dropped it in. "I need this."

Mattie turned her head to look at A's face, puzzled. "Need what?"

"This." She raised her arms in an expansive gesture. "I need to be able to get outside every day. To smell the fresh air, to walk for miles in solitude, to sniff for snow or get drenched in an afternoon shower. I want to be able to take the nymphs for long, long walks and let them run until they are exhausted. I'm tired of living in Denver. The traffic gets worse every year and the drivers get nastier. It's hot as hell in the summer. My yard burns up. My flowers die and the grass turns to straw. I don't want to live there anymore."

Mattie made a small sound of disappointment. "Where are you going? Back East? California? I'm going to hate it and the kids will too. Atticus and Cate will be disappointed."

Artemis grabbed hold of Mattie's elbow, dragging her back on to the road to continue walking. "I don't want to move to the East. Are you kidding? I just want to get out of the city. I want to move to the mountains, but it's so overwhelming to try to find a place. I have classes to teach, my book to write and a long term consulting contract that means I have to be in an office at least twice a week. I'm in and out of the Red Carpet Club so often they call me by name. I want a nice quiet, remote place to go home to when I get off the merry-go-round. Great views and enough land that the girls can have a fenced in yard to come and go when I'm not home. Do you have any ideas?"

"As a matter of fact, I do, but it may be more than you want to take on. Maria wants to sell Whitewater Ranch. I told her I would help her, but I've been afraid to list it, for obvious reasons. Perhaps you would like to take a look at it. I have to get back to work on Monday, but we could drive over there tomorrow if you like."

Artemis paused for a moment, listening to her internal voice. "I don't know, Mattie. It's land with an awful history. What do you know about it?"

"You're right. It belonged to the White family for over a hundred years. During the Twenties it was headquarters for the KKK. The original house burned down about five years ago. The firefighters couldn't get to it because of all the security. I understand they rebuilt it a couple years ago and it's reported to be very nice. There are several outbuildings, but I don't know what they were used for. There is also a meeting hall where the

Whites had their services, or rallies, or whatever they call them."

"Cate mentioned that. What was the Klan doing out here in Colorado?"

Mattie stooped to pick up a pinecone, which she sniffed, then let drop. "I did a bit of research on it when I was working on the case. In 1925, Clarence Morley became Governor of Colorado. He was anti-Semitic, anti-Catholic, anti-foreign, anti-everything. For many years he and a fellow named John Galen Lock ran a political machine that dominated state politics. One of their staunchest supporters was Elwood J. White. He came to Colorado around the turn of the century, bringing his wife and children. He was a bigoted old fart who ruled with an iron fist. He's the one that came up with the symbol of the Cross and One—compensatory phallic symbolism that it is. The story goes that one of his daughters wanted to attend school in defiance of his wishes. He struck her so hard it killed her."

"She's probably buried around there somewhere. If we go there, we'll probably encounter her ghost." Artemis scanned the horizon, wondering where the girl was buried and if the grave were marked. "How many acres?"

"More than a hundred."

"That's a lot more than I had in mind, Mattie. I don't see myself running a ranch, or starting a cult. I was thinking more like ten acres, with a view."

They walked on in silence for a half hour or so. Mattie considered the failing light and the threatening sky. She turned and started back. Artemis followed her, head down, watching her own feet pace the gravel road. Both were thinking hard.

"I think we could divide it into parcels of thirty-five acres or so. Would that be too big for you?" said Mattie.

"I don't know. I never had that much land to take care of. What does one do with thirty-five acres?"

"Pretty much what you're talking about. Live on it. Walk on it. Watch the mountains grow older. Cate has fifty acres. What does she do with it?"

"Takes in strays. Raises children, grandchildren and abandoned relatives. Welcomes visitors. Provides nourishment and healing for anyone who turns up. Gives parties. Creates a sanctuary. But I'm not nearly as generous as Cate... or as powerful." Artemis's eyes filled with tears that ran down her face and turned icy. She scrounged in her pockets for a tissue. "You know, ski jackets should have a place on the arm where you could insert one of those little packets of tissue. That way you could just wipe your nose on your sleeve."

Mattie laughed and hugged her cousin with one arm. There was an emotional catch in her throat when she spoke. "Try not to get snot on me, if you don't mind." She swallowed and released Artemis. " Listen. Cate didn't take you and Atticus in like strays. She believes, and so do I, that the Great Mother sent you to us as a gift. At first, the four of us made a family. PZ and Chrys came along, and we were six. Now, Luna and Flora make eight. More than once I've heard her offer a prayer of gratitude for each one, including you, Atticus, my two brats and me. Her place *is* a sanctuary, but it's more than that. It's a temple."

"I know that," said Artemis, straightening her shoulders. "I really do. I was just indulging in a bit of self-pity. Every year this time, I think about Leigh, my 'mother'," gesturing with her fingers as quotation marks, "giving birth alone and then dumping us on Cate. It's a gruesome story and upsetting, to say the least. 'Too twisted for color TV,' as they say in Texas. Come to think of it, it would be perfect for TV."

Mattie didn't have an answer. Arm in arm the two women walked back to Las Sombras. The afternoon cast long shadows on the mountain—the evergreens black, the aspen standing silently in the darkness like white skeletons. The house, however, was ablaze. The jack-o'-lanterns had been relit, including PZ's barfing pumpkin. Tiny white lights twinkled once again in the trees, a reappearance of the fairy visitors. As they approached, a large dog came bounding down from the front porch like something out of a horror flick." It made straight for Artemis, jumped up on her and started licking her face.

"Lightning! Get down! Where did you come from?" The front door opened and two more dogs leapt on her. "What in the world? Down, Moon Doggie. You too, Streak. Sit." The three dogs obeyed the command immediately. Lightning, however, just touched her butt to the ground, then leapt up in inexpressible joy at finding her mistress. "Sit and stay!" Lightning sat, but quivered under the strain. The three of them gazed at her with adoring attention.

"Surprise!" yelled PZ and Chrys, jumping out from the side of the house.

"I thought you two were at a hayride or dance or something. Mattie's supposed to pick you up later."

"We were," said Chrys. "But now we're here for your birthday party. Uncle At picked us up and we got to ride with the dogs."

Atticus came out the front door. He came down the steps. "Happy Birthday, Sis."

"You, too, you sneaky, lying scoundrel. It's probably closer to *your* birthday than mine. What are you doing with my dogs? You didn't put them in the back seat with the top down, did you?"

"They loved it. I had to bring them to the party. We can't celebrate without the nymphs."

"Another party," groaned Artemis. "You know how I feel about parties. The only thing worse than one party is two."

"Or more," said Atticus.

"It's only family," said Mattie.

"Were you in on this?" asked Artemis, turning to glare at her cousin.

"Of course. And you proposed a walk right on schedule. I didn't even have to think of a distraction. Obviously I did it with mind control."

"Obviously," said Artemis. "Just what I wanted for my birthday. A controlled mind."

"Come on! Come on!" said PZ, jumping up and down. "It's cold as a witch's tit out here. Let's go in."

"PZ!" said Chrys. "Witches' tits are not cold."

"As you both should well know," said Mattie. She grabbed her twins and wrapped her arms around them. They responded by hugging her fiercely and running for the door. Mattie turned to Artemis and Atticus, who both ducked out of her reach. "You two are emotionally retarded," said Mattie.

"Yes," they replied, in unison.

The warmth of the house was welcome after the chilly walk. Artemis and Mattie stripped themselves of coats, hats, and gloves, headed into the family room. Luna was putting together a salad on the kitchen counter.

"What's that delicious smell?" asked Artemis.

"Roast Beast Soup," announced PZ "My favorite."

"Mine, too," said Artemis. "With veggies?"

"Of course," said Cate. "What I used to call refrigerator soup."

"Refrigerator soup? Yuk! What's that?" asked PZ.

"Well, when your mother was a little girl she came home from school one day with a note from her teacher. The first grade class was putting together a cookbook. Each child was asked to name a favorite dish and Mattie told them that hers was 'refrigerator soup.' Her teacher was writing to request the recipe, which was her polite way of asking what in hell I'd been feeding the child. I had to admit that most Mondays I stood at the door of the refrigerator and scrounged around for leftovers to make soup."

"You were really a dork, Mom," said PZ. "Refrigerator soup!"

"Well, tonight, we have a veritable refrigerator harvest. I made soup from leftover prime rib and vegetables," said Luna. "I hope you're hungry, because there's lots of it."

Flora appeared from out of the pantry, carrying chips, pretzels, and the last pumpkin cheesecake. "Hey, Aunt A. Happy Birthday to you and Uncle At."

"Flora! It's really great that you're here. You had us scared to death last night! Are you out of the doghouse yet?" asked Artemis.

"Yeah, Mamacita let me out, but not for good behavior. I think she felt sorry for me when she saw my car."

"What!" said Mattie, Atticus and Artemis.

"Yeah, somebody vandalized my car last night. I guess that's what I get for leaving it behind the McDonald's on Halloween. Someone must have been really mad that they couldn't get a Big Mac."

"What did they do?" asked Atticus.

"Slashed all four tires. Broke the windows. Cut the upholstery and did something to the engine. Probably sugar in the gas tank. The Punkin is pretty much totaled. I loved that car." Flora's face was distorted with pain. "The insurance won't help much. I'll never find another Punkin, and all my savings will have to go toward another car. If I get a scholarship to college, I can go, but I won't be able to eat while I'm there."

Artemis, Atticus and Mattie stared at each other.

"What did you say about a pumpkin?" asked Mattie.

"Not pumpkin. Punkin. P U N K I N. That's what *mi padre* used to call me when I was a little girl. That's what I named my car, because it's my orange carriage. The worst part is that I never got to wear my Cinderella costume and arrive in a punkin."

"Did you have any white mice?" asked PZ. "Lizards?"

"No," said Flora. "I don't think it's a very good idea to leave mice in the car."

"I could have kept them for you," he said. "I like mice. Lizards, too. "

"You kids set the table," said Luna. "And go get the cakes out of the shed."

"Why the shed?" said Chrys.

"I hid them there yesterday before the big twins got here. Kept Artemis and Atticus from finding them and you two from eating them." She smiled at Chrys and gave her a wink.

"PZ might have, but you know I wouldn't," said Chrys.

"No, you would have decorated them," said her brother. "Put leaves and lights on them."

"Hush," said Flora. "Let's go. Then you two can help me set the table."

The young people went out, the girls going first, and PZ exiting behind with his usual slam.

"Luna! What do you think about all this?" said Mattie.

"I told your Mother this morning. I'm so relieved that the car was all that got butchered. I knew something was threatening my Flora last night. The cards never lie. It was divine intervention that sent her to the hospital with Rosa." Luna chopped a red bell pepper into a wet confetti. "You should see the car. It didn't look like vandalism to me. It was hatred."

"Cate, why didn't you tell us?" asked Artemis.

"Well, you were asleep when Luna called, and I really didn't want to ruin the birthday. I just want us to have a good time together. I figured we could talk about it tonight, afterwards. Besides, I don't want to discuss it around the kids. Particularly around Flora."

"Well, I know why we kept getting pumpkin images last night," said Artemis.

"That's a leap of logic. There are pumpkins everywhere, all over the house, by the side of the road, in the cheesecake," said Atticus.

"Riiiiiight," said Mattie and Artemis.

"You're being a contrarian," added his sister. "Yeah, the symbol *could* have referred to any of those things. However, it is fairly certain that it was referring to Flora and her car."

"It is not. That's my point. This stuff is *never* certain. Which is why it is useless. Besides, hindsight is twenty-twenty. What good is it if you don't understand until afterward?" Atticus folded his arms, leaned back in his chair.

"That's only one piece of the puzzle," said Cate. "Of course you're right, Atticus. Such information is not very helpful if we can only understand it after the fact. However, we've all been receiving information. There's more going on than just a prank. I think we need to work on it. We're not through yet."

Mattie stormed around the kitchen, her eyes flashing. "I'm sure as hell not through. Listen, somebody attacked her car, and might have intended to attack *her*. I'll be surprised if this isn't the work of the Whites. They seem to have a particular animosity for beautiful, young Mexican women. I intend to find out who did this and fry them for it."

"Ah, Mattie. Often wrong, but never in doubt," said Atticus.

The door flew open. PZ whirled in, followed by Chrys, holding a chocolate cake, and Flora, carrying a caramel one. "Ta Da!!"

The grown-ups clamped their lips together, stopping their discussion in midstream.

"What?" said Chrys, stopping short. "What's going on? It feels all yicky in here."

"Nothing, my dear," said Luna. "Just set them down. We'll light the candles after dinner."

"You know," said PZ. "Chrys and I *hate* sharing a cake. We always get two, so we figured you guys should get two,...too."

"And there will be more left over that way," said Artemis.

"That too," said PZ.

"Just what you need," said Mattie. "A double dose of sugar."

"Yep," replied the boy, licking the finger he dipped in both chocolate and caramel icing.

"Mom," said Chrys. "You changed the subject. Why is everybody so uptight in here? Did we do something?"

"No, honey," said her mother. "We're just upset about Flora's car. But we'll find out who did it. Let's eat soup."

"Okay. And open presents," said Chrys.

The group coalesced to get dinner on the table. As if by magic, the table was set, the bowls were filled with the steaming soup, and a pile of packages materialized on an extra chair. The atmosphere of tension gradually melted into familial warmth. PZ downed two bowls of soup, two helpings of salad and four pieces of cornbread in the time that everyone else ate one of each. Chrys lit the candles and PZ helped blow them out. He cut the cakes into huge slices and Chrys dispensed them.

"Any ice cream?" asked PZ. On a dinner size plate, he had a slice of each cake.

"Forget it. Artemis polished it off for breakfast," his mother said. "Tomorrow is the return of Mother Rule. Your sugar intake is about to take a sharp downturn."

"All the more reason for ice cream tonight," he replied. His mother just stared at him until he looked down at his plate and began to eat what he had.

"Open your presents," said Chrys. "These are from PZ and me. Actually, I ordered them online. I used Mom's credit card to pay for them, but I wrapped them when they got here. Now PZ thinks he should get half the credit."

"It doesn't cost a thing to share credit and there's plenty to go around," said Cate.

Artemis had a book on Celtic mythology. Atticus had one on quantum physics. Both were delighted. There were many packages holding more books, leather gloves, new briefcases for both, and various cold weather gear. Mattie reached under the table for a brown manila envelope, which she handed to Artemis.

"What's this?" said Artemis.

"Just something to remind you of our mission."

"Our mission? Should I choose to accept it?" Artemis wrinkled her brow at Mattie, as she opened the metal clasp. She pulled out a stack of bumper stickers. She laughed as she read the message printed in gold medieval lettering, "To Reclaim That Which Has Been Lost."

Atticus groaned. Mattie and Cate applauded. The others blinked in confusion.

"I don't get it," said Flora. "What's been lost?"

"When Artemis was writing her dissertation, we would sit at this table for hours, listening to her tell us about her research," said Cate. "It was so interesting that sometimes we'd be here until dawn. She was especially incensed by the misogyny she unearthed."

"Who's Ms. Ogeny?" asked PZ.

"Shut up, dufus," said Chrys. "Nobody you'll ever know."

"Artemis wasn't the only one that got on her broom about what she was studying," said Mattie. "I was in law school. That's when I decided to become an advocate for women's legal rights."

"Artemis feels that in our culture, certain aspects of the human psyche have come to be considered inappropriate or evil. That judgment is often projected on to women. Am I being accurate here?" said Cate.

"Yes, if somewhat simplistic," said Artemis. "An individual may decide that parts of himself, or herself, are unacceptable. It may be something like sexual urges or the desire to have one's own way. Instead of accepting these aspects of ourselves, we have often branded them as being evil. Some people spend the rest of their lives repressing those desires.

Artificial snoring sounds came from PZ.

"These aspects of ourselves fail to mature and often become pathological," Artemis continued, ignoring her nephew. "This is a kind of self-mutilation, often supported by the values of the family or a society. A therapist works with a client to help reclaim those aspects of self that have been rejected, to heal and incorporate them in a mature, healthy way. No part of ourselves is inherently good or evil, but human abilities may be used in a myriad of ways, some of them being truly wicked and some being extremely benevolent. Mostly, our actions are somewhere in the middle on the scale of good and bad."

"So, I'm not ever bad," said PZ. "Just immature."

"I think," said Chrys, "that you are actually both. She said that you weren't 'inherently evil.' She didn't say you never pull it off."

"Ignore them," said Mattie. "Finish telling Flora."

"Well, culturally, the same thing happens. For political and economic reasons, certain human behaviors are valued and others are deemed unacceptable. In a patriarchal society, for example, it is politically expedient to devalue the power of women, to claim that women and children are the property of the father figure. The ability of the female to reproduce is a threat to the idea of a male creator. Consequently, feminine sexuality is portrayed as dirty or evil. To take another example, Christianity was accepted by the Romans for political, not religious reasons. Their emphasis on one god, their insistence on the construction of churches, the sacraments of marriage and baptism and the threat of excommunication, all made it much easier to govern and tax people. Patriarchy is always about control."

"Is that what you do, Aunt A? Are you trying to be a therapist to a culture? That's sounds impossible," said Chrys.

"I suppose you could look at it that way, Chrys. A cultural mythologist listens to what's going on in much the same way that a therapist listens to an analysand."

"What do you hear?" asked PZ.

Artemis laughed. "The same things you hear. What people say. What we buy and what we believe. I pay close attention to the kinds of advertising that is dominating the airwaves, to the movies and television shows that are popular. Then I try to see beyond the surface and figure out what beliefs are behind them."

"Shrink to the world," said Atticus. "How unassuming of you."

"Shut up, Atticus," said Mattie. "If you close your mouth, something might get in through your ears. What *you* might be able to reclaim is genuine intelligence instead of the artificial kind you worship."

Artemis, ignoring this sibling sparring, continued. "We have become addicted to the idea that there is one true perspective and the others are all false. This makes for great discord. One economist may say that 'What's good for business is good for America.' The ecologist may hold an opposite opinion. 'Anything that's good for business is bad for the world.' Both assertions are false. Both economic and ecologic concerns have varying effects on our world, some more positive than others, some more detrimental than others. It would be much simpler if we could classify things as good and bad, but it is fallacious thinking."

"Phallicious thinking," said PZ. "Hmmm."

"Then why do people want to think that way?" asked Flora.

"Two reasons that I can think of right now. One, it's easier. The other is that we all like to believe we are right about things. It's a part of human nature to want to see ourselves as good, better, best. It takes maturity and self-discipline to understand the limitations of being human," said Artemis.

"That's what's called a 'beginner's mind.' Beginners don't think they know everything already. Beginners don't spend all their energy on being right. They are trying to learn something," said Cate.

"So, what has been lost, exactly? And who lost it?" Chrys leaned forward in her chair, her chin in her hands.

"Well, what Mattie is referring to is the feminine perspective. In a society that persists in thinking in dualities, then the perspective of one sex must be favored over the other. In a patriarchy, which all monotheistic societies are, it has to be the male perspective. Do you see what this does to the feminine perspective?"

"Yeah!" said Flora

"It makes us wrong," said Chrys.

"What has been lost," said Mattie, "is the ability to value feminine perspectives as equally insightful. Artemis and I think this is worth reclaiming."

"However," said Artemis. "It isn't exactly accurate to say that we have lost anything. In our drive to reduce everything to a set of opposites, we have ignored our ability to transcend dualism, to be pluralistic, to consider many facets of truth simultaneously. It's difficult for us to hold the opposites without valencing them, to appreciate that while things may appear to be contradictory, they in fact, are just different perceptions of reality. Do you know the story of the blind men and the elephant?"

"Yes," said PZ, Chrys, Mattie and Atticus, with an emphasis that discouraged retelling of the story.

"No," said Flora.

"Then those of you who have heard it will, of course, want to hear it again. The possibility exists that you may be further enlightened."

They groaned.

"Once upon a time there was a group of blind men who went to the zoo. They wanted very much to know what an elephant was like, so they convinced the keeper to allow them into the cage. The first man grabbed hold of the elephants tail. 'An elephant is like a snake,' he said. 'Hairless, long and thin.' 'Ah, my friend. You are so wrong,' said his friend, who had his hands on the elephant's leg. 'Not thin at all, but thick like a tree trunk.' And so this went, with one man describing the tusks, another the ears, a third the slablike sides. There was much arguing, for each was convinced that he was absolutely right. There was no doubting the truth of his experience. Finally, one wise man said, 'What if none of us is wrong and all of us are right?' It is from that observation that the blind men came to understand. While their perceptions were true and were truly reported, their collective observations were more accurate. Insistence that your perception is the only right and true one is a sure fire way to be blind to a greater understanding. Furthermore, we can never, any of us, know completely. Not an elephant, nor the universe, nor the nature of reality."

"You gave her the abbreviated version," said Atticus.

"I had to. I was under a lot of pressure from my critics," replied Artemis. "When a culture, a nation, a religion, or a person, insists that there is only one way to see things, only one true god or one right way to govern, only one truth, then that narrow-mindedness is crippling. It limits the possibilities. What we have lost, I believe, is what the blind men learned. Each one of us perceives differently. It is important that we honor those differences rather than go to war over them."

"Is that why dumbass Robbie Barswell says we are 'pagan babies' and that we're all going to hell?" asked PZ.

"Talking to Robbie Barswell is my idea of going to hell," said Chrys.

"It depends on what you mean. Unacquainted as I am with Robbie Barswell, I suspect that he is a devotee of the one god, one truth school of thought," said Artemis. "Our 'religion,' if we could call it that, finds divinity in all of creation. You could call it a kind of polytheism, or you could call it monotheism, in the sense that we believe that all is one. I personally think that every religion is a collective set of observations, an accumulation of stories told by blind men and women. That doesn't mean that all of these perspectives are equally useful. Some poor souls are more challenged than others."

"Take Robbie Barswell, for example," said Chrys.

"Or the Whites, for another," added her mother.

"And that, little Flora, is the gospel according to Artemis," said Atticus.

"And a fine one it is," said Cate. "One I embrace with enthusiasm."

"Which means you may have one of my bumper stickers for your car," said Artemis. "Would anyone else like one?"

"I would," said Flora. "In case I ever get another car."

Artemis passed them out, but Atticus held up his hand to stop her putting one at his place. "I am not putting a bumper sticker on my Porsche."

"Fine, brother. If you don't want this one, I have another one I'll put on when you're not looking."

"And what would that be?"

" 'My other car is a broom.' "

CHAPTER 14

Buzz
November 2

    Buzz was spraying silicone on the last row of tires. He liked them to gleam—not a speck of dust on them. He wiped them down and admired the shine. Already this morning, he had straightened the cardboard signs, cleaned the windows, swept and dusted. He always did the tires last, in case any dust got stirred up during his cleaning. Tires are our bread and butter, he would say to himself.

    When she drove in, he shoved his dust cloth under the counter. He thought for a minute he was dreaming, as he watched a pair of long stockinged legs in black high heels came sliding out of a big silver Audi. He felt like he was watching a goddess emerge from the sea. The sun was behind her, nearly blinding him when he stared, but he could appreciate her long, lean silhouette. She put on the jacket to her black suit, strode across the parking lot, and opened the glass door. A little chime announced her presence. Behind the cash register, he was frozen. When she took off her dark glasses, she stared right into his eyes. He had a hard time getting his breath.

"Yes, ma'am," he stammered. "Can I help you?"

"You certainly can," said Artemis, giving him a warm smile. "And I would really appreciate it if you would. I want to buy some tires."

"You have come to the right place," he said, knowing at the time that it was a silly thing to say.

"So I see."

"Just pull around to the bay and . . ."

"They're not for me," she said. "They're for a friend of mine who had her tires slashed. They had to tow her car. I don't really know what size tires she needs, but maybe you could go over there and see."

"Well, ma'am. I'm the only person here today. I don't see as how I could leave."

Artemis moved closer, leaned on the glass counter and rested her elbow on the top, her chin in her hand. Her grey eyes were boring into his. "What's your name?"

"Buzz," he said.

"Well, Buzz. The car is at the Exxon station, just across the street. Maybe I could stay here and watch things for the five minutes it would take you."

He couldn't bear the intensity of her look. At the same time, he couldn't bear to break the eye contact. "No, ma'am. I couldn't do that, but I tell you what. We work with them all the time. I'll just give ole Jake a call and see what he says. He can tell me right off what he needs."

"That would be fine," she said, backing off and giving him a bit more space. "I appreciate it."

He dialed the number from memory, thinking that somehow that might impress her. "Jake, I got a lady here says she wants to buy tires for a car that had all four slashed last night. Do you know which one I'm talking about?" He hoped she didn't hear Jake's reply, because he called him an idjit and said of course he knew. He didn't have more than one car in the shop with four cut up tires. "Well, then that's fine," Buzz said. "Can you tell me what kind she needs?"

When he hung up, he clicked his pen and nodded at Artemis. "I got them in stock. Jake said he'd put them on for you while he was doing all the rest of the work you ordered. I'll run them over there as soon as my business associate comes back from his appointment." He thought that sounded better than saying he would have to wait until Buddy got back from the dentist.

"You do mean today, don't you?" said Artemis.

"Yes, ma'am. In about an hour or so."

"That's fine," she said, handing him a credit card.

"I'll need your name, address and tele-phone number," he said.

"Why?"

"Company policy," he said.

She complied, although a little voice in her head suggested that it wasn't a good idea. "Thanks," she said, putting back on her glasses and turning to leave.

Buzz snatched up a tire gauge and ran after her. "Ma'am?" he called.

"Yes, Buzz?" she said, a bit startled as he caught up with her.

"You are entitled to a free pressure check with that purchase."

"Well, when Jake gets them on, you can go over there and check them."

"I meant your own tires, ma'am."

"I think they're fine," she said.

"Well, better safe than sorry," he said. "It won't take but just a minute and it might save you being stranded on the highway. A beautiful woman such as yourself, it wouldn't be good at all for you to be stranded with a flat tire." He rolled up his sleeves, flexing his biceps as though the operation of a tire gauge required considerable physical strength. He sprinted out to her car and applied himself to the task. The three dogs scrambled for a view of him, but refrained from barking.

"You're very muscular," she said.

"I work out every day, "he said. "In a line of work such as my own, sometimes you have to have a lot of muscle power."

She smiled at him, and nodded. That was when he saw it. He had just finished with the right rear tire, when he looked at her bumper. There, in gold lettering on a white background, were the words, "To Reclaim That Which Has Been Lost." He caught his breath and stood up. He stared at her. Surely this meant she was one of them. He wished he had his ring on so he could flash it at her. She would know what it meant, he was sure. This was the kind of woman he had been dreaming about. God was finally answering his prayers.

"What else can I help you with?"

"If everything's all right, Buzz, I've got to be going. Thanks for your help." She opened the door, sat down and pulled those legs in after her.

He tried to think of something to say, but his imagination failed him. "Wait," he said, but she only waved and backed out of her parking space. He considered running after her, but thought it might make him look foolish.

"Good girls," she said to the dogs. "Now lie down in the back seat and stay quiet." Artemis dialed her cell phone. "Hey, Mattie. Well, it's not as bad as she thought. There's no sugar in the gas tank. They're going to put new tires on and check it over. He says he can get the glass repaired too. I don't know about the upholstery. I haven't gotten that far." She listened for a moment. "Well, at least it will be drivable and Flora's college fund doesn't have to go for a new one. I'll let you know what your share of all this is. We'll stick Atticus with some of it too."

She merged on to the interstate and started the steep descent down to Denver. The road was packed and she needed to pay careful attention to the reckless drivers weaving in and out between cars. "I'm going to take the nymphs home and do a few things this morning. Stop by around noon. We'll grab lunch and drive up and see this ranch. The more I think about it, the better I like the idea. I'll see you then, Cuz."

CHAPTER 15

Hank
November 2

Sunlight turned the dusty window shades a golden orange. A brilliant light cut through the small cracks in the paper. The room was as dark as the deteriorating shades could manage with the midmorning daylight beating down on them. The walls had once been papered with stripes of rosebuds and filigreed bands, but the white background had turned to a parchment color and there were holes where the gauzy backing showed through. On one wall, coffee-colored stains blossomed, evidence of a roof leak. An incongruous cork dartboard hung on the far wall with hundreds of pinholes in the surrounding wallpaper attesting to misses. The sagging old Sears Roebuck bed was unmade, a dirty yellow chenille bedspread dragging on the floor. Above the headboard hung a black velvet painting, a lurid image of a naked woman with brown-skin. She was thrusting her breasts forward by way of erotic invitation, her hands on her buttocks. Hank lay on grimy sheets, a beer bottle sitting on his chest, his dirty socks propped on the wall, head resting on a wadded pillow jammed against the footboard. He stared at the image, simultaneously aroused and infuriated.

Damn picture. He didn't know why he kept it. He ought to burn it. He fumed when he remembered. She had called him redneck scum. He would never have to worry, she had said, about any Latina messing with him. He was so ugly she'd rather fuck a pig. Then she said something in Spanish. Ace wouldn't translate, but it had made him laugh so hard he damn near bust a gut.

Hank didn't give a crap what Whitey said. The only thing those Meskin whores understand is a fist and a boot. That time in Matamoros, when that whore had said something about him in Spanish and then laughed.

Well, he'd taught her to laugh at him. Every time she looked in the mirror, she would remember what it had cost her to disrespect a white man.

CHAPTER 16

Artemis and Mattie
November 2

The road went on and on, twisting and twisting again. Afternoon light twinkled through the pines as Artemis took the curves with a lot more speed than the law allows.

"If you don't want recycled enchiladas on your upholstery, you'll slow down."

When Artemis looked over at her, Mattie's face did have that pre-vomit ashen color, so she shifted down and her speed dropped by about five miles an hour or so.

"The deer aren't out yet," said Artemis. "You have to be really careful in the morning and at twilight. The elk, too. They'll just step out in front of the car."

"Bizarre as this may seem," said Mattie, "I thought you might slow down because you're making me carsick. Why don't you do it for the squirrels? I really don't care, as long as you stop taking the curves on two wheels."

"Okay, okay. It's just that I love my car. It handles like a dream. You should feel it on ice and snow. It hugs the road. Amazing."

She let up on the accelerator and slowed to the legal limit. Mattie unscrewed the plastic lid from a bottle of water and took a long swig. She closed her eyes for a moment, took a deep breath and the color returned to her face.

"It's around here somewhere. Slow down," said Mattie.

"I'm already letting the tortoise win. If you don't want to miss it, then it's a good plan to keep your eyes open."

They rounded a curve and Mattie pointed to an inconspicuous dirt road consisting of two deep ruts with a weedy streak down the middle.

"Are you sure? It looks like an old logging road or something. Too humble for such an inflated group."

"Just wait. This insignificant little dirt road is part of their security. You have to know where to look in order to find it."

"How elitist."

"That's putting it mildly," said Mattie.

Artemis winced as the bottom of her car scraped. "If I'm going to drive this road every day, some modifications will be required. How long is this crappy ass thing?"

"Long."

Artemis frowned. The canopy of trees grew progressively denser and the light dimmer. They drove for ten minutes or so, inching along to protect the car from the large rocks in the roadbed. An occasional shaft of sunlight pierced the shadows. When a black squirrel darted across the road, Artemis managed to avoid him by coming down hard on the brake.

"I think I'd have to buy a Hummer, Cuz. How much longer are we going to do the 'Westward Ho' thing?" Artemis said.

"Who you calling a Ho, girl?"

"Funny. I'm turning around the first chance I get."

Mattie gave her an 'I know something you don't' smile. The road took a sharp turn to the right and they popped out of the trees. A wide meadow opened up before them and the road became a two-lane asphalt drive. A hundred yards ahead, two stone pillars flanked a pair of ornate silver gates. Glittering on each gate was the ranch's brand, a running W. On either side of the pillars was a twelve-foot high cyclone fence, stretching across the meadow and disappearing into the woods. At the top of the fence, electrified razor wire acted as a deterrent to intruding climbers.

"Great Goddess!" said Artemis.

"This is as far as I've ever come. The fence surrounds the whole property. I'm told that the main house is about a half mile ahead."

Artemis dropped her jaw in a display of amazement. Mattie jumped out and punched a series of numbers into a keypad. The gates slowly rolled aside. Mattie got back in and turned to grin at her cousin.

The drive was lined with big boulders, stretches of rock retaining walls, landscaped areas of trees and shrubbery. Artemis wondered what it would look like in the summer with the wildflowers blooming. At the crest of the hill, they could see the house in the distance, a large contemporary, made of Arizona sandstone stacked in precise layers, framed with pines, and sitting atop a ledge of rock. A river ran near the house and disappeared into the forest. The elevation afforded them a broad panoramic view. In the distance was a big parking lot, a picnic area with tables in rows that looked like it would seat a hundred. A huge stone barbecue stood beside it, large enough to cook a side of beef. There were several outbuildings in the distance, their function indeterminate. Near the house there were a couple more structures. One undoubtedly a garage, but the other, a small stone building with a tin roof, was a mystery.

"The house is incredible," said Artemis. "I was expecting some kind of atrocious architecture, but it's really great. How big is it? It looks huge."

"I don't know. I've never been in it. I've seen aerial photographs, but that's it. I would say that there's plenty of room for you and your girls."

"Yeah, I'd say so."

They parked in front of the house and walked up a long stone walk with an occasional riser. A pair of gates, smaller versions of the ones at the entrance, blocked the entrance to a courtyard. An identical keypad on the wall lit up when Mattie touched it. Once again she knew the secret code and the gates rolled back to admit them. The plantings were all dead. The fountain was dry. A bizarre life size bronze statue of several figures stood just inside the gates. A man, dressed in turn-of-the-century clothing, had both his arms raised to the sky, his hands clutching a Cross and One. On his face was an expression of exaltation. Kneeling on the ground beside him was a woman and three children, their heads bowed and eyes closed.

"That gives me the screaming mee-mies," said Artemis. "Sort of tests my philosophy of honoring all points of view."

"I suspect that what we have here is a statue of Granddaddy Elwood J. White, original owner of the land and Hater Baby extraordinaire. Grand Whajamajig of the Royal Order of Assholes."

"Well, what am I supposed to do with it?"

Mattie shrugged and pointed to a mat the size of a twin bed, sitting in front of the double front doors. "What about these Ws scrawled all over everything? What will you do about that?"

"W can stand for witchcraft, just as well as it stands for White."

"True, true, Cuz."

Mattie pulled out a key from her pocket and they pushed open the doors. The ceiling in the foyer ascended twenty feet. The floors were white limestone, polished to a soft sheen, but cold as gravestones in the unheated house. Mattie felt the walls until she found a bank of switches. When she flipped the switches, an obscene tangle of antlers hanging from the ceiling sprang to light.

"Got to go," said Artemis, pointing upward to the fixture.

"First thing," replied Mattie.

They wandered around the front rooms of the house. Most of the furniture had been removed, but enough of the decorating remained to leave a lingering flavor. There were framed barbed wire collections, lariats and whips hanging on hooks, and a half dozen glass-eyed animal heads. In the living room a massive Cross and One hung in front of a stone fireplace that rose to the ceiling.

They found five bedrooms with connecting baths. A library with empty shelving didn't appear to have ever held books. The kitchen gleamed with stainless steel appliances—a Vulcan stove, double ovens, a pair of dishwashers and a wide refrigerator with the doors standing open. The kitchen had been designed to cook for crowds.

Artemis couldn't imagine living in this huge house, with its history of hatred, its massive masculinity, its reek of testosterone. She walked down a wide corridor, feeling the chill of the stone penetrate her feet and enter her heart. She opened the last door in the corridor and stepped into what might have been an office. The late afternoon sun was streaming through a wall of glass that faced the mountains, dusty with snow. The floors, the baseboards and doors were a warm, rich cherry wood. It was an empty room, but in her mind's eye she saw her desk facing the view. She imagined a pair of big armchairs sitting in front of the fireplace, holding her snoozing greyhounds. She pushed opened the double French doors and the sound of rushing water filled the room. A broad deck overlooked an oxbow in the stream, reflecting the November sky. A silver omega.

"A?" Mattie's auburn curls appeared around the doorframe and she stepped out into the sunshine.

"Yeah?"

"What do you think?"

"I think we should all live here. You and the kids and I."

Mattie joined her cousin at the railing. She stared, first at the view and then at Artemis, whose eyes never left the water.

"Artemis," she said. "You're practically a hermit and my kids aren't exactly unobtrusive. You can't just tell them to sit."

"It would mean your kids could stay in school up here. Not have to go back to Denver."

"It would mean my commute gets a lot longer."

Artemis shrugged. "Mine too. So, we'll work on our Spanish or listen to all of Proust on CDs."

"The collected works of Carl Jung," said Mattie.

"You like him better than I do."

"You know more about him than I do. Do you suppose that the collected works are really on CDs?"

"I hope not."

They stood side by side, watching the mountains turn indigo. Silently they admired the view, the smell, the magnificence of the moment.

"I want *this* room. All to myself. Off limits to the twerps and their friends. Admission by invitation only," said Artemis.

"Okay. There's probably some security gizmo already rigged to vaporize anyone who trespasses. What do you suppose this room was for?"

"I don't want to know. Now, it's for me to write in and think in and just be in."

"Okay," said Mattie. "That's what it's for. Besides, there are more than enough bedrooms. Lots of room for animals. Enough of everything for privacy, but I can't make any promises about the twins."

"Close to Cate, but not too close." Artemis's eyes crinkled when she smiled at Mattie.

"PZ and Chrys can visit Las Sombras, but Cate gets her life back. It would make my kids happy and I think it'll make me happy too."

"Are we getting ahead of ourselves?" asked Artemis. She wrapped her arms around herself and shivered.

"Let's see the rest of it."

The pool was a dark charcoal colored material. Empty now, but it would be spectacular when full of water. Mattie found a switch for the concealed lighting that ran along the edges and illuminated the semicircle of steps at the shallow end. In the corner was a hot tub of the same material. The area was enclosed on three sides with waist high planters of stone. Great urns, in sets of three sizes, were grouped in the corners.

"This is perfect for star-gazing," said Mattie, lying on a bench, looking up into the sky. She watched dark clouds on the horizon that seemed to foretell precipitation. The rock slabs chilled her back and she sat up with a shiver. "Or weenie roasting," she said.

"Somemore squishing," said Artemis. "Atticus could sit out here and pontificate to his heart's content."

"Do you suppose Atticus could ever have a contented heart?" Mattie tilted her head and smiled doubtfully.

"Not really," said Artemis. "But I can practically see his face in the firelight, enraptured with his own discourse."

"The rest of us snoozing."

"There's even a guest room for him." Artemis walked around the pit, looking into the charred circle.

"Or anyone else we want to invite."

The two walked the perimeter of the house, peering in windows, tugging at outside doors. They were all locked with two or three bolts. They returned to the front door and sat side by side on a step.

Artemis's brow was furrowed. She frowned. "What does she want for it, Mattie?"

"I don't know. She's never laid eyes on it and never wants to. I'll need to get it appraised. It would have to be a fair offer."

"Do you think we could swing it together?"

"Maybe. Let's find out. Like I said, we may want to sell off some of the land."

"What are those other buildings we saw?"

Mattie wrinkled her brow in thought. "I had a list, but it's in a file back at the office. There's a chapel slash meeting hall. There's a big garage, for trucks and farm equipment, I suppose. A dormitory that sleeps fifty or more. At one time their membership was quite large. There are several other structures, but that's all I remember."

Artemis shivered. "We would have some serious purification rituals to perform. I don't even want to think about what's gone on here."

"Do you want to see the rest of it?"

"No, I'm overwhelmed already. Let's find out what it would take to buy it from Maria before I get any more emotionally involved." Artemis stuck her hands in the pockets of her jacket and started back for the car. She withdrew into thought, wondering how she could possibly be drawn to a piece of land with such a history. For over a century this soil had sustained those who stood for all she found evil. She wondered if their words would echo in her head if she occupied the space. Would she hear them espousing a faith that branded women as wicked, that demonized their femininity and considered their sexual power to be filthy rather than divine?

Would her dreams be haunted by angry diatribes? Would her meditations be invaded by images of persecuted daughters and wives, of small boys molded into miniature replicas of their hate-mongering forefathers? How could she fall in love with a place where wickedness had seeped into the ground like blood on a battlefield? Then she heard it, as clearly as if it were spoken, but it wasn't. You have fallen in love, because only love can heal such hatred, said the silent voice that spoke inside her head and heart. You, it said, are here as a healer. In the process, you will be healed as well.

Mattie, oblivious to the torment going on in Artemis, busied herself in the ritual of departure. She fished the keys out of her pocket, turned the three locks, and tested the doors to make sure they were secure. At the keypad, she punched in the code and watched the pair of gates slide shut.

The air in the car was warm and stale. Artemis lowered the windows to let a fly out, which made Mattie's wild mane slap her face. Gathering her hair into one hand,

Mattie pressed her window's button. She turned her signature stare on her cousin, who ran the rest of them up and turned on the heating.

"I don't know what I expected," said Artemis. "But it wasn't this. Something with an *ominous air*—ugly, institutional, or military. Instead, it just feels vacant. Empty, in a clean sort of way, like the property itself is waiting for new owners."

"I think it's waiting for us."

"That's pretty scary." Artemis watched a rabbit scamper for a hole in the rock wall. "I found the omega that's been appearing in my dreams."

Mattie didn't answer. She watched the big gates move aside automatically. Driving through, Mattie turned around in her seat to watch them close. "Do you still have the feeling of danger?" she asked.

"Yes and no," said Artemis. "Somehow this property is tied into it. But I don't feel threatened or warned off. To the contrary, I'm attracted to it in a way that I've never been attracted to any place before. Well, I felt this way about the Grand Canyon, but I didn't want to take up residence."

"This reminds me of Cate's story of finding Las Sombras."

"It does, doesn't it? I guess I hope you're right, that it's just like that, and that we have found a home for the rest of our lives."

"Maybe we have, Cuz." Mattie leaned back in her seat and closed her eyes. "Maybe we have."

They carefully made their way back out and over the bumpy narrow road. Artemis steered around the rocks, mentally calculating what it would take to make the road Audi friendly.

Mattie looked over at her and said, "I think it's a good idea to leave the road unpaved. Very effective camouflage."

"From whom are we hiding? The Whites already know all about it. Besides, it gets my car dirty. Think how muddy it'll be in the spring."

"Why don't you get another car?"

"I like the car I have. We're paving the road."

"Okay. We'll pave the road."

The sun was moving down behind the horizon when A turned onto the highway. A doe and her two fawns leapt across the road. Artemis paused to let them pass in safety, and to admire their grace. Mattie played with the radio, finding a jazz station she liked. Artemis wrinkled her nose in distaste.

"Which bedroom do you want, Mattie?" Artemis turned down the volume with a control on her steering wheel. "You can have first choice, because I'm taking that room with the fireplace and the view of the river."

"Okay. I'll take the one with the French doors that open on the pool. The bath has a steam room. If I get too hot, I can step out into the snow and cool off. Yum. That'll be wonderful after a day in court and a long drive home."

"Done. We don't want the kids to be able to sneak out anyway. I bet there's some kind of built in surveillance we can activate when they get to be teenagers."

"Which isn't far off," said Mattie.

"The antler chandelier goes."

"And all those stuffed heads."

"We'll have a burial ceremony for them," said Artemis.

"We'll put Chrys in charge. She'll have a blast. She can make up the ritual. Even invite friends, if she wants to."

"Good. Almost as much fun as barfing pumpkins." Artemis bugged her eyes and stuck her tongue out in imitation of PZ's creation.

"He'll probably form a rock group and name it that."

"With your luck, they'll become famous and you'll become the barfing Mama."

The rest of the way home they dreamed and schemed. Mattie speculated about logistics—selling her house, financing the purchase. Artemis imagined herself writing in front of her fireplace, surrounded by books, looking out on the mountains and the river. Mattie's voice receded in her consciousness with only snippets penetrating. She heard something about painting the walls taupe, and another mention of eggplant and green. Not quite an avocado (too Sixties or was it the Seventies?) but more the color of a Granny Smith apple. Maybe some red or a turquoise....

During Mattie's dialogue, A was transported. Her eyes were glued to the road, but her mind's eyes were admiring the mountain view from those windows. She imagined them dark purple on a fall day, the broad ochre meadow, the oxbow river a string of liquid silver. She imagined snow, first lightly capping the mountains, then covering them and the lands around. In the dead of winter the shadows would be dark blue, the snow a sparkling white and the river frozen over. The thaw would come, filling the stream to capacity, carrying frigid water down from the mountains. Then summer, when the meadow would be a field of wildflowers on a carpet of greens—yellow green, blue green, grey green. Back to autumn with glowing golden aspen leaves fluttering on white branches. The year would begin again with the mysteries of Samhain and the nip of November promising another winter of white glory. Through it all, through each and every season, the wandering, singing stream would make its distinctive horseshoe shape, a lively, rippling flow right outside her window.

Artemis snapped her head around at Mattie. "Silver Bow."

"Silver?" said Mattie. "Well, that's an idea. I hadn't thought about silver. It would make a nice accent. You mean, like Mexican Silver, or aluminum? I'm starting to sound like Cate. She's so much better at all this than I am. Chrys will have some great ideas, I'm sure."

"We'll call it The Silver Bow." Artemis gripped the wheel with determination. "We're sure as hell not going to call it Whitewater Ranch."

"The Silver Bow." Mattie arched her back against the seat, tilted her head and eyes upward in thought. She inhaled deeply, then let it out with a decisive puff. "I like it. Okay. But what do you think? Red or Turquoise?"

"For what?"

Mattie's rolling eyes were her answer.

CHAPTER 17

Whitey
Later that day

Whitey propped his cowboy boots up on the wagon wheel table and leaned back on a brown leather sofa that was way too large for the den in the tract house. Across the back of the sofa, branded into the cushions, was a string of running Ws. In the corner stood a wide screen television, the word MUTE in green letters at the bottom corner of the screen. A boy in an orange and white uniform sprinted across bright green grass marked with white stripes. He crossed the goal line two steps ahead of his pursuer and performed a jubilant victory dance before throwing the football to the ground.

Whitey took a swig of bourbon and water, staring at the screen vacantly. His mind was also in the big room with the view of the mountains and the bend in the river. Instead of dreaming of the future, however, his thoughts were in the past. He remembered himself sitting behind a big desk, pouring Jack Daniels into a heavy crystal glass with a stack of ice cubes that made a cracking sound when the liquid hit. The taste of the whiskey took him back, back to an autumn afternoon when everything had looked promising. There had been elk in the meadow and Hank had talked about the opening of hunting season. Ace had been leaning back in his chair, bragging about the boots he had just ordered in Santa Fe and how much it was going to cost him to have the Cross and One appliquéd into the leather. It was the first time Whitey had ever invited Buzz up to the house. He'd been to meetings at the chapel, but never before had he been included in the unwinding time that took place afterward. The boy had been so excited he'd nearly wet himself. He's a smart kid, thought Whitey. A hell of a lot smarter than those two halfwits, Hank and Ace. Buzz had designed the surveillance system and it was as sophisticated as anything the by God CIA could come up with. Buzz could work those sumbitch computers. He could find stuff, track down information. Buzz had created a website for the Whites and now their sacred message was available to the world. He could even tell Whitey how many people had been reading his inspirational essays online. Whitey couldn't imagine how in the world he did that, but he did. Yeah, Buzz was smart all right. Whitey just wished he wasn't such a suck-up.

They had smoked cigars. Not the kid, of course. He was into physical fitness and wouldn't touch tobacco or alcohol. Whitey could still remember how good those cigars had smelled and tasted. Cuban. Flown in on Worthington's private plane. He'd brought four boxes of Habana Monte Christo No. 4s and Whitey had put most of them in his humidor—temperature and moisture controlled. It had been a good day. He'd been particularly eloquent at the meeting that afternoon, discussing the divine order of things and God's plan for the purity of the races. He'd told the story of Cain and Abel to a packed house, and of Eve's violation of God's law.

Eve was the source of Evil. Yep, it had been a good day, all right, and the fellowship of the men in his den had been warm and friendly. They watched the sunset and made plans for a big rally the next weekend. The bourbon flowed like the creek before them and the air was hazy with blue smoke that matched the mountains in the distance. Hank and Ace reported on their surveillance of John Kincaid's wife and when they had turned on the television, by God, there the woman was, big as a watermelon, on the evening news. She was all weepy over her husband and how she wished he could be there for the birth of her mud baby. She knew it was going to be a boy, she told the reporter. She was going to name him Juan, after her husband John. Jesus, but Hank had gotten mad. Ever since he'd gotten into it with that whore in Matamoros, he had a thing about Mexican women. Whitey tried to tell the boy to control himself, but there was no reasoning with Hank when he was drinking.

Whitey reached for his glass, rattling the ice cubes in frustration. He poured another slug. He had loved that room. When he built the house, he planned it first. He put his Daddy's big old desk in it, and his Granddaddy's gun case. His two golden retrievers, Zachariah and Micah, always slept on the floor beside him while he wrote his messages. Whitey downed the drink and slammed the glass down on the tabletop. For all he knew, that Meskin whore was sitting in his office right now, watching *his* river roll by in front of *his* mountains, while he sat here in this ticky tacky tract house on a pissant quarter acre of land with Micah and Zach pacing the cyclone fence outside. Well, he thought, if she's sitting in *my* house, breathing *my* air, she's doing it without her precious Juanito, by God. She won't be there for long. He reached for the portable phone and punched in a number.

"What you doing, boy?" He waited for the answer. His eyes glittered with that kind of dim-witted fanaticism that accompanies the combination of alcohol and anger. "Listen to me. You and some of the boys work out a schedule. I want you to start watching the entrance to the ranch." He listened with impatience. "Twenty-four, seven, that's what....Don't you think I know that, you peckerhead? I said *watch.* We don't need any more interaction with the police. Don't go on the property. You hear me, boy?" He clicked the phone off and dropped it on the table with a clunk.

CHAPTER 18

Flora
November 3

"So, I like, totally freaked when he told me we were going to a topless bar." Sharon rocked back and forth on her heels, waiting for a customer to walk into McDonald's. Beside her, Flora was refilling the straw and napkin dispensers.

"Omygod, so, like, what did you say?"

"I said, 'Like, I don't think I'm going, Dude. I won't even go to Hooters. I'm like the world's biggest feminist.' And he just sat there, staring at me like I was, you know, nuts."

"Well, I can't believe he...."

"Wait, wait. So, he goes, 'What!?' And I go, 'What *what*? I'm not going to a topless bar, not even with you.' And he goes, 'Topless? I said tapas bar. You know, like, food.'"

"Oh My God. Did you just die?"

"No. I said, like, 'You should speak more clearly, Dude. You almost lost me there.'"

"You are so cool, girl."

The two girls were waiting for the afternoon rush. Sharon, a friend of Flora's, was filling in for the recovering Rosa. Both of them were allowed to leave school fifteen minutes early to go to work. They barely had time to put on their uniforms and stow their book bags before a horde of hungry kids came pouring in, demanding burgers, fries and shakes.

The afternoon was warm for early November. A white pickup on oversized tires careened off the highway and screeched to a stop in front of the MacDonald's. Flames adorned the doors and the sides of the bed, but some sort of symbol on the hood had been spray-painted out. The back windshield had the usual small boy pissing in the lower corner, and "Social Misfit" in big letters scrawled across the glass. Four boys in their late teens got out and swaggered toward the door. Three of them wore muscle shirts, leather pants and motorcycle boots. The third wore an identical outfit, but he also had on a black leather jacket. Flora noticed that he seemed to be sweating profusely and she wondered if he was so proud of the coat that he refused to take it off. He and one of the other boys commandeered a row of tables.

Two of them approached the counter to order. One wore a kerchief knotted around his shaved head. The safety pins in his ears, nose and lip made Flora wince with imagined pain. The other was devoid of piercings, but his forearms and neck were covered in blue, red and black markings. On his right bicep, a nicotine patch obscured a symbol etched into his skin. He stood, insolently scoping out the two girls. He shook a cigarette from a pack of Camels, lit it with a flick of his lighter and blew the smoke directly into Flora's face.

"There's no smoking in here," she said.

"Four number fours," he said. His eyes were flat. He took a deep drag and exhaled in her direction once again.

Sharon punched in their order without a word. Flora turned and filled a sack with burgers and fries. She stacked four cups and set the whole order on the counter.

"You didn't ask us if it was 'for here or to go'," he said, in a mocking tone.

Flora looked directly into his eyes, her gaze unwavering. "I made it to go. Wishful thinking, Butch," she said.

He rippled his pecs. "I bet it is," he said, with as much sexual innuendo as he could muster. He picked up the bag, ignoring the paper cups. He left his friend to pay.

"You *know* him?" whispered Sharon.

"He's in my homeroom," said Flora. "Not that he bothers to attend that often."

The boys shoved four tables together and sprawled out, propping their feet in chairs, dropping cigarette ashes on the floor. The one with the kerchief went out to the truck and returned with a six-pack of beer, which he plopped down in the middle of one of the tables.

"When does the manager get back?" asked Flora, leaning close to Sharon.

"He said he had to pick up his dog at the vet," Sharon answered. "I'd guess it'll be at least a half hour."

"Can you handle this for a few minutes?"

Sharon looked at her with terror in her eyes. "Hell, no. I'm not doing a thing about it."

"Not those assholes. Just handle the customers. I won't be gone but a minute." Flora picked up her handbag on the way out the back door. She stood leaning against the brick wall, watching cars pull in. A group of teenagers got out of cars, chatting about homework and football. They entered the restaurant, then turned around and came out as quickly as they had gone in. Wheels screeched as they drove away.

Flora dialed the police. Patiently she told her story, but was put on hold. She had her back to the parking lot when Butch's tattooed hand reached around her to snatch the phone. She was too fast for him. She clicked the end button and stuck it in her pocket.

"What are you doing out here, Señorita Flora?" His voice was snide, his face too close to her own. "I don't think it's your break time. You shouldn't leave your friend all alone in there. We might need some *service.*"

Flora's eyes flashed anger but she controlled her tongue. She managed to sidestep him when he turned to watch a couple of SUVs pull into a nearby parking slot. They were driven by young mothers, their vans full of kids. The diversion gave Flora an opportunity to dart past him, through the back door. She turned the bolt.

Soon the tables were overflowing with grammar schoolers, slurping soft drinks and dipping fries into the catsup. The skinheads were drowned out by the happy noises of children released from an interminable day of geography, verb tenses, multiplication tables and the solar system. The youngest displayed manila paper with crayon drawings of turkeys made from their own handprints. The cigarettes and beers drew dirty looks from the mothers, aggravated but unwilling to take issue with the offenders. Butch swaggered in and took a seat giving Flora a smirk.

The parking lot continued to fill. The dining area seemed to explode with backpacks and notebooks, empty lunchboxes and dirty sneakers. Flora was efficiently sacking fries and burgers, when she heard a familiar voice.

"I'll have a double order of pumpkin cheesecake with a side of *dulce leche*."

"PZ!" said Flora, turning to give him a smile. "What's up? Hey, Chrys. If you two want that, you'll have to head back to Las Sombras. I'm afraid the cuisine at Casa de Mac won't live up to Cate's culinary standards."

"He thinks he's so funny," said Chrys, rolling her eyes.

"Sometimes he is," said Flora.

"This isn't one of them. Can we have two small cokes and two small fries?" Chrys held her money in her hand, counting carefully. "He doesn't have any of his allowance left, of course. So I have to pay for us both."

"You wouldn't want me to *perish*," he said.

"Only your thoughts," said Chrys.

"I'll pay you back."

"No, you won't. You never do."

"Okay," he said, grinning.

Flora filled their order and returned a few cents change. Chrys leaned forward and whispered. "You see that creep that just sat down with the skinheads? The one that thinks he looks like a boarder dude?"

Flora glanced over at a chubby boy of twelve or so who had pulled up a chair in a desperate attempt to look like he belonged with the skinheads. Butch gave him a punch to the arm, forceful enough to be painful. The kid grinned with pleasure and took a cigarette from a pack lying on one of the tables.

"I see him," said Flora. "C.I.T. Creep in training."

"That," said Chrys, "is the infamous Robbie Barswell."

"No wonder you think so highly of him," said Flora.

PZ had grabbed the tray and was headed toward a table full of his friends. A couple fries were hanging out of his mouth.

"Hey, Warlock." Robbie's voice carried over the noise. "Where you going? To a meeting of the coven?"

PZ turning to face him, calmly munching his fries. He swallowed. "Male witches are not called warlocks, you ignoramus. You've been watching too much television in day care."

"Oh, yeah? Well, you know what they call witches like your grandma?"

PZ turned his back and kept walking.

"Satan's whores." Robbie's voice had risen to a yell. "Do you know what they do with Satan's whores, warlock? They fry them. Drown them. Use them for firewood. And that's what's going to happen to your whole family, warlock. It's just a matter of time." A few small children remained oblivious to the confrontation, but Robbie had the attention of most of the room. Chrys stood frozen at the counter. "My daddy says," Robbie yelled, "that your mother is another one, just like your grandma and she's going to pay for what she did to the Whites. My daddy is never wrong."

Robbie turned in triumph to the collection of skinheads, expecting to see admiration on their faces. Instead he was surprised to see the beers disappearing below the table. Butch jammed his glowing cigarette into his beer bottle and shoved it behind his back.

"Hello, gentlemen," said the officer who came walking through the door. "Let's all take a little ride." Robbie slid down and tried to duck under the table. "You too, pipsqueak." He lifted the boy by his collar and nodded in the direction of a patrol car.

The boy in the leather jacket sent a vicious look toward Flora and Sharon. He muttered, "Which one of you two greasy bitches called the cops?"

"I know which one," said Butch, leering at the girls. "And I'll be back. In the meantime, work on your wishful thinking, Flora."

CHAPTER 19

Buzz
A few days later

Buzz backed his truck into the woods, down a rutted road across from the entrance to Whitewater Ranch. When he was satisfied that he could see without being seen, he impatiently slammed the transmission into Park and killed the motor. Beside him on the front seat was a grocery sack containing a quart of milk, a banana and a couple power bars. He opened the cold carton and took a deep drink, his Adam's apple bobbing as he swallowed.

He was miffed. Hank had drawn up the schedule, giving Buzz the undesirable slot of sunset to sunrise, and leaving the daylight hours to be divided between Ace and himself. Big deal. Whitey ordered round the clock coverage like there were still dozens of Whites taking orders from him on a daily basis. Since the loss of the ranch, most of his followers had drifted away. There were still a faithful few who attended the services at the old church, but it wasn't like it used to be. It would be again, though. Whitey said so and Buzz believed him.

He didn't drink coffee. He didn't touch caffeine of any sort. Nor did he drink alcohol. He tried to avoid sugar. He'd been tempted by the smell coming from the bakery in the grocery store, but he disciplined himself. He believed in discipline.

It seemed to Buzz that the instant the sun went down, the temperature dropped. He clutched at his old coat, grateful for the curly wool inside the sheepskin. The coat had been Granddaddy's. Buzz remembered him wearing it while they repaired barbed wire fences. "Bob War," he'd called it. "Greatest invention known to man. Changed the face of the range, son, and the course of history."

He sure missed the old man. As long as he'd been around, Buzz's daddy had towed the line. After he died, though, the whole thing had gone to hell. His mama hated the old frame house where they all lived. The dust blew in through the screens in the summer and through the cracks in the winter. She complained about the grimy coating that covered everything despite her efforts to keep a clean house. Air-conditioning was what she wanted, and a dishwasher, a new stove and a new refrigerator. Their old refrigerator had a broken latch. They kept it closed with a pile of bricks on the floor. She used to get so mad when she'd have to move that pile to get milk or eggs when she was cooking.

A blue Subaru came down the highway, casting light beams through the trees. It didn't even slow down in passing. Buzz sighed at the futility of his vigil. He slumped down in the seat and peeled the banana.

One day, after Granddaddy died, (She sure wouldn't have done it while he was alive.) Mama heaved one of those bricks right through the kitchen window. He'd been sitting at the kitchen table, doing homework, he remembered. It made a huge crash and broken glass went all over everywhere. Into the sink, on the floor, across the counter and into the pot of beans she was getting ready for the stove. Then she just walked out, leaving an onion half chopped on the counter, with splinters of glass on top of the little white pieces. Buzz cleaned it up, nailing a piece of masonite over the hole.

His Daddy had gone to the bank and borrowed the money for "Mama's Dream House." Not a hundred yards from the old house, they'd built a three bedroom brick ranch. Buzz didn't have to share a room with his sister after that. Mama made biscuits in the new oven and curtains for the windows. She seemed happy for a while, and the fights between his parents had stopped. Then things got much worse. They weren't making enough money, his Daddy told her. They'd been okay until they had a mortgage to pay. She'd said fine, she'd get a job.

When he thought about that, Buzz got tightness in his chest and his eyes burned. She told him that she'd gotten a job in Denver, working for an insurance company. She was really happy, standing in the kitchen in her bra and slip, pressing her dress.

For about six months, she had commuted. She got up at five to make the long drive and didn't get home until after dark. When it got to be fall, she said it was going to be too much to cope with in the winter. For what she was spending on gas, she could get an efficiency apartment in Denver. She would come home on weekends. Dawn went with her, because the schools are better and a girl needs her mother.

They only came back home a few times. By Thanksgiving, it was all over. She filed for divorce. He and his Daddy moved out of the dream house, back into Granddaddy's. They rented out the brick ranch to a family from their church. Buzz started working at the tire store after school. It took him a long time, but he finally saved enough to buy a new refrigerator. His Daddy was glad because he didn't have to move those bricks every time he got himself a beer. Buzz had moved out after graduation, into his own trailer. It had seemed too childish to keep on living with his Daddy. It sure was lonesome, though.

Buzz shook his head, trying to clear it of sad memories. He hated sitting in this car, cooped up, doing nothing. He should be home right now, working on his online courses, doing his pushups, cooking himself a pot of soup for the week. He hadn't done the research for Whitey yet. He'd promised to get an address on that Punkin girl. He wondered why Whitey wanted it.

Hell, he could be at home finding out about Artemis. He'd memorized her name and address, along with the curve of those legs as she got out of her car. He had her phone number, too. Maybe he would call her and ask her out to dinner, if he could save up enough to take her to a nice place. A woman like that would expect a first class meal, for sure.

Artemis. That's what the Greeks called the Goddess Diana. He'd learned that somewhere. Lady Di is what he liked to call her, in his mind. Just like Lady Di, she was pure and good. He'd never believed any of those stories about Diana. Her husband had treated her badly and she had to leave him. But she never would have had sexual relations with that foreign guy. The press made that up. He was sure of that. She had been beautiful and kind and good to children. She was the perfect white woman.

He knew what her bumper sticker meant. It was obvious. "To Reclaim That Which Has Been Lost." It might refer to the ranch, but he figured it had a deeper meaning. It meant that she believed in the old ways, that old time religion. It's time to return our nation to its Christian roots and reclaim the white man's rightful place. She wanted to reclaim her birthright, and his, too. She would make a wonderful wife.

When they got married, Buzz decided that he would change her name to Diana, or maybe just Diane. "Artemis" sounded too foreign. He liked plain names. She would be changing her last name, anyway. So she could just start out with a whole new name in a whole new life as *his* wife. They could move into the house next to Granddaddy's, the dream house. *She* would appreciate it, unlike someone he would prefer not to think about. He would need to find a better job, which he felt sure he could as soon as he finished his online degree. She'd have to quit work. No woman of his was going to work. It led to really bad things. Women should stay home and take care of the family. Buzz didn't want a really big family. Maybe two kids, or three, if the first two were girls.

Another car came down the lonely highway, going slowly, as if searching for something. He abandoned his woolgathering to do his duty. He didn't really expect anything of consequence. This was a waste of time. He'd stay up all night, watching for intruders that never came, and he would be dead on his feet at work tomorrow.

For a minute, he thought he'd fallen asleep and must be dreaming. It was a car just like hers, turning on to the road to Whitewater. When he saw the bumper sticker, he knew. What in the hell was going on? What did she have to do with the ranch? She must be trying to get it back. Maybe she was somebody's daughter, or one of the Whites that he'd never met. Maybe Whitey's wife's kin.

Please, he sent up a quick prayer. Don't let her be somebody else's wife.

Whitey had told him explicitly not to go on the property. But Whitey didn't know about Lady Di. He couldn't let her go in there alone, this perfect specimen of femininity. He thought about some of the protective devices he had installed and wondered if they had all been disarmed.

Buzz slipped out of his truck, careful not to let the overhead light illuminate the cab. He was glad he was wearing running shoes instead of boots. He could track almost soundlessly, a skill he practiced on weekends, behind the house.

Buzz hung back, checking the road for signs of life, particularly any signs of the law. Confident that he was unobserved, he sprinted across the road and followed her taillights as they eased down the bumpy road. Buzz chuckled to himself. He'd designed that road himself, set those boulders in the road to scrape the bottom of cop cars and nosey strangers. He sure hoped she didn't ruin that nice vehicle. The Whites mostly drove pickups and SUVs, with the exception of Whitey and his big old Cadillac. Whitey knew just how to steer around those boulders. Buzz had taught him.

She pulled up to the gate, stuck her arm out the window and punched in the code. He couldn't see into the car, but the sight of her arm was arousing. That proves it, he thought. She has to be one of us if she knows the code. Maybe she's a distant relation. Not many women know the code, outside of Whitey's family. Not any, that he knew of. He couldn't ask, though. Whitey would eat him alive if he knew he'd disobeyed orders.

As he watched her taillights disappear, he considered following her into the compound. Better not, he decided. He needed to find out more. He didn't want to run the risk of being seen, or reported to the boss.

He made his way back to the truck, pondering the possibilities. She sure wasn't part of that Mexican crowd. Of that he was sure. What should he report in the morning? He didn't want Hank or Ace to know anything about Lady Di. Those two would go after her like hound dogs after a coon. Buzz thought he would just keep some things to himself for the time being—at least until he could do a bit more investigating. If she was related to Whitey, he might be able to find that out some way. Maybe she wasn't. Maybe she was just an angel trying to get their property back for them. She seemed to have plenty of cash, he thought. Maybe she had bought the property back and intended to donate it, anonymously, to the Order of the Cross and One. If she owned the property, he could find out easily enough.

Buzz climbed back into his truck and chugged the last of his milk. He put his feet up on the seat and settled back against the driver's door, keeping one eye on the ranch road. He threw the banana peel out the window. The smell was bothering him.

An hour later, when Artemis and Atticus drove out, Buzz was asleep.

CHAPTER 20

Atticus and Artemis

Atticus was deep in thought. Artemis kept glancing away from the road at his face, barely illuminated by the dash lights.

"Well," she said. "What are you thinking?"

Atticus looked over at her, returning from his mental meandering. "Oh, several things. I was thinking about the security system. It's state of the art, but a lot of it is jerry-rigged. Somebody pretty smart designed it and put it in. But right now, we don't know how to operate it and the former occupants are unlikely to tell us. There might even be booby-traps."

Artemis shook her head. "I don't want to know about that stuff. It's too complicated and reeks of paranoia."

"Yes, you do. There are good reasons for you and Mattie to learn how to use it. Those guys can play rough. If you don't believe me, talk to Maria. And we still don't know who went after Flora. Might have had something to do with Mattie's battle with the Whites, or it might not." He pulled on his bottom lip, considering. "I think I can figure out the system. I'll get a couple of guys from work out here to help me. Once we do, we're going to change all the codes. The four of you are going to learn how to use it before you move in."

"Okay, okay. You win. But what do you think about it? Isn't it just amazing? You couldn't see much of the river or the mountains. You'll have to come back in daylight. The view is great. Did I tell you that I'm going to call it The Silver Bow? Isn't that a good name? I knew, when I saw that oxbow in the river, that I'm supposed to live there. I kept getting that image, over and over, and I had no idea what I was looking at. Now I do. Now I know. You really were a toad the other night, when we were scrying. I don't know why you have such a...." She trailed off. Atticus wasn't paying attention to her.

"Here's what we are going to do," he said. "You and Mattie and I are going to form an LLC, limited liability corporation in order to buy it. That way the title won't be in your names. We'll call it Silver whatever you said."

Artemis was flabbergasted. "You want to live there, too?"

Atticus stared at her. "No, of course not. But if you and Mattie want to sell off part of it, why not sell it to me? Eventually, I might want to build a house of my own out here. If we go in together, that makes it easier for the two of you to afford it. Plus, we don't have to rush into subdividing it. I think it might be smart to keep a low profile for the time being. Let some of the publicity die down."

Artemis grinned at him. "Okay, you're not a toad. You're a good guy. Are you just being the protective brother, or are you really interested in the property?"

"Artemis, my love. I've lived around witches long enough to know they don't need patriarchal protection. It's a sound investment. Over time, it could be lucrative. I need a place to put some cash and it feels like a good time to put money into real estate."

Artemis noticed that he had said "feels like a good time," but she decided not to tease him about such a lapse of rationality. Instead, it "felt like" a good time for gratitude. She said, "And it would be a big help to your sisters."

"I think it's good for PZ and Chrys to be living out here. Mattie's controversial, and extremely combative. She's always going to be highly visible. This gives the kids a chance to get out of the limelight, which seems safer to me."

"Maybe if PZ had his own stallion, he would quit pretending to be one," said Artemis.

"Don't count on it," said Atticus. "PZ definitely gallops to the tune of his own drummer."

"Plenty of room for it out here," said Artemis. "What did you say about building a house?"

"Forget it," said Atticus. "No time soon. Maybe just a cabin for romantic weekends."

"With your computer," said Artemis.

CHAPTER 21

Las Sombras

"That's a fantastic plan!" Mattie's face glowed with excitement. "I'll draw up the documents tomorrow. How do you like 'Silver Bow Enterprises'?"

"Could we leave out the 'enterprises' bit?" said Artemis.

"Do you like 'Silver Bow, Incorporated' better?"

"I suppose. Just do it and don't tell me the name. That's why I'm not an attorney."

"Atticus, you're a genius. And generous. This accomplishes two things. First, it helps conceal the ownership from prying eyes. Secondly, it buys us some time. We can explore the property and come up with a good plan."

Atticus wrapped his hands around his steaming mug of apple cider. "I think there might be a few surprises, maybe even dangerous ones. The property has been in the hands of supremacists for a long time. I want to be very careful in exploring it. Maybe bring in some equipment."

"Everything Atticus does requires bringing in equipment. So manly. So techy." Artemis threw out her chest and thrust her jaw forward.

"Okay. As you're falling twenty feet into a hole, remember how snide you were."

Artemis gave him a nudging shove with her shoulder. "You're right. The place reeks of paranoia. I just like to tease you about your bells and whistles obsession. I'm sure the place is riddled with James Bond gizmos. If I have my way, we'll rip them all out."

"If I have my way," said Atticus, "we'll rearm them and use them to protect you from the Great White Hope. Heroism is a dangerous thing."

"One man's heroism," said Mattie, "is another man's terrorism."

They were sitting at Cate's table, drinking hot cider and eating oatmeal cookies.

Mattie scraped a few crumbs into her napkin, crumpled it and dropped it on to her plate. She watched the gas fire flash an orange glow in the big firebox.

"The food has gotten even better since Luna joined the family," said Atticus.

"I think Cate got tired of cranking out three meals a day," said Mattie.

"Speaking of...." said Artemis.

"Cate took the kids to pick up Flora, and Luna is taking a nap in the guest room. They're going to stay here tonight. Cate and Luna still have the heebie jeebies about that car vandalism, and I have to say, I agree. It could have been a Halloween prank, but it could have been personal. We still don't know. By the way, where's her car?"

"I parked it in Cate's barn," said Atticus. "Artemis dropped me off and I drove it up here. Chrys wanted to put a bow on it, but I put an end to that idea. It's not in that great a shape. A bow would only emphasize how pathetic it looks."

"It runs," said Artemis. "It has a windshield and new tires."

"The upholstery is slashed. Not to mention that it wasn't in that great a shape before the Halloween Horror got to it," said Atticus.

"I'm sure you enjoyed driving it," teased Artemis. "Did any of your techie geek friends see you?"

Atticus pursed his lips, refraining from answering her.

"She'll be thrilled," said Mattie. "It may not be as classy, but she loves it just as much as you love your Porsche. We'll figure out something for the upholstery. In the meantime, she can get to school and to work."

"I do not 'love' my car. It is a machine," said Atticus, primly. Mattie and Artemis burst into laughter—Mattie with her head down on the table, Artemis arched back in the chair looking skyward. Atticus's face grew sullen while he waited for the laughter to subside. The fact that they had gotten to him brought on a fresh wave of hilarity. He pushed his chair back and stormed to the sink with his cup and plate.

"We're home!" PZ's voice preceded him into the room. He and Chrys had Flora sandwiched between them, each with an arm through hers. She looked worn, but was trying to smile through her weariness. Her uniform was stained and wrinkled. Her eyes had lost their usual sparkle. Artemis would have said that her energy was grey.

Cate came straggling in, picking up PZ's coat where he dropped it. She smiled a "got a secret" smile at Mattie that lasted only a moment. "Sit down, sweetheart. You look exhausted. Chrys, get her a cup of cider and PZ can go upstairs and find Luna. We need to call a family meeting."

"Why can't Chrys go upstairs?" PZ whined. "I'm tired, too." The fact that he was bouncing up and down, pretending to dribble, undermined the believability of this statement. "And I have a lot of homework I haven't even started. Plus I have to call Tim. He and I...." PZ's voice shriveled to nothing when his mother gave him one of her infamous looks. Without another word, he abandoned the imaginary basketball and bounded up the stairs, making a thundering noise as loud as if he had actual hooves.

Flora wilted into a chair. Chrys handed her a mug and set a plate of cookies in front of her, along with a napkin with a witch flying across it. Flora took a sip of the hot drink and gave Chrys a smile by way of thanks.

Mattie got up to stand behind her chair. She wrapped both arms around the girl, resting her chin on her head. "What's the matter, Florita? Did you have a rough day?"

"*Si, Senora. Muy malo.* School was okay, but at work...." She put her head in her hand, the cup on the table. "The skinheads came in this afternoon and the manager was gone. They just act like, I don't know what. I don't understand why...." The tears started to run down her face. "Sorry," she said. "I think I'm still upset about the death of Punkin. She was just an old clunker, but I loved her. I know it's silly, but 'punkin' was my Daddy's pet name for me. He said that his mother called him 'punkito' when he was a child. I think maybe it means 'little pumpkin.' She died when he was very young, and he said that calling me 'punkin' was just a bit of my grandmother. Now both of them are dead. I just like to remember him by calling my car that." The tears came faster and sobs prevented her speaking.

Luna had been standing in the doorway, watching her daughter. "Do you know why he was called 'punkito'?" she said.

Flora swung her head back and forth.

"Because his initials were PNK. He was named after his father, who was called 'Punk.' She called him, little Punk, or 'Punkito.' It has nothing to do with pumpkins, sweetheart."

"What are you talking about?" Flora looked at her mother in alarm. "My father's name was Paulo Lopez. What are you telling me?"

"Only that he changed his name. His name was Paul Nathan Kincaid, Jr. His father married a beautiful Hispanic woman named Luz Lopez."

"I have a grandfather?" Flora's voice was tight and angry. "I have a grandfather you never, *ever* told me about? Why didn't Dad tell me about him? I can't believe this. I thought I could trust you! I thought both of you were always honest with me!"

Luna crossed her arms over her chest and clenched her jaw. "I don't know if the old bastard is dead or alive. He was a racist, a narrow-minded pig. He called his wife 'Lucy,' which he pretended was short for Lucinda. He was ashamed of her ethnicity and tried to hide it. He never allowed Spanish to be spoken in his presence, although she taught her sons. When she died, he forbade them to use our beautiful language, and ordered that they never mention that she had come from Mexico. Paulo wanted nothing to do with him and neither do I. When Paulo left home, he changed his name to Lopez to honor his mother. The old man was furious when we married. After that, he never had any contact with either of us. He refused to come to your father's funeral and he has no idea you even exist. Believe me, he wouldn't welcome you into the family, Flora, even if you tracked him down. It's best you forget all about him. I didn't see any reason to tell you this, until you started talking about 'punkin.' Paulo called you that because he loved you *and* his mother. It grieved him that she never got to meet you."

"So you named me Flora Luz Lopez."

"In memory of your grandmother," said Luna.

"I'm sorry, Mama," said Flora. "It's just been an unbelievable day. I'm sure you did what you thought was the best." She wiped her face with her hands. "He doesn't sound like much of a grandfather, anyway."

The room grew silent in sympathetic misery. The women sat motionless, but PZ and Atticus began to fidget.

"Um, Flora. I need your help with something. Would you mind coming out to the barn with me?" Atticus stood, taking his jacket off the back of his chair.

Flora gave him a look that said she thought he was insensitive. "I'm sorry, Uncle At, I don't think I can do another thing. I just need to rest a minute." Her voice quavered.

"Oh, just take a walk with us. You don't need to do anything right now. Just look at something," said PZ, grabbing her hand and pulling the girl to her feet. It was clear that Flora didn't want to go but politeness prevented her from refusing.

Mattie wrapped the girl in a jacket that hung on a peg near the back door. The wind was penetrating. They all put their heads down and ran for the barn. PZ was still pulling a reluctant Flora along. Luna and Chrys caught up, grabbing hold as well.

Atticus pushed back the bolt and opened one of the barn doors with a screeching sound. Artemis felt along the wall until she found the light switch.

There on a bed of hay, like an egg in a nest, stood Punkin, looking as good as she could, considering. She had been washed and waxed. Her new tires gleamed. Chrys had thrown a Mexican blanket over the slashed upholstery. Proud and unbowed, Punkin was ready to embark on another journey.

"*Mia Madre!*" Flora was jumping up and down with an enthusiasm that rivaled PZ's. Her joy was so infectious that the twins joined in. Soon they were a threesome, holding hands and bobbing up and down, screaming their pleasure. The two girls wound down, but PZ continued until his mother shushed him. "Who did this for me?" asked Flora, the tears returning. "I am so happy."

"We all did," said Artemis. "We just couldn't bear the idea of a Punkin dying on Halloween. Witches can't stand for that. So we performed a little resurrection spell."

Flora threw herself on each of them, giving them a hug and a loud smack. When she came to PZ, he accepted the hug, but ducked out of her arms before she could kiss him. *"Mamacita,"* she said to Luna, "the gods smiled on us when we found *Senora Cate y su familia."*

"Si muchacha. Los dioses deben amarnos mucho."

Flora got in the car, and finding the keys in the ignition, started it. "Can I drive her around?"

Luna and Cate exchanged looks. "No, we have some things we need to talk about first. Maybe later."

"Can I just drive her up to the house then?" Flora's eyes had a gleam in them once again. Her mother nodded and the twins scrambled in. "And maybe just around the driveway," said Flora, as she pulled out of the barn. "We'll beat you to the house anyway."

Luna, more restrained than her daughter, took the hand of each of the benefactors. "I can't thank you enough," she said. "Flora is right. Our lives changed for the better the day we found you, Cate, and your family. I don't know how I can possibly pay you back."

"You already have, as far as I'm concerned," said Mattie. "All we did was turn a pumpkin back into a coach. You've had Chrys and PZ to manage all year. By my calculations, I'm still in your debt."

Atticus and Artemis chose to say nothing. They merely gave each other the faintest of smiles and started walking back to the house.

Cate looked at Luna and said, "We have great kids. Let's figure out how we're going to protect them."

CHAPTER 22

Whitey

"We gotta protect the American Way of Life," said Whitey. He was reclining across the back seat of his own Cadillac, legs stretched out, wearing his Stetson and smoking a Cuban cigar. His ample belly, hanging over a large silver buckle, was full of Maine lobster, Texas beef, Idaho potatoes, Tennessee whiskey and California wine. He was feeling expansive. "I consider it my God-given responsibility to protect future generations from evil. Foreigners, with dark blood and them crazy religions. Women running all over, bossing men and having babies that don't belong to nobody. It takes a strong man to rein in 'at kinda dangerous activity, but I'm just the man to do it. You take the Cross and One. We had a real good thing going until that Meskin whore and her witchbitch lawyer cleaned us. Let me tell you, Brother Joseph, this fight ain't over.

I'm formulating plans to restore my family's rightful heritage. We are a family that walks with the Lord. The legacy of the Whites and those who follow them will live throughout eternity." He thoughtfully considered the ash on his cigar.

Joseph Worthington, sitting beside him, nodded the kind of agreement that pontificating drunks require. By contrast, his stomach contained a green salad, grilled chicken breast and many, many ounces of water, poured from a gin bottle and served in a martini glass with a twist of lemon. "You are just the man to do it, Reverend White," he said.

"Whitey. All my boys call me Whitey, Brother Joseph. And I thank you for your support. It means a lot coming from a man of your stature. Buzz, here, he's been handling most of the surveillance at Whitewater ranch. Hell of an intelligence gatherer, my Buzz. He's also got a line on a little Mexican gal that works at the McDonald's. They're all tied up together, you know. I figure that she might lead me to that bitch that sued me. She has disappeared."

The two men watched the back of Buzz's head bob up and down in agreement. He was chauffeuring the two of them back from the airport. They were returning from the Broncos/Cowboys game, played in Texas Stadium. They had flown to the game in Worthington's private jet and been served dinner on their return.

"Tell Brother Worthington what you found out, son."

Buzz was thrilled to be asked. "Well, I ran a check on her license plate first. The car belongs to a Mrs. Luna Lopez, but her daughter's name is also on the title. Flora is a senior in high school and it looks like she might be the valedictorian. Well, that's what Brother Matthew's wife said. She teaches the girl advanced calculus. If she's that smart, I started wondering who she belongs to. This is where it gets interesting."

"Go on, son," said Whitey.

"Her Daddy's been dead for a long time. His name was Paulo Lopez. He was a policeman, got shot during a routine traffic stop. But...," he paused for emphasis, "when

I did some more research on the Lopez guy, I discovered that he changed his name. His name used to be Paul Nathan Kincaid, Jr. That's as far as I've gotten."

"Can you imagine a white guy changing to a Mexican name? Don't make no sense to me," said Whitey. "Was Lopez his wife's name before she married him?"

"No," said Buzz. "Lopez was his mama's name."

Worthington was sitting up straight and, leaning forward, placed a hand on Buzz's shoulder. "Where did you get this information?"

"On the net, sir. There was a lot about Paulo Lopez after he died. *The Post* had a long article. That's where I found out he'd changed his name."

"Can you get me a copy of all this?" The strain in Worthington's voice made Buzz glance in the rearview mirror.

"Sure he will," said Whitey. "Buzz, you get all that stuff over to Mr. Worthington tomorrow. You hear?"

"Yes, sir," said Buzz, frowning.

"Why you want this stuff?" asked Whitey. "It's just another boy making mud pies. Can't do much about it now."

"Oh, like you say, it's just stuff we need to keep up with," said Worthington. He leaned back, affecting a casual air. "By the way, Buzz. How many children did this Paulo Lopez have?"

"Just the one, sir. Just Flora."

"Thank you, Jesus!" said White.

"I agree completely," said Worthington.

Buzz drove up the long drive to the Worthington home. He pulled in front, got out and opened the Cadillac's back door.

"Thank you for a mighty fine evening, Brother Joseph," boomed Whitey. "Too bad the Broncos took a licking. That was a wonderful dinner, though. And that little gal that served it was just delicious." He chuckled at his own wit.

Worthington was too distracted to reply. He got out and hurried toward his house. Turning, he spoke to Buzz. "Get that stuff on Lopez here early," he barked. The large oak door slammed behind him.

Whitey hadn't even noticed Worthington's abrupt departure. His eyes were half closed, his words sliding off his tongue and dribbling out. "You done good tonight, son. Now get me home to Mrs. White. I'm tuckered out."

"Whitey, I need to tell you about this woman who's been out to the ranch. I think she might be trying to help us," said Buzz. He had decided he better mention her, just in case one of the other guys had seen her too.

"Not tonight, boy," mumbled Whitey, just before he began to snore.

CHAPTER 23

Joseph Worthington

Joseph Worthington sat at his desk punching in a telephone number. While he listened to it ring, he tapped his family crest ring on the desktop.

"Hello?" The sleepy voice slurred the word, and then exploded into coughs.

"Wake up!" barked Worthington. "Are you drunk?"

Savannah's drawling voice preceded her down the hall. "Joseph, honey. How was the game? Are you just devastated that the Broncos lost? I hope it didn't ruin your nice evening with the boys." She swished into the room, dragging the grimy hem of a full length, peach colored peignoir. Leaning seductively on the doorjamb, she said, "I'm about ready for bed, honey. I thought you might like to join me."

"Get out of here," he snapped. "I'm on an important call."

"Okay, darling. I'll just wait for you upstairs." The syrup ran off her voice and she made bedroom eyes at him.

"Damn it, Savannah. Didn't I tell you to get out?" She disappeared around the corner.

"Hello? Who the fuck is this?" The voice on the phone was now angry and impatient.

"Shut up, Ace."

"Oh. Sorry, Mr. B. I thought it was some kind of prank call."

"I had to get rid of my wife. Don't you ever speak to me like that again."

"Yes, sir. What can I do for you?"

"Do you know anything about some Mexican girl that geek that drives Whitey around is investigating?"

"Well, yeah." Ace told him the story of their visit to McDonald's. "It wasn't nothing, boss. She's just a kid. Whitey got uptight because she was talking to a rich white guy. So Buzz took her plate number and found out who she is. Hell, you don't care about that shit, do you?"

Worthington reached across his elegant mahogany desk and pulled a pad and pen toward himself. "Do you remember the license plate, by any chance?"

Ace found this hilarious. He couldn't stop laughing.

"What is so funny?"

"Nothing, Mr. B. Just a private joke." Ace was snorting his laughter, trying to stop and choking instead. "Yeah, I remember it. I thought it was pretty funny that she had a license plate that said 'PUNKIN' on Halloween. She's pretty round and ripe herself."

"Did you say pumpkin? Spell it." Worthington had his hand poised over the paper, but when he heard the letters that Ace spelled out, he threw the pen across the room. "Get over here by eight in the morning."

"Sorry, boss. I got to relieve Buzz in the morning. Whitey ordered round the clock surveillance of Whitewater."

"Who pays you?"

"You do, boss."

"I sure do, and very well at that. That old fool thinks he's going to get his ranch back, but it isn't going to happen. You just let Buzz handle things in the morning. He's the one that loves to kiss that old buzzard's ass. Stop by the boy's house first thing in the morning and get his research on that girl. Then get over here." With that, Worthington slammed down the receiver. He sat motionless, cursing under his breath.

CHAPTER 24

Artemis
The Silver Bow

Within a week, Atticus and Mattie had worked their magic. Silver Bow, Inc. was the owner of the property formerly known as Whitewater Ranch. Mattie decided to wait until her children had a winter break before moving in, but Artemis put her house on the market and sold it the next day. The purchaser was anxious to occupy and she was anxious to vacate.

Almost all of her possessions fit into the big room overlooking the river. Her living room furniture formed a small seating area. She positioned her dining room table facing the windows and it became her desk. On the wall she hung a large hand-painted sign, "Silver Bow Ink." She had tried putting her bed and dresser in the bedroom, but the two pieces seemed so forlorn that she stuck them in the office with the rest of her furniture. She liked waking up to a view of the river. The house felt immense and she preferred camping out in one room to rattling around. Occasionally she went to the kitchen for a drink or to zap frozen food in the microwave.

Artemis barely opened her eyes, aware that morning was coming but had not quite arrived. She caught sight of the oxbow, this morning a dull pewter ribbon of water forming the omega of her imagining. As the last morning star twinkled its final twinkle before finishing the night shift, she watched the creek emerge from shadow. Color was gone from the meadow—the stoplight yellow of the aspens, the blue green spruces, the yellow green of cedars and the green black pine silhouetted along the mountain ridges. The grasses had turned brown. The flowers had all disappeared. A silvery patina covered everything. The frost on blades of withered grass took on tiny sparkles as light crept out of darkness. The water ran, swift and cold, reflecting the November sky. There might be snow up there, molecules of frozen hydrogen married to oxygen, icy flecks momentarily paused in a swollen cloud cover before a minor shift in temperature or wind released them to drift down and transform autumn to winter. She snuggled deeper into the covers. Resisting the call to daily activities, she inhaled cold air that came through the window she left cracked every night. It was good for sleeping, frosty air around the cocoon of down that kept her body warm. She floated in twilight consciousness, the solitude delicious. She wondered what it would be like when the house was full. Would she hate it? Would she wake up to PZ thundering down the hall or Chrys shouting to her mother for a clean shirt? Oh, she would handle it. If they were too loud, she would soundproof the room, or move into one of those yet unexplored outbuildings. On second thought, no. She was never going to move out of this room. In sixty or seventy years, maybe. They would work it out. It would be fine. Maybe. What about when they became teenagers? That wasn't far off. Would that be a problem? Would there be hip hop blaring in PZ's room? He was just the kind of kid that might like rap. What if it was the kind that talked about "hoes"? Once, walking down the street, she had heard sounds blasting from this red automobile full of boys. "Forty-five to the head, and the Motherfucker's dead." What if PZ played *that*! She would have to do something about it. She couldn't have that in her house. No, PZ wouldn't play that. What was she thinking! What if Mattie got all workaholic manic and didn't come home? Would she expect Artemis to take up where Cate had left off? No, it would be fine. She could manage Mattie. If it got to be a problem, well, Mattie would have to hire a housekeeper. Artemis pulled the pillow over her head, as if she were able to block scary thoughts with a sack of feathers. To tell the truth, it was the thought of living near Atticus that really disturbed her. He could hear her thinking. There were times when she couldn't tell whether it was her mind or his that was jabbering away in her head. When they were kids, he could look across the room and give her the answers on the geometry quiz without so much as a flicker of an eye. She knew when he lusted after a girl and could silently telegraph to him a "Go for it!" or a "You don't have a snowball's chance in hell." During college, when they were thousands of miles apart, he would call as she walked into the dormitory after a brawl with her boyfriend. She knew immediately the night he wrapped his car around a tree, and she knew how long he had to live before the ambulance arrived. For her whole life it had driven her crazy, living her life in two bodies. In the past few years, it seemed like they were creating some separation, but if he moved out here, the proximity might make it worse. Would make it worse. It might be like the two of them wrapped around each other in the crib again, breathing each other's air. She could be making a huge mistake. Stop it, she thought. What if Atticus is listening right now? She threw the pillow across the room and sat up.

"Let's go for a hike," she said to the three hounds curled up at the foot of her bed. Lightning took this as an invitation to come lick her face, but Moon Doggie and Streak feigned sleep until she threw back the covers.

They leapt off the bed and raced to their bowls in anticipation of breakfast.

"Atticus says that we can't go poking around the property until he checks for booby traps. But there's a trail that picks up at edge of the ranch and heads into park land. Let's try that today. Then we'll come back and I'll pound out another chapter of my book. Sound like a good plan?"

She filled three bowls from a large sack of dry dog food and stood back to watch them perform their comedic morning ritual. Each of the dogs gobbled the contents of her own bowl. Then, in a furious scramble, they checked the other bowls to see if any morsels still remained. Finally convinced that there was nothing more to be had, they finished with a drink of water and plopped down, satiated.

"You three are 'so predictable,' as Chrys would say. Just let me put on some clothes and we'll go."

The morning was clear, crisp and cold. Artemis zipped her down jacket and pulled a fleece band up around her ears.

She followed the road until she came to the gate.

"Okay, girls. Let's see if we can trip the detector and get it to open without a vehicle. She approached the mechanism and waved a hand in front of it. Nothing happened. She motioned with both arms, up and down, jumped back and forth, and finally ran up and down the road. With a soft purr, the gate slowly parted.

"Don't know what I did, but it worked. Let's go." She began a slow jog, looking for a path.

Buzz could scarcely believe what he was seeing. He sat on an old folding stool, concealed in the woods, watching her run down the road. Whitey didn't know that Hank and Ace had stopped coming to take their turns at surveillance. It would hurt the old man's feelings, so Buzz fabricated reports from them. Each night he kept a vigil, until it was time to go home and get ready for work. He tried camping, but he was afraid to build a fire and at night the temperatures dipped below freezing. His truck hidden across the road, he slipped through the woods to a spot where he could get a view of the gate. He relied on a thermos of hot herbal tea and power bars to get him through the night. A week without sleep was getting to him. It was hard to find the time for his workout and run. Sometimes, when the tire store was deserted, he catnapped behind the counter. If the front door jingled, he would leap to his feet and pretend he had been attending to something. So far, he had been able to discipline himself to the task, but he was getting tired of it.

He couldn't believe that she had moved into that big house all alone. His investigations revealed that a corporation now owned the property. Silver Bow, Incorporated. He assumed she worked for them, but his schedule had not permitted any further research. This was the first time he'd ever seen her on foot and he wondered what to do. Checking his watch, he made a decision.

Buzz could move like an Indian, or at least like he thought an Indian would move. He had read somewhere that he should call them "Native Americans." He had no idea what that meant. He wanted to be like the Indians in the westerns. In the reruns of "The Lone Ranger," they said that Tonto could move through the forest without making a sound, a skill Buzz had practiced since he was a Cub Scout. He thought he probably could move as swiftly and silently as any Indian brave ever did. He didn't know exactly how Whitey felt about Indians, but he could imagine. Therefore, he never discussed his Indian skills with Whitey. He could probably track, too, but he had never had the opportunity. He never could seem to find anything to track other than tires. That was boring.

Buzz slipped behind the pines, keeping her in his sight. He watched her breasts move as she walked. He disapproved of women who go braless, but he was enjoying the show. Her legs were encased in black spandex, muscular calves and thighs, on up to tight buns. A really nice butt.

"I'm feeling better already, girls," said Artemis. "It was just the morning phantods, spooking me. Those evil little demons of the underworld are trying to ruin it for us." She stretched out her arms, tilted back her head and went into a spin. "It doesn't get any better than this, ladies. Enjoy!" The dogs barked and frolicked. Lightning began chasing her own tail, while Moon Doggie and Streak ran up and down the trail. Artemis ran after them.

It wasn't that easy for Buzz to keep up with her. He could sure tell that he hadn't been training this week. She slowed to a jog, and he ran deeper into the woods, planning to get ahead of her. Pausing, he inhaled deeply until his breathing was normal. With an assumed casualness, he began strolling toward her. Within moments he met her on the path. The dogs started leaping in the air, barking.

"Sit," said Artemis. "No barking." They obeyed. "Well, hello, Buzz" she said. "Nice morning, isn't it?"

"Good morning, Ms. Diana," he stammered. "I mean, Ms. uhm...."

"Oh, you're a student of mythology, I see. Diana, goddess of the forest. It's Artemis, actually, but Diana was her Roman name.

Not many people know that. In fact, Diana was my name until my aunt changed it."

"That's great!" he said, thinking, it will be easy for you to change it back.

"What's great?" she asked.

"Oh." His cheeks, already pink, turned to fuchsia. "It's great to see you."

Artemis thought he was a bit strange, but he seemed harmless enough. "Well, thanks. The nymphs and I are trying to get in a walk this morning before I have to get to work. Nice to see you, too." She started down the path and he turned to follow her.

"Mind if I join you?" he said. "I usually turn around here anyway. It's private property beyond that gate, so I can't go any farther. I like this walk, though. I try to stay in shape. It's hard, but it's worth it. Don't you think? I work two, sometimes three jobs. Hard to find the time to exercise. Do you find it hard to find the time?" He abruptly stopped when he heard himself rattling.

Artemis smiled at him. "I make the time. I love being outside and the girls need to run. It's the reason I moved to the country."

"Oh? Do you live around here?" he asked.

"Yes." She didn't volunteer any further information. "What kind of jobs do you do, besides selling tires?"

"I'm in the security business. I install security systems, surveillance, research, that type of activity."

"Really?" she said. "That must be interesting."

They walked for another half hour. She listened to him tell her about new devices that could stun intruders, record conversations, spy on babysitters and teenagers. Artemis said little, but she didn't mind listening to him.

"I need to turn around," she said. "I have a lot to do today. It was nice walking with you." She gave a whistle to round up the dogs, who were marking bushes and reading messages left behind by other travelers.

Buzz scrambled to think of a way to continue the contact. "How are your friend's tires? Do you need me to come by and check them? And how about that Audi of yours? You know, with the weather coming and all, you ought to put on snow tires."

She smiled at him. "You're probably right. This is the first winter I've lived up here. I'll stop by and you can put some on." She turned and jogged away from him, followed by her canine entourage.

Buzz stood, bewildered. He couldn't tell whether he had blown it, or initiated a relationship. She had seemed interested. She hadn't told him to leave her alone or anything, but she'd gotten away. Maybe she would come in for those tires. He would be better prepared by then. He looked down at his watch. He didn't have time to go home and change. He would have to shave in the men's room at the tire store and wear the same clothes all day. He hated that, he thought.

Artemis jogged up to the security pad and entered the gate code. Moon Doggie and Streak raced by her, headed for home and doggie biscuits.

Artemis put two fingers in her mouth and gave a loud whistle. "Lightning!" She looked down the road, expecting to see her zooming toward her. The greyhound was nowhere in sight. She yelled a bit louder, her tone tinged with impatience. "Lightning. Come here!"

The gate began to return to the closed position. Artemis frowned and jogged back down the path. "I mean it!" she said. "Get in the house!" The dog had disappeared.

She retraced her steps, but decided the dog had gotten off the trail. Perhaps the idea of giving Gris Lightning plenty of room to run had its downsides. She tromped through the woods, calling the puppy's name and growing increasingly anxious. Out of the corner of her eye, she caught a blur of movement. Turning, she began to sneak up on the canine hindquarters sticking out of a hole. The dog was digging frantically, throwing dirt into the air.

"Lightning! Sit!" The dog obeyed, grinning at her mistress and reeking of skunk. "Gods, you smell horrible!" The expression on her face led Artemis to believe that Lightning thought it had all been a grand adventure. "You have been a bad dog!"

Artemis stared at the hole where the skunk had sought refuge. It was large, about five feet in diameter, disappearing into black oblivion. She wondered how deep it was, and if it had any purpose. It looked dangerous to her, but it was on park land and she couldn't do anything about it. More pressing was the problem of the stinking dog. She grabbed Lightning by the collar and dragged her away before the skunk returned to do anymore damage.

Artemis was sitting on a built-in bench in a little mudroom off the kitchen. She unlaced her running shoes, a portable phone clenched between shoulder and chin.

"I stayed on the trail, At. You are such an old grandpa. It isn't exactly a fourteener," she said, referring to those mountains whose elevation exceeds fourteen thousand feet.

"You wouldn't even call it a hike. More like a stroll." She threw her shoes beneath the bench and pulled off sweaty socks. "There's no point in carrying a cell phone. It doesn't work up here." Listening absently, she sniffed the socks and made a face at the smell. "Well, I'm sorry your alarm bells were ringing, but it has been a relatively uneventful morning at the Silver Bow. Lightning had an unfortunate encounter with a skunk and that took a good hour to clean up. Other than that, there's a heron fishing the creek and the deer have eaten more of the landscaping. I'm not going to stay locked up in the house until you and your team of Super Geeks come out here and get the paranoia gear working." Leaving her shoes under the bench, she began to peel off clothes, layer by layer. "I know you are busy. I know you spent last week on this and you're playing catch up. I know, I know, Atticus. You've told me. I would know even if you didn't tell me. What's with the Big Brother routine? This place is like Fort Knox. There's nobody here but three dogs and a witch. As PZ would say, 'Chill!'" She padded down the hall in her

bare feet, stripped down to thermal underwear. "Look, I think I may have found someone to help you. There's this weird kid who
works at the tire store, the one that helped us
with Flora's car. He seems to know about this
kind of stuff. Just call him. I don't know his
name, but I doubt they have a huge number
of employees. Hold on." She pulled the silk
underwear over her head. "I have to spend the
morning writing. Let me know if you don't
get him and I'll try to track him down this
afternoon. I've got to buy groceries anyway."
She turned the water on in the shower. "Well,
no. Not groceries like Cate buys groceries.
Just junk to microwave. I may not cook, but I
do eat. Got to go, Atticus. I can't take a phone
into the shower. It might fry me or something." She disconnected, dropped the phone
on the counter before pulling off the last of
her clothes and stepping into the hot water.
"Ahhh!" she said.

CHAPTER 25

Whitey
Later that afternoon

Whitey came sauntering into the tire store, the Stetson brushed and his boots gleaming. An electric heater was glowing orange, making the showroom too hot with the afternoon sun streaming through the windows. The fat jingle bells tied to the glass door brought no one to the counter. Whitey reached back and gave the door a shove, setting up another clanging. Still no response.

"Boy! Where you at, boy?" He approached the counter and slammed an open palm down on the top. Buzz came rolling out from under, blinking and stammering. "What the hell you doing?"

"Gosh, you scared me to death, Whitey. I was just hunting for some tape for the cash register." Buzz's face was bright red. He seemed to prefer a view of the linoleum rather than meeting the old man's eyes. He tucked his shirttail in and straightened himself.

"You was not. You was sleeping. I thought you took your job seriously. You lose this job, son, and you'll be back working for your old man. I thought you was saving for some more education. You keep on pissing around like you been and won't nobody give you a job. You hear me?"

"Yessir. I hear you. It's just that I've been watching the ranch and my Daddy's got me digging postholes. I can't seem to find the time for sleeping. But I won't do it again, sir. I promise."

"I coulda been a customer, son. Then where would you be? Rolling out from under the counter like some drunk behind the Lonely Bear. You ain't been drinking, have you?"

"No, sir. Certainly not, sir. I would never drink on the job. Well, actually I never drink anyway."

"Well, see that you don't. You got the integrity of the Cross and One to uphold. You tell Ace to cover for you and you get some shuteye tonight. You hear me?"

"I will, sir."

Whitey pulled off his hat and waved it in front of his sweaty face. Buzz's eyes widened and he ran to unplug the heater. He moved the magazines from a grimy white plastic chair and dragged it over for Whitey to sit in. The old man lowered his butt like royalty taking a throne.

"What I come for," he said, "is to find out what you know about this woman that has taken up residence on my ranch."

Buzz colored again with the fleeting thought that Whitey might be able to detect his personal interest in the Lady Diana. "Well, sir. As a matter of fact, I managed to strike up a conversation with her this very morning. She came out of the compound and I pretended that I was taking a morning jog."

Buzz told Whitey about his encounter with Artemis.

"Did you watch her go back in?" Whitey asked.

"Not exactly, sir. It might have looked like I was being too aggressive."

"Well, I just wondered if she used the old code. That would be a good thing to know."

"She's still using it. I checked that out. The code hasn't been changed. I tested it myself," said Buzz.

"Well, that was a peckerhead thing to do. You could get arrested for that. If any one of us sets foot on that place and gets caught, there will be hell to pay." Whitey leaned forward, thrusting his face at Buzz.

"I won't get caught."

"I told you not to go on the property. Didn't I?"

"You did."

"Well, I mean it."

Buzz stood looking at him for a minute. "Well. There's something I need to tell you."

"Get on with it." Whitey gave an impatient shrug to indicate he had many pressing matters to attend to and needed to quit wasting time. In actuality, he had none.

"This afternoon I got a call from this guy. He said he was calling on her behalf."

"What did he want? Tell you to stay away from her, did he?"

"No sir. He wanted to ask me to work on ranch security. He wants me to check it out and get everything in working order."

This had the old man's attention. He jumped to his feet and shouted, "How the hell did he know you was the one to call about that security?"

"He doesn't. When I was talking to her this morning I told her I was skilled in that area. She must have told this guy. I don't know. Maybe he's her boss. Maybe he works for Silver Bow, Incorporated. Anyway, he called me here at the store. Seems he is worried about her staying out there alone and wants all the security measures activated. He asked me if I thought I could do it, and I told him I would have to take a look at it first."

This tickled Whitey. He laughed so hard he began wheezing, then started to cough. He pulled a yellowed handkerchief out of his back pocket and held it to his mouth with a hand freckled with age spots. His ring finger still showed a white line where his Cross and One ring had been for decades.

"You are cagier than I thought, boy." Buzz beamed. "You found yourself a way to get inside. By invitation to boot. Damn clever."

"Thank you, sir."

"Tell me, son. What does this woman look like?"

Memories flooded Buzz's mind. A long slim leg snaking out of the Audi. The streak of silver hair blowing in the early morning wind. Cheeks and lips, scarlet from the morning chill. The curve of her firm buttocks as she jogged away from him. "She's attractive. Slim, athletic, kind of classy."

Whitey nodded. "Why don't you try romancing her some? Take it easy, though. Don't move too quick now or you'll scare her off. Women are like rabbits. Quick to run. Easy to scare and delicious once you catch 'em." He amused himself.

"Sir? Do you think I could slack off the surveillance a bit? I mean, if I'm going to be inside?"

Whitey considered this for a moment. He looked at the bags under the boy's eyes. "Sure. I'll tell the boys that you got it handled. In the meantime, go home and get some rest. You look like hell." Whitey settled his hat on his head and started for the door. "When you going out there?"

"First thing in the morning. I figured you would want me to get right on it. Well, I gotta dig some more holes for Daddy, but I can do that early. I told them I would be out there by nine."

"Good. Find out what they are up to and report in as soon as you get back."

CHAPTER 26

Las Sombras

"So I told her. Madisdater. And then she says, 'What's your brother's name?' So, I told her PZ and she goes, 'PZ what?' and I said 'PZ Madison' and she goes, 'How can his last name be Madison and yours be whatever it is you just said?'" Chrys waved a chicken leg in the air to emphasize her point. "So, I said, '*Madisdater*, and if you think about it, you'll figure it out.'" She took a bite and, with her mouth full, "Duh!"

PZ jumped in. "The woman was *freaking out*. She told Chrys that we were twins and she was going to list us both under the same 'surname.'" He wiggled his fingers in the air, making quotation marks. "So Chrys told her, 'Fine. Use Madisdater,' and I said, 'No way. My name is PZ Madison.' Silly cow could *not* get it. Why would I be called Madisdater?"

"And why would I be called Madison?" Chrys laid the leg down and spooned another helping of mashed potatoes on her plate. "Then she goes, 'Who was your father?' and we like said…"

In unison, they chimed, "Ask Mattie."

PZ swallowed a gulp of milk, giving himself a mustache, which he wiped on his sleeve. "She wanted to know what PZ stood for, too."

"I told her that she didn't want to go there." Chrys jumped up and started clearing the table. "That was great. What's for dessert?"

"Yeah. What's for dessert?" PZ wiped his plate with the last half of a bread slice and stuffed it into his mouth.

"That's why, Cate, that PZ and I are not enrolled in the Art for Kids program. It's a frigging bureaucracy and I'm having nothing more to do with it." Chrys grabbed the empty chicken platter and flounced to the sink.

"Not to mention," PZ mumbled around the wad of bread. He swallowed. "Not to mention the moron quotient."

Cate chuckled. "Sounds like Art for Kids isn't ready for you two. That's okay."

"Chrys is an amazing artist already, and I haven't got a drop of talent. So, either way, we're better off outta there." Both arms raised over his head, PZ held his plate up for Chrys to take. She ignored him and collected her grandmother's glass and dirty napkin.

When Chrys took her mother's plate, Mattie looked up from a document she had been reading. "PZ, get up and put the dishes in the dishwasher."

"I gotta make a diorama about the first white settlers in Colorado."

"What the hell is a diorama?" asked Mattie.

"Well, I was hoping they could tell me at Art for Kids, but Chrys got us kicked out of there." PZ wadded up his paper napkin and shot it toward the kitchen counter. It missed entirely, which he pretended not to see. "So I guess I better go look it up, or something." He pushed back from the table and stood up. His mother laid a hand on his wrist. When he turned to her, she gave him a look that made his stomach contract. "I tell you what, Sis. I'll help you clean up the dishes, if you will help me with my diorama."

"*Help me do the dishes!* It's your job as much as it is mine. And I'm not helping you. You know perfectly well what a diorama is and you've had two weeks to do it."

"Would somebody please tell me what it is?" Mattie stuck her pen behind her ear.

"Dumb. Dumb is what it is. It involves cutouts of pioneer people and wagons and junk like that. I did mine ages ago." Chrys folded her arms over her chest.

Her brother mimicked her. "*I did mine ages ago.*" He wobbled his head and added a limp wrist for greater effect.

"PZ, you finish up. Chrys has done her share," Cate said. "She helped me fix dinner."

PZ shrugged and walked to the sink. It was a battle he fought periodically, but never won. He never expected to.

Chrys sat down at the table and fixed a stare on her mother. Mattie, reabsorbed in legal jargon, was slow to sense her daughter's request for attention. She glanced up. "What is it, Chrys? I'm trying to read something important here."

"Mom, I need to talk to you for a minute. It's about Flora."

"What about Flora?" said Mattie.

"Nothing has happened to her, I hope," said Cate, a tinge of alarm in her voice.

"Nothing new," said Chrys. "You know that she is, like, brilliant, don't you?"

"I know she is very talented academically," said Mattie.

"Well, the thing is. She really wants to go to Stanford. She's got terrific grades. Her test scores are nearly perfect and she's been president of about a million organizations. I think she'll get in. She's applied to a bunch of places, but she really has her heart set on Stanford. Only, she thinks that she hasn't got a chance because of the money."

"Well, maybe we can help her find a way," said Mattie.

"I think I know a way, but I need your help."

"Okay. How can I help?" Mattie reluctantly closed the file folder, giving her daughter her full attention,

"I need to talk to Maria," said Chrys. "Will you give me her number, or an address where I can write to her?"

"Honey, I can't tell you that. It's confidential and it would put you at risk. Why do you need to know?"

Chrys twirled a curl around her finger. "Well, you know, Maria's got a lot of money now. I thought maybe she would give some to Flora for college."

Mattie tilted her head. "Well, she might. I don't know. You mean, because both of them are Mexican-American women?"

"I mean, because Flora is her niece." Chrys used that "isn't it obvious?" tone that kids use with adults when they get the opportunity.

Mattie gave her daughter a bewildered look. "What did you say?"

"Maria is Flora's aunt, Mom. You know that."

"I do not know that. How could I not know that?" Mattie's eyebrows were pulled down into a V over her blazing eyes.

Cate said, "Mattie, didn't you know that Luna recommended that you represent Maria?"

"Yes, of course. But I didn't know they were sisters. They're *not* sisters."

"No," said Cate. "They are sisters-in-law. They were married to brothers."

"Duh. Like, where you been, Ma?" PZ squirted dishwasher soap into the little cup on the dishwasher door, but managed to get it all over the floor as well. Cate gave him a frown. He wasn't sure whether it was about the mess on the floor or the sass he had just given his mother.

"What brothers? John Kincaid and Paulo Lopez were brothers?"

"Yes. Don't you remember talking about Punk Kincaid the other night?" said Cate. "He was not only Luna's father-in-law. He was Maria's as well. Paul, Jr. hated his father for the way he treated his mother. When he left home, he changed his name to Paulo Lopez. Lopez was his mother's name."

Mattie thought back to the days when Luna had taken care of her infant twins. In her last year of law school, Mattie decided to have a child. Mattie being Mattie, she calculated that it would take her several months to conceive. She planned to give birth after she passed her boards, stay at home for six months, then open her own practice. However, magic being what it is, she delivered about two months before graduation. And, magic being what it is, she had twins. At the time she had referred to them as the "Be-careful-what-you-ask-for twins." Now, she often remarked that if you wanted to make the Great Mother laugh, tell her your plans. At Cate's suggestion, after the delivery, they had moved to Las Sombras. About that time, Patrolman Paulo Lopez was shot while apprehending a speeder. Luna came looking for a job and Cate thanked the gods for sending her. Flora had just turned seven. For five years they all lived together in Cate's big house. Mattie, who usually worked eighty hours a week, eventually bought a house near her office in Denver. Luna found a cabin a few miles down the road from Las Sombras. Over the years, she and Cate had become best friends. They now ran a business out of Cate's house, so she still came to work five days a week. Sometimes, on weekends, she just came to visit. In theory, Cate lived alone. In practice, the house was still the center of life for her large family.

"Mom. Don't you remember the father/daughter banquet that Flora went to when she was in the eighth grade?" said Chrys. Mattie gave her a confused look. "Cate and Luna made the dress? Blue with white organza? Her first real high heels? She looked, like, totally gorgeous."

Mattie shook her head. "Sorry, honey. I must have been involved in a case."

"Well, she went with her Uncle John. I can't believe you don't remember. Maria like gave me that dress and I'm going to wear it when I grow into it. Of course, I'm not going to any father/daughter banquet, but that's okay. I'll wear it to the Beltane party. The blue matches my eyes. Perfectly."

PZ came and sat down, carrying a tub of ice cream and a handful of spoons. He plopped them down in the middle of the table.

"Where are the bowls?" asked Cate.

"I thought we could just eat out of the carton. That way I won't have to wash any more dishes."

Cate shook her head at him. "Why don't you and Chrys fix yourselves some? You can take it into the library and start working on your project. I need to speak with your mother."

"Cool," said PZ, gathering up a spoon and the carton.

"Get a bowl," said Mattie. "Two bowls."

"What a moron," said Chrys to her brother.

"What a suck-up," said PZ.

While Chrys scooped the dessert, PZ bumped her butt with his hip and shoved his shoulder in her back. She ignored him. "Get napkins," she said. He laughed, grabbed his bowl and ran out. He was followed by the three dogs and his sister. "I'm not making your diorama for you," she hollered after him. "Besides, I have to study for a math test I have next week."

The room seemed strangely quiet with their departure. Mattie and her mother sat for a moment, enjoying the lull.

"Mom?" said Mattie.

"Yes, dear."

Mattie looked at her mother with soft eyes. "How can I thank you for all you have done for us? I don't think I could have managed without you."

Cate smiled. "Oh, I imagine you would have managed, but I think it was better that I helped out. We have created our own little village to nurture our children. Most of the time, when you and Atticus and Artemis were little, I had to manage on my own. Well, with the help of the gods. I wanted your children to have more. I wanted you to have an easier time of it."

"I wouldn't say I've had an easy time. I've taken the space you gave me and crammed it with my career. It was my choice, but you gave me the opportunity."

"Exactly," said Cate. "Chrys and PZ will need the same and I expect you to be there for them."

"I should have enough money by then to pay for whatever they need." Mattie looked longingly at the legal documents.

"Money cannot buy what they need, although it can help. Without money, I couldn't have brought Luna into our home. Nevertheless, you won't be able to buy what you are required to give. You must re-direct your attention, your passion, your gifts and your time."

Mattie stared into a candle still burning on the table beside a small vase of chry-santhemums. "Time is the thing I have the least of these days."

"Therefore that is the thing you will have to give up. It is the nature of the journey. You surrender what is precious to you in order to appreciate the sweetness of life. We most appreciate what we pay dearly for."

"Like labor and delivery."

"Labor and delivery are just the deposit. You keep paying for the joy of children until you leave them behind. If you are fortunate, you get to leave this life before they do."

"Can't I buy time? Hire some help?"

"No. You can't buy time. You can pay others to give of their own. However, each of us has twenty-four hours in a day. No more. No less. The number of years we have varies. Every day, your children have the same amount of time that you do. We all have choices about how we spend it. I've given you some of my time so that you could study and practice law. You tell *me* why you give your time to the study of law."

"Because," said Mattie, "the law is a tool for justice. It isn't a perfect tool, but it is the best one I have found. I like the idea of restoring balance. I think the man who killed Maria's child should pay for his actions."

"Do you know who killed the child?" asked Cate.

"No, not exactly. But I know that he was a member of the Cross and One. I know that he was sent to harass her. I don't know whether he deliberately killed the child, or whether it just happened as a result of the beating he gave her. Maria says that several men assault-ed her, but she doesn't know how many. One of them shoved her into her car and another blindfolded her. She doesn't know where they took her. They said disgusting things to her, tore her clothes off, grabbed her breasts, put their hands on her belly. When she was completely hysterical, she says that they all left but one. When they were gone, he stuck his fingers into her vagina, then stomped on her. He kicked her in the belly, and left her with the wish that she would bleed to death."

Cate stared into the candle herself. "You're right. If you wish to restore balance," she said, "you have to find out who this man is."

"I failed, Mother. I don't know who he is and I doubt I will ever find out," she said. "The best I could do was to go after the Whites."

"The Whites have, for almost a century, fostered hatred. The Great Mother, working through you, stripped them of the land they have abused and She has made the three of you the stewards of it. You don't really own it, you know. You have assumed responsibility for the care of it—a relationship not unlike that of yours with your children. The earth will sustain you and you will care for it. I think, my dear, that it is time for you to move to a higher plane. You are being called to greater responsibilities. You must look up from your books and papers and see what is going on around you. You and your children are leaving my house and it is time. Luna and I won't be around to listen to the rhythm of your lives. I am turning that job over to you."

"Mother, I can't take on anymore. I'm worn to a frazzle as it is."

"Mattie, your fatigue is a sign that your life is out of balance. Restore harmony and the fatigue will disappear."

"Do you mean give up my work?" asked Mattie. Her glittering eyes were starting to flash fire.

"That's not what I said." Cate, unperturbed, gave her a soft smile. "You'll figure it out."

Mattie blew out the candle and shoved back her chair. "You're a big help. Artemis told me that she doesn't intend to take up where you leave off. I think that all of you are abandoning me. I thought this would be easier. Now I think it's going to be a nightmare."

"Perhaps. Often people feel it is nightmarish when they are forced to grow. You've buried yourself in work. It's time to come out and face the demons. The law is only a tool. You have been using it as a hiding place."

Mattie's face was a storm. Her wild hair seemed to flame and her eyes were like lightning. "This is so unfair of you."

"I cannot change the conditions of existence for you, my beloved. Just think about what I have said as you enter this new phase of your life. Your children need more attention than you have been giving them."

Mattie had a momentary sulk before calming down. "Is that what you wanted to say to me?"

Cate smiled. "No. It just came to me. Must be the Great Mother using my mouth again. I wanted to talk about the Silver Bow. Luna and I would like to perform a purification ceremony and then a blessing of your new home."

"That would be very nice," said Mattie in a conciliatory tone. "It would mean a lot to us. Thank you."

"Fine. Then we will plan it for Friday night. I'll call Artemis and see if that works for her."

"Artemis is holed up, working on her next book. It'll be good for her to have some company. I doubt if Atticus will want to attend, however."

"Fine. I'll tell him he has to take PZ to the movies or something. We'll have Witch Night at the Silver Bow."

Mattie relaxed a little. "That will be a lot of power under one roof."

"We'll do it under the stars. Oh, and Mattie. Call Maria and talk to her about Flora. I think you are being led."

"What do you mean?"

"Mattie, my dear. You have been absorbed in your work for so long that you have neglected your powers. You are being divinely led. Mine isn't the only mouth the gods use to speak. Follow the guidance you are receiving. It isn't over yet, regardless of what the law says. Something is threatening. Luna and I both think so. We'll do our part and you do yours."

Mattie wrapped her arms around her mother. "You are truly a Good Witch. I was blessed the day you became my mother."

"Ah, my dear. No more than I."

CHAPTER 27

Artemis
The Silver Bow

Artemis threw a pen across the room. "Damn, damn, damn!" It took a bounce and rolled to a stop. She pushed her chair back from the table where she was working. The first six tones of "God Bless America," were pealing loudly through the house. It was the first time she had heard the doorbell, and it wasn't pleasing her. Who could be ringing the damn thing anyway, she wondered. Atticus and Mattie both have keys. One of them must have lost it, or left it somewhere. Annoyed, she stomped through the empty house and threw open the front door.

Buzz stood there in all his geekiness. "Good morning, Ms. Diana."

She stared at him, wondering whether to slam the door. "How did you get on this property?" she snapped.

"Atticus gave me the code," he said.

She looked him over to determine if he could be carrying a weapon. It was possible, she supposed, but she couldn't see where one could be concealed beneath his clean T-shirt, snug jeans and running shoes. "What do you want?"

"Atticus wants me to go over the security system."

"He didn't tell me that."

"He's meeting me here."

Artemis stared at him for a moment. "You can start by walking around the property. See what you find."

Buzz took a step forward, as if to enter. "I'll need to find the control room first."

Artemis gave him a look so fierce that he stepped back. She slammed the door.

Buzz sat down on a bench just outside the front door. That didn't go very well, he thought.

Artemis punched in the single digit that dialed her brother. "There's a Super Geek on my front porch. Did you send him?"

"Hello, my dear sister and soul mate. Is it the Super Geek that you yourself selected because you didn't want any of my employees prowling around?"

"You should have checked with me first. I'm right in the middle of a chapter and I don't have the time to play 007 with you two nerds."

"Oh, but you would make such a lovely Octopussy, my dear."

"And you will make a glorious Mr. Toad. Where are you?"

"Driving through the gate. Go back to the Muses and I'll handle everything." Atticus parked his Porsche beside the front door.

Buzz leapt to his feet. "Good morning, sir."

"How did you get in here?"

"Ms. Artemis let me in, sir."

Atticus gave him a hard stare, examining him from head to toe. "Well, let's see what we can find. I warn you, though. The security around here appears to be highly sophisticated. Do you think you can handle it?"

"I think so," said Buzz, picking up a toolbox that was sitting on the ground beside him. "Let's take a look inside at the control panel."

"Why do you think it's inside?" asked Atticus.

"Well, it doesn't make sense to put it outside. If you had an intruder, you would want to be able to control things without an encounter. Sir."

The gate to the courtyard was standing open. Buzz paused a moment, staring at the empty pedestal where the sculpture of Elwood J. White and his family had been. He quickly looked in another direction.

Atticus used his key to let the two of them in the front door. He called, "Arrrrr-te-mis?" His voice echoed through the empty rooms. "A? Are you here?"

"No," came the answer from the back of the house. A door slammed.

"She's busy," said Atticus. "Not that she's all that warm and fuzzy when she isn't."

They wandered from room to room, opening closets and cabinet doors. In front of the fireplace was a haphazard pile of animal trophies. The glass eyes of elk, deer, bison and antelope gazed emptily at the ceiling. Buzz's eyes flickered over the large wooden Cross and One that had been removed and was leaning sideways against the wall. The antler chandelier was a collapsed mess in the middle of the front hall and bare wires hung from the ceiling. When they came to the kitchen, Buzz walked directly into a large walk-in pantry.

In a moment he said, "I found it." When Atticus peered around the door, one whole wall of shelves had swung open. Behind was a floor to ceiling panel of knobs and toggle switches. A headset hung on a peg beside a speaker. A dozen small television monitors stared blankly down at them. Atticus considered them for a minute or so. Then he looked at the boy.

"What do you think this means?" he asked, cautiously.

"It means that there is a lot here and it's well concealed," said Buzz.

"Can you figure it all out?"

353

Buzz grinned. "Without doubt. I can probably get it all working in a couple of days. I'll have to do it when I can get off from the store, though. I'll need a key."

"I would have to talk to Artemis about that. Wait here and I'll see what she says."

"Does she work for you?" asked Buzz.

This struck Atticus as immensely funny. "No. If anything, I work for her and have for years and years."

The color drained out of Buzz's face. He tried, but failed to keep the emotion out of his voice when he asked, "Is she your wife?"

"No. She's my sister," said Atticus, over his shoulder as he left the room.

Atticus knocked lightly on the door to Artemis's room. He slipped inside and closed it behind himself. His sister turned around in her desk chair.

"He lied to me," they said in unison. "He said you let him in."

"How could I let him in?" said Atticus. "I wasn't even here."

"He said you gave him the code," said Artemis.

"Well, I didn't. Which means he knew it."

"Or was smart enough to figure it out. Or wire around it. Could *you* have figured it out?"

"Maybe, but it would take me a while. Did you leave the gate open?"

"I might have. You know I hate this security shit. But if I did, why didn't he just say that? Why lie?"

Atticus sat down in one of the leather armchairs, staring unseeingly at the magnificent view. "He wants a key."

"Nope," said Artemis, her arms folded across her chest. "We should have checked him out before we hired him."

"There's nothing here to steal and he seems to know what he is doing. I think I would feel safer if we got the security system working. Then I'll change the code. Are you afraid of him?"

Artemis screwed up her mouth, turned her eyes upward and consulted her inner senses. "Not really. He strikes me as the lost puppy type. Needy, but not dangerous. Maybe he was just overly eager this morning. Let's do this. Tell him to call before he comes to work. If it's convenient, I'll let him in and keep an eye on him. Wonder how he got in this morning."

"Tell you what," he said. "I think I'll just hang out here today and work with him. That way I can familiarize myself with the system and watch him at the same time. Maybe I can learn something about him."

"Ah, James Bond meets Sam Spade. The falcon is probably hidden inside that butt ugly sculpture I dragged out of the front courtyard. It's down by the fire pit. I can't figure out how to get rid of it. How hot does a fire have to be to melt bronze?" She changed her voice, giving a bad imitation of Peter Lorre. "If you find the falcon, don't let him see it. It's worth a fortune." Artemis whirled around in her chair and went back to her computer.

Atticus clamped his jaw in exasperation. "Lock the door behind me."

"Will that keep you out?"

He almost slammed the door when he left.

The two men worked all day. They followed wires and located hidden cameras. Atticus thought Buzz demonstrated an uncanny ability to unearth the devices and reactivate them. By late afternoon, the two of them stood in the pantry watching the live monitors. Not a thing moved around the pool. No embers smoldered in the fire pit. No one stood at the front door. No car was parked outside the front gate. One monitor revealed an empty courtyard and the vacant sculpture pedestal. They could see into the garage, the empty chapel, the dormitory bunks with mattresses of blue and white ticking rolled into bundles.

"Wonder what that is," said Atticus, pointing to a dark blurry image on one of the screens.

"The shed," said Buzz. "A shed, probably. Someplace with no windows, because there is no natural light."

Artemis appeared in the doorway with a canned soft drink in each hand. "'The problem with the world is that everyone in the world is a few drinks behind.'"

Atticus rolled his eyes as he reached for the cold cans. He handed one to Buzz. "My sister thinks she is an impersonator. Your Bogart is worse than your Peter Lorre, A."

"Thank you, Atticus. I appreciate your encouragement and you are welcome for the room service."

Buzz popped the top in his soda. "Thank you, ma'am. I was getting pretty dry. We have about finished in the house, but I'll need to come again to finish outside. I'm afraid I can't come until Friday after work. I have some chores for my Daddy I need to finish up. Today was my day off, and he was some kind of mad that I didn't finish his new fence. Would Friday do for you?"

Artemis considered the matter. Cate and Luna would probably be cooking and getting ready for the ritual. She felt like it would be better to have them around when Buzz was working. "What time do you think you could get here?"

"I only work until four that day. It will take me about a half hour to get here."

"Fine. I'll be expecting you."

Atticus looked at his watch, pulled his cell phone out of his pocket. "I am supposed to be on a conference call. I'll leave you two to clean up." He made a dash for the outside door as he was dialing.

"Buzz. On Friday I will meet you at the gate and let you in." Artemis gave him a hard stare that made him wriggle. "You are not to let yourself in again. Do you understand?"

His face reddened and he became absorbed in returning his tools to the box. He mumbled something.

"What did you say?" she asked him.

"Pardon me, ma'am. I said that you don't have to wait at the gate. You can activate it from inside. When someone punches the button at the gate, it will ring the doorbell."

God Bless America, thought Artemis. Terrific.

"You just punch this and the gate will open." He indicated a green button. There's another one in, uhm, in the room you are using for your office."

Artemis stared him down and her voice was low and dangerous when she asked him, "How did you get in here today?"

Shamefaced, he said, "Oh, I was just showing off. I used a device I have that can open garage doors, automated gates and stuff like that. It isn't really legal, but they aren't very hard to come by."

"Are you a professional burglar or something?"

No ma'am. It belongs to the tire store. Sometimes we have to use it to get in garages and parking areas. People will give us the keys, but forget about the gate. Like I said, I was just trying to impress you." Buzz thought all this was a plausible lie. He had read about such devices in some of the magazines he received. His boss at the tire store would have hung him on a nail if he had heard it though.

"Well, don't do it again. Put that thing back before you get arrested for breaking and entering. And how do you know there is another opener in the office?"

"I don't know exactly where it is. I just assumed that it might be there."

She stepped back and crossed her arms, indicating that it was time for him to leave. Before he closed the toolbox, she tried to get a good look of what was inside. She couldn't see anything other than screwdrivers, wrenches and a hammer.

"Did you bring a coat?" she said. "It's getting chilly."

"I'll be fine. I've got one in the car." He paused, delaying his departure. "Do you mind if I ask a question?" he said.

"You can ask. If I don't want to answer it, however, I won't."

"I notice you don't wear a wedding ring. Are you single?"

Artemis laughed. "Oh, yeah. I am single and determined to stay that way."

He didn't quite know what to make of this. He picked up the toolbox and headed for the door. "The good Lord meant for us all to go through life two by two" he muttered in a sullen tone. "'Be fruitful and multiply,' the Good Book says."

"Is that so?" she said, urging him down the hall.

He hesitated on the threshold, debating whether to say anything else. "'And God blessed them, and God said unto them,

Be fruitful, and multiply, and replenish the earth, and subdue it: and have dominion over the fish of the sea, and over the fowl of the air, and over every living thing that moveth upon the earth.'" He scanned her face for her reaction. "Genesis 1:28," he added, helpfully.

She gave the door a firm shove against his foot, leaving him no alternative but to exit. He backed out, keeping her in sight as long as possible. Artemis turned the deadbolt and started back to her office, shaking her head.

Atticus came in through the kitchen and met her halfway down the hall. "That guy knew entirely too much about this place."

"Every word that came out of his mouth was a lie. 'Dominion over,' my ass. What do you think he's up to?" Artemis looked at her brother, her head tilted to the side.

"I don't know. But I don't want you out here alone with him," said Atticus.

"I'm not afraid of him. He seems harmless, but he's a terrible liar. I'll be glad when he gets finished. Then you both will go away and leave me alone."

CHAPTER 28

Mattie
The same day

"Hello, Maria. How are you doing?" Mattie was leaning back in her chair, at her desk in her office in Denver. Her auburn mane was firmly contained in a clip at the back of her head. She wore a dark brown suit with an ochre silk T underneath. The trousers slid up her leg where she had them propped on her desk, revealing brown socks and comfortable loafers. She took a gulp of coffee from a black mug with a witch on a broom superimposed over a glowing orange moon. Outside her office windows, it was a grey day, threatening snow. The clouds hung low over the office buildings and the fog was so dense it obscured the streets below. She listened patiently to her client, nodding as if the woman could see her. Occasionally she made a sympathetic humming sound. "Sounds like a good job. How do you like the people you work with?" The door to her office opened and a young woman poked her head around the door. She gave her boss a quizzical look. Mattie shook her head and pointed to the phone. Her assistant nodded and closed the door. "Well, why don't you at least have lunch with him?" She reached for a legal pad and a pencil. "I'm not suggesting that you marry anyone. I'm suggesting you have lunch with a nice man. Then, maybe even dinner." She smiled at the response. "Okay. Do whatever you like. I just want you to find a way to be happy. Listen, honey. I need to talk to you about something else. Have you ever heard of a Paul Nathan Kincaid? Punk Kincaid?" The response was so loud that Mattie had to pull the receiver away from her ear. She dropped her feet to the ground and began to write on the yellow pad. "Hold on. Let me get this down. Okay, I'll tell you why I'm interested."

The phone conversation went on for well over a half hour. Mattie said, "I'm going to call you back in a day or two. In the meantime, think about Flora and Stanford. By the way, consider a wild time in the coffee shop with Sr. Sexy Eyes. Not all attorneys turn people into stone. Just this one. *Bendiciones. Puedes caminar con los dioses"*

Mattie hung up the phone and stared out the window, thinking. "Ling?" she said, in a voice loud enough to be heard by her secretary. "Can you come in here a moment, please?"

The door to her office opened and the young woman came in. "You could use the phone. You don't have to yell."

"Sorry," said Mattie. "Comes from growing up in a noisy household, I expect, or from living with PZ." She tore off her notes from the phone conversation and handed them to the woman. "Would you type these up for me, please, and see what you can find out about this guy. All I have is a name and the fact that he lives in Charleston, South Carolina."

"Be glad to," said Ling. "And I don't really mind about the yelling. I'm used to it by now. When you're mad you don't yell. You glare."

✵ ✵ ✵

Mattie looked up from the open folder on her desk and shouted "Ling?" There was no response. She repeated herself. "Ling!" She's training me, thought Mattie. She wants me to use the phone. Mattie dialed the extension number and could hear it buzzing in the office next to her own. Puzzled, she put the receiver down. The glower on her face dissipated when she turned her attention to the windows. The hovering clouds had disappeared. A crisp oval of a moon gleamed in an inky sky. She stood and walked to the windows, looked down on the street below. Neon decorated the windows of restaurants where men and women entered arm in arm, seeking the comforts of Bacchus and the assuagement of emptiness in their bellies. A wave of loneliness swept over her as she watched a couple embrace and kiss before entering the glitzy steak house across the street. There was still traffic, but the rush hour had long since passed. She stared back at the moon and heard her mother's voice. "You have been absorbed in your work for so long that you have neglected your powers."

"Damn," she said. With a sigh, she looked at her watch. It was past eight o'clock. "Damn, damn, damn." She stood up, closed the folder and went for her coat. On the floor, propped up against her briefcase was another fat folder with a purple post-it attached. "Boss. Here's everything I could find on PNK. Let me know if you need anything else. I'll see you in the morning. I recommend you go home between now and then. Ling." Mattie picked it up and was amazed at the number of pages it contained. She stuffed it in her briefcase, threw her raincoat over her shoulders, turned out the light and locked the door behind herself. The sound of her walking echoed in the corridor as she passed empty offices. She rounded the corner and slammed into a security guard. She didn't recognize him, but he wore the uniform of the company that provided security for the building.

"Sorry," she said. "I hope I didn't hurt you." He shrugged by way of an answer. "You must be new. I don't believe I've seen you before."

"No," he said. "This is my first week."

"Well, I'm Mattie," she said. "Unfortunately, you'll often find me working late. What's your name?"

"They call me Hank," he said.

She made her way to the elevator and was surprised that he walked with her. He didn't say another word and she couldn't think of any polite chatter to fill the void. She noticed that he had an untanned band on his left hand and surmised that he had recently divorced. They waited for the car to come. Like a thunderbolt, a wave of revulsion ran through her. She turned to look at him and felt an urgent need to get away.

"I'll ride down with you," he said.

"Oh, wait a minute. I think I left the door to my office unlocked. Would you mind walking down there and checking? I really don't have time."

The elevator door opened. She backed in, blocking his way. For a moment, she thought he was going to shove her aside. He had been looking down at the carpet, but when he turned his eyes toward her, she was startled to see hatred in them. She flashed him a glance that made him recoil. The door began to close, leaving him standing outside. She pressed P3 and then reconsidered. The parking garage was below ground and she wanted to phone Cate's house. Cells don't work very well in that concrete cave, she thought. She got out at the lobby. The clear fresh air hit her when she pushed through the revolving door onto the street. The phone rang only once and PZ picked up.

"Hi, Mom," he said.

"Hi, Mom," said his sister, picking up another extension.

"You missed dinner," they said together. "It was pot roast."

"With carrots and potatoes and onions," added Chrys. "I made oatmeal cookies."

"I'm sorry. I was so absorbed in my research that the time got away from me."

"Chrys got a C on my diorama." PZ said.

"That's because you didn't finish it. I showed you how to put it together and even cut out some of the pictures. You didn't do *anything*," said Chrys.

"I can't believe you made a C diorama. That must be the first C you ever got in your life. She got an A+ on hers, but she got a C on mine."

"I think that's cheating, PZ. Next time, let him do his own work, Chrys," Mattie scolded.

"I thought he *was* going to do his own work, but he just turned in the part I did."

"Well, I don't want her to help me if she's going to get a C. I figured she would get an A, like always."

"Tell Cate I'm going to stay down here tonight. I have to be at work early in the morning."

"She said to tell you, no," Chrys said.

"Why? No, what?" Mattie asked.

"I don't know, no what. When the phone rang, she like said to tell you no."

Mattie laughed. "Okay. Tell her I'm on my way." She clicked off and turned the corner into the parking garage. She walked the ramp down two levels and headed for the lonely black Jaguar in the far corner. She unlocked it with the remote on her key. Shoving her briefcase and coat on the passenger's side, she slid in and closed the door. As she was pulling out, she saw Hank loitering near the elevator and she locked herself in.

CHAPTER 29

Las Sombras

It was ten o'clock when Mattie walked into Las Sombras. Three dogs and a boy were asleep in a pile on the sofa. Chrys sat at the table, reading a Harry Potter book. Cate was curled up in an easy chair, staring into the flames of the fire. Mattie walked over to the sofa, sat down and took the top half of his lanky boy body into her arms.

"Time to go to bed, honey."

"No," he murmured. "I'm watching the game."

Mattie looked at the blank television screen and smiled. "It's over," she said.

"Who won?" he asked her, his eyes still shut.

She looked at her mother, who only shrugged. "The Cowboys," said Mattie.

PZ cracked one eye at her and frowned. "They weren't playing."

"Okay," she said. "They'll win on Monday."

PZ stood up and stumbled sleepily toward his bed. The dogs followed close behind. He stopped, turned and headed back to his mother. He threw his arms around her and hugged her mightily. "I love you, Mom," he said. "You, too, Cate. You, too, Hermione."

"You, too, Dudley."

PZ's eyes were tight squints as he tried to find his way to his bed without waking totally. His bare feet made little slapping noises on the stone floors.

Chrys closed her book, stuck her finger to hold her place while she gave her mother a hug. "I'm going to finish this chapter and then go to sleep. It's good to have you here, Mom. Can I paint my room in the new house purple?"

Mattie kissed her forehead. "We'll talk about it. Don't stay up too late reading."

Chrys, her book open, was reading and walking in the general direction of her room. "Uh huh," she muttered.

Mattie went to the cupboard and got out a wineglass. She poured herself a glass of red and put a bowl of leftover pot roast in the microwave. She grabbed a cup towel from the counter, took a spoon out of the drawer and waited for the ding to tell her she could eat. Slumped over her food, she downed it hungrily. She realized she hadn't eaten since the night before. It was no wonder she was famished.

"What kept you so late?" asked Cate.

"I had a killer day. I don't even remember leaving my desk to pee. I talked to Maria."

Cate rose and came to sit with her daughter at the table. "What did she say?"

"Well, first she said that she would be delighted to send Flora to college. She and I discussed setting up a trust."

"I thought so," said Cate. "I had a feeling that's what she would say."

"She also told me a bit more about Paul Kincaid. I had Ling do the research and she left me a huge folder."

"What does it say?"

"I don't know. I was going to take it to my house and read it, when you told me I had to drive all the way out here." There was a note of resentment in Mattie's voice.

Cate just looked at her. Mattie's defiance seemed gradually to melt. Tears came to her eyes and overflowed. "There's just not enough of me, Mom. When I'm at the office, it seems that everything is pressing and urgent. When I'm around my children, I realize that I'm missing their childhood. Wasn't it just a week or so ago when they were in a double stroller? Artemis is rattling around out there at the Silver Bow, waiting for me to move in with my entourage. There are wires hanging out of the ceiling and dead animal heads lying around on the floor. No one knows how to operate the security system. The whole house is empty except for A's 'room of her own.' The furniture I own will fit in the foyer. I need to set up a trust for Flora. I need to go over Maria's case again and see if there is any way to find the bastard who killed her child. And Chrys wants to paint her room purple."

"Let her," said Cate.

"What? Let her what?"

"Let her paint her room purple. At first tell her you don't think it's a very good idea. Then, reluctantly, tell her it's okay. When it's painted, tell her you are amazed, but she's right. It looks wonderful."

Mattie wiped her eyes on the cup towel. "This sounds vaguely familiar. I seem to remember going through this when I got my ears pierced. I had to beg for weeks."

"Exactly. Kids their age need to find something to do that they think the adults disapprove of. They *have* to push against us. It's part of growing up."

"But purple!"

"Mattie, it's only paint. It's not drugs. It isn't a tattoo. It's not running away to join the circus. Purple paint is a blessing. Be grateful and scratch that problem off your list."

Mattie grabbed her briefcase on her way to the kitchen to pour herself a second glass of wine, and one for her mother as well. "Thanks for saving me some dinner. I was down to my last drop of energy." Mattie pulled three folders out and plopped them on the table.

Cate sipped at her wine. "There's no point in reading those old files," she said. She pointed to two tattered folders, one pertaining to the criminal charges against the Whites and the second to the civil action that followed. "If you were going to find the answer in there, you would have already. Haven't you been beating that dead horse long enough?"

"I don't know where else to start," said Mattie.

"Didn't I tell you that you were being led? Have enough faith to follow. What came your way today?"

"This," said Mattie, picking up the folder labeled PNK.

For the next hour, the two women poured over the documents, making notes and munching oatmeal cookies. Mattie finished the last page and laid it on the facedown pile.

"Ling is amazing. I can't believe she found all this in one day."

Cate tried to conceal a knowing smile.

"What? What's that know-it-all smile about, Mother?"

"It's about recognizing that you don't have to do everything yourself. You're surrounded by very competent people. When you ask for help, usually you receive it. Your responsibility is to say thank you, to those who help you and to the gods for providing."

"Do you think the gods would buy my new furniture?"

"Well, they might but you probably wouldn't like what you get. Too much gold. Heavy Mediterranean influence. A bit gaudy for your taste."

"Might mix nicely with an antler chandelier. Sort of eclectic tacky."

"Do you like the way your office is decorated?"

"Actually, I do," said Mattie. "Ling got a very talented woman to do it over last year. It's nice."

"Ask Ling to give her a call, and don't you have a woman in your office who just passed the bar?"

"Yes. Serena. She's this gorgeous black chick who wears the most amazing clothes. I asked her how she did it on her salary and she said her mother made them all."

"Ask her to prepare the trust for Flora. You can go over it to make sure it's perfect."

Mattie's automatic response was to shake her head. Cate looked at her, silent.

"Okay. I'll give her a shot at it. I guess it can't hurt."

Cate smiled and raised her eyebrows, gracious in victory. "Why don't we go to bed now? We can work on this in the morning."

"I can't. I have to be at the office by eight. Let's just make a list of what we know about the old geezer."

Cate shrugged, conceding. "First," said Cate, looking at her notes, "he's dead. He died of peritonitis about the same time John did. I don't have anything about the will. I doubt if he left anything to his sons, whom he despised and hadn't seen for years."

"There's a note here from Ling that says she will get that information tomorrow. There seems to be some controversy about probate." Mattie pulled out a copy of a newspaper clipping with a very grainy picture of a football player in the Sixties, one leg lifted as if he were running, his right hand wrapped around the ball. The face was hard to see, but his fierce grimace was evident. "At SMU, he played football. Quarterback, it says. He was called 'Punk' by his teammates."

"He married Luz Lopez in Matamoros in 1965," Cate read, her bejeweled glasses riding on her nose.

"Sounds like a drunken escapade to me."

"Maybe. But Luz didn't have Paul until three years later. John came along the next year. She died when Paul was ten and John, nine."

Mattie looked up at her mother. "Maria told me that John's father sent them away to school two weeks after their mother died. He and Paulo ended up at a military school in South Carolina. They were sent to camp in the summers and hardly ever saw their father."

"Which explains why they both detested him," said Cate.

"Mother!" Mattie snapped. "I haven't shipped my children off to boarding school."

"I never said you did, honey. You're being overly sensitive."

"I thought I detected a barb in that."

"If you did, it wasn't I who put it there. Now what else?"

"Maria said that John was crazy about his mother. His old man tried to conceal their Hispanic heritage and forbid them to ever speak Spanish. He forced them both to learn French and told them to say their mother was from Dallas."

"Luna said that Paulo changed his name right after college. His father was furious and vowed never to speak to him again. She never met him and doesn't think Paulo even told his father he was married."

"Well, Maria and John went to see him before they were married. He threw them both out and refused to come to the wedding. Maria sent him a note when she found out she was pregnant, but he never answered her."

"Which is not surprising." Cate leaned back in her chair. "What else?"

"The brothers moved to Denver together. Paulo was married to Luna, but John was single."

"I suppose Punk never knew about Flora, which was a good idea. I don't think he would have been pleased. What's in all the rest of that stuff?"

Maria rifled through the papers. "Most of this is about PNK, Inc., home office in Charleston. Kincaid had his fingers in a lot of pies—primarily real estate and communication. There's a bit of oil and gas, but most of that dates back to his Texas days. 'Punk' was CEO and there's a list of officers. The President is a man named Joseph W. Worthington III." She looked up at her mother. "That name rings a bell."

Cate sat up and stared at her. "That's the guy who's married to Savannah. You remember. Rhett Butler and Scarlett."

"You mean the jerk that nearly crushed my hand? The guy that tried to hassle Luna into giving his wife a second reading?"

"The very one," said Cate.

"Could there be more than one Joseph W. Worthington III?"

"Oh, sure. Particularly from Charleston, where they just use the same names over and over. Once, when I was visiting a friend in South Carolina, I met Winston Jefferson and his cousin, Jefferson Winston. Win had a daughter he named Mary Winston Jefferson. They called her Winnie."

"Who, no doubt, will have a daughter called Mary Jefferson Something," said Mattie. She laid her head down on the table. "Gods, I am tired. I have to go to bed, Mom. I'll see what I can find out about Joseph the hand mauler tomorrow."

"And about Punk's will." Cate gathered up the wineglasses and the empty plate with only a few oatmeal crumbs left on it. "I'll ask Luna if she can tell us anything more."

Mattie started peeling out of her clothes as she stumbled toward the hall. "Did you hear about the diorama drama?"

"Sure I did. PZ loved telling it."

"I should have named that boy Hermes," said Mattie. "Good night, Mom. You're the best."

CHAPTER 30

Mattie

On Friday morning, Mattie came back from her eleven o'clock meeting to find another report from Ling sitting on her desk. Beside it, on a paper napkin, sat a tuna on toasted rye and a cold bottle of sparkling water. Picking up the phone, she rang the desk in the outer office. "You are too amazing, Ling."

"Thanks, boss. There were a few calls while you were out, but I thought I would wait to give them to you until after your lunch."

"Anything urgent?"

"Yes. Your tuna sandwich. It shouldn't sit out too long."

Mattie took a bite and remembered to taste it. She loved tuna fish, with celery and mayonnaise, lettuce and tomato and fresh rye bread. She even took another bite before opening the file.

Paul Kincaid's will was long, legally intricate, and detailed. There were various beneficiaries such as political groups and institutions of higher learning. However, regarding the major assets, the terms were clear, if surprising. He left the bulk of his estate to his sons. If they were deceased, the money went to their descendents. In the event that Paul Kincaid had no living heirs, his personal estate would go to the PNK Foundation and PNK, Inc. would go to the Joseph W. Worthington III. Ling had attached a separate memo listing the Board of Directors of both legal entities. Joseph Worthington was the Executive Director of the PNK Foundation.

The old man died a couple days after John. Paulo had been dead for several years. Mattie wondered if anyone had informed Punk when either were killed. According to Luna, he was never told about her marriage, nor did he know of the existence of Flora. However, John and Maria had visited him before they married and Maria had written him about her pregnancy. He might have changed the will had he known that both his sons were dead. Perhaps he didn't have time.

Ling buzzed Mattie's phone. "Yes?"

"Your mother's calling."

"Thanks," she said, punching up a line, putting her mother on her speakerphone. "What's up, Mom?"

"What are you doing?" asked Cate.

"Eating a tuna sandwich and trying not to drop mayo on the front of my suit." Mattie leaned forward just in time to prevent a loose lettuce leaf from hitting her skirt. It landed on the paper napkin.

"Luna and I are headed out to the Silver Bow to start getting ready for tonight. I wanted to remind you that you are expected to show up no later than six o'clock. This is not a request. It is a maternal mandate."

Mattie pulled a desk calendar toward her and examined it between slurps of sparkling water. "I have it on my calendar. I may even get there early. Did you talk with Ling, because she seems to have rescheduled a couple of things?"

"I certainly did. She said you didn't have anything that couldn't wait. She's a nice girl and you overwork her."

"Correct on both accounts," said Mattie, with a mouth full.

"Let her go early. Please come on out here. There's lots to do."

"Anything I need to pick up?"

"Yes," said Cate. "I faxed Ling a list."

"Great," said Mattie, her tone sarcastic. "Okay, I'll see you sometime before six."

"That is an excellent plan. Flora is bringing Chrys when they get out of school. PZ is spending the night with Atticus. I think they're going to a football game, but I'm not sure. Counting you and Artemis, there will be six for dinner." Cate hung up with a click.

Mattie got up and walked to Ling's desk. She was working on a document on her computer. "Did my mother...?"

"I called the Magnificent Market. They will deliver everything by four." Ling never looked away from her screen.

"Have I told you today how terrific you are?"

"Yes," said Ling. "Which is why you won't mind that I'm leaving at four-thirty. I have a haircut."

"I don't mind at all. In fact, leave earlier if you want to."

"I have to wait for the delivery guy."

"I think I can handle that," said Mattie.

"Great," said Ling. "I have a hot date tonight. I'll go buy something new to wear." She stopped typing and looked up. "Thanks."

"No, thank you. I understand my mother called and gave you a bunch of orders."

"Nah. We had a conference. For a witch, she's really nice."

CHAPTER 31

Whitey's house

"I saw her last night, I tell you. She said she works late most nights. I tried to get into her office, but the door was locked." Hank wore the uniform of a security guard, but he was sitting in Whitey's kitchen, drinking a beer.

"You're the security guard. Don't you have a key? I want you to get in there and find out what's going on at my ranch. Find out where that Meskin girl is. That lawyer woman will have records and it's for sure she knows where that Maria bitch is." Whitey turned his bottle up and part of his beer ran down his face on to his shirt. He wiped his mouth on his sleeve and took a puff from his glowing cigar.

"She sold the ranch," said Buzz. "I already told you that, sir. She sold it to a company called Silver Bow, Incorporated." The only one not drinking, he stood leaning against the kitchen counter with a glass of water in his hand.

"Why don't you forget about that Meskin?" said Ace, tipping his chair back and balancing his fancy boots on the table edge. "She's long gone and there don't seem to be no point in trying to track her down. She's doing the taco tango with some greasy guy, living it up, boss, with the money she got from selling our ranch."

"*My* ranch," said Whitey. "Warn't no *ours* about it."

"I got a whole ring of keys," said Hank. "Not a one of them opens the door to her office."

Whitey sulked, smoked, drank and sulked some more. "Who is that woman that's living out there, Buzz?"

"I told you everything I know about her."

"Well, when you going back out 'ere?"

Buzz put his glass in the dishwasher. "I'm supposed to be out there now," he said. "I said I would come today if I could."

"Any progress in the romance department?" asked Whitey.

"No, sir. But I haven't given up," said Buzz. He reflected on his odd conversation with Artemis regarding her being single and decided she was probably just teasing him.

"That's the spirit, son. Ask her if I can buy that statue of Granddaddy and Grandma. It breaks my heart to think about it sitting out there with nobody to take care of it. She don't know that it is a holy relic and will probably sell it cheap. Now get on about your bidness."

Hank, Ace and Whitey watched Buzz throw his napkin in the trash and leave by the back door.

Ace lifted his bottle toward his mouth, but paused in mid-air. "That boy plum gets on my nerves," he said. He finished the job and took a big swig. "The other day he damn near threw me through the front windshield. Said a squirrel ran across the road. A squirrel!" Ace made a derisive sound. "You heard anymore from Worthington?" he asked Whitey.

"Not lately. He said he had something important he was working on. Seems there is some kind of problem with his bidness. He'll work it out, though."

"I expect he will," said Ace.

Hank said, "I'll get a key to that office, boss. It's just some kind of mistake that it ain't on my ring."

CHAPTER 32

Buzz
The Silver Bow

Buzz climbed into his old pickup, still thinking about Lady Di. The door creaked when he opened it and he made a mental note to give the hinge some lubricant. He would need a new truck when he married Diane. Maybe a big black one with a double gun rack. The single rack in the back of the old Ford held one of Granddaddy's rifles. Ace kept it loaded in case of trouble. Lady Di had told him she was "single and determined to stay that way." Was she being modest? Humble? Humility is a good trait in a woman. Modesty, he mused, rare these days. She doesn't want to appear too eager, he guessed. The thought pleased him immensely.

It was close to four by the time he pulled up at the gate to the Silver Bow. He punched in the first two numbers of the code before he remembered that he wasn't supposed to know it. The intercom button brought no response. He tried again. He sat for five minutes trying to decide whether to let himself in or not. She had warned him against it and he didn't want to spook her. He'd almost blown it the last time. He waited some more, beginning to wonder if anything had happened to her. She had no business staying up here alone.

A girl was trotting toward him, coming from the house. He didn't recognize her. She ran like she enjoyed it, her head thrown back and her chest thrust forward. She stopped on the other side of the gate, breathing hard and smiling at him.

"Artemis said open it with that gizmo you used last time. She can't remember how to open the gate from the inside," said Chrys.

For a moment, Buzz panicked. The "gizmo" was entirely fictional. "Who are you?" he asked.

"Chrys," she said. "I'm her niece." She wrapped both hands around the bars of the gates, staring at the guy in an old pickup with a gun rack and spray painted spots.

Buzz climbed out of the truck and ambled over to her. "Do you know the code?" he asked. She shook her head. "Well, tell her that I gave it back, just like she said to." He told the girl where the button was located to open the gate and she ran back toward the house. He felt stupid standing beside his truck, waiting, when he easily could have let himself in. Maybe he should have just said he would use the "gizmo" again, but she might ask to see it. Telling lies was so hard. He couldn't keep up with them and it didn't seem like a good idea to write them down. He sighed impatiently. The gate began to slowly open.

He parked under a tree near the house, grabbed his toolbox from the bed of his truck and got out. Chrys was grinning at him from the front door. She beckoned him in.

She started bombarding him with words. "My Grandmother and Luna, that's her friend, are like cooking this big feast 'cause we're having this totally awesome ceremony tonight to like bless our new house. We're going to like cleanse the house and grounds of bad energy. My Mom is gonna come home from work early and we're going to have a big fire and stuff like that."

Buzz stood in the foyer, listening intently to everything she said. She looked over her shoulder as she started toward the kitchen. "What do you need? Artemis said to ask you."

"I guess I'll start in the kitchen," he said. "See what isn't working and go from there."

"Well, come on, then." She scampered away, but paused at the pile of animal trophies. "We're also going to have a funeral for these guys. Poor things."

Buzz paused beside the large Cross and One that lay in the middle of the empty floor. "What's going to happen to this?"

"Dunno," she said. "Burned, I guess."

He recoiled. "Can I have it?"

Chrys shrugged. "Probably. I gotta stir the soup. It's pumpkin. Did you ever have pumpkin soup?"

He shook his head, but she was already disappearing into the kitchen.

The room was redolent with the smell of spices and roasting meat. In the center of the large kitchen was a makeshift table, an old door on a pair of sawhorses. Around it were six folding chairs. Flora was laying out sage colored placemats and matching napkins. At the island stood Luna, chopping onions and celery. Cate was tasting a spoonful of the pumpkin soup.

"It needs a bit of allspice, I think. Maybe a sprinkle of mace. Did I bring any?"

"I'll look," said Chrys. She opened a big wicker hamper and stuck her head in so far you couldn't see it anymore.

"Where's the silver?" asked Flora. "And the glasses? In the cabinets?"

"Are you kidding?" said Chrys, emerging. She fished them out of the hamper along with the spices for her grandmother. "This is what's in the cabinets." She flung open a door. There stood six bowls, one wineglass and two coffee cups. "This is all the dishes Artemis owns. Can you believe it?"

"Why so many bowls?" asked Flora.

"To feed the dogs," said Chrys, opening another cabinet that held large bags of dog food.

Cate looked up from her tasting spoon and spotted Buzz. "Who are you?" she asked.

"I'm fixing the security system," he said. He scanned the room for any sign of Artemis, but she seemed to be missing. "I just need to get into the pantry." He nodded in the direction of a closed door.

"Help yourself," said Cate. "When you're finished I'll give you a bowl of my soup."

He gave her a dubious look, followed by a slight nod.

"What do we call you?" asked Chrys.

"Buzz," he said.

"Is that short for something? I can't think of anything that would be short for. Buzz-ard? Buzzle? Buzzillo? Is that English?"

He smiled. "It refers to my haircut," he said, rubbing a hand across the stubble on his head. "I've worn it like this all my life."

"It's kinda cool, I guess. Is it a nickname? Who gave it to you? When did you first get that kind of haircut? Did they call you something different before that? Cause it doesn't make sense to call a baby 'Buzz' if he was born like bald or something." Chrys followed him nearly into the pantry and leaned in the doorway. "Can I watch?"

"My mother named me Luke. It's not a name I care for," said Buzz, opening his toolbox and setting it on one of the deep, empty shelves. He pushed the panel that revealed the security monitors.

"I have this totally annoying brother, he has a nickname, too. His name is Pegasus, but I couldn't say that when I was a baby, so I like called him Pega-zeus. Ya know, like Zeus. Anyway, we call him PZ now. I don't remember when I started called him PZ, but everybody does now. Usually, I think, it's like somebody's mom that gives them a nickname, but I gave my brother his. If I had known how annoying he was going to be I'd have called him Weasel Butt or something. Did your mom give you your nickname?"

"No," said Buzz. "I think it was my father, when he gave me my first haircut with these clippers he has. I don't think I was much older than two or so." The monitors flickered on. He turned dials and adjusted sound levels.

"Chrys, let that poor man do his work and quit pestering him with questions," Cate called. "Come wash the lettuce."

Chrys gave him a wave and whirled around. "Is there a salad spinner?"

"What do you think?" said Flora.

"There's some paper towels," said Luna, pointing with her knife. "On the counter behind the sack of bread."

Buzz worked in the pantry, listening to the women cooking and joking with one another. He wondered about the ceremony they were planning. He fretted about the fate of the Cross and One. Primarily, however, he wondered where Lady Di was.

Chrys stuck her head in again. "Buzz, would you mind helping Artemis carry something?" she said.

"Not at all," he said. "Where is she?"

He followed the girl down the hall, where Artemis was struggling with the head of an elk buck with broad antlers. She wrestled with it, unable to steer down the hall and stay on her feet at the same time. Buzz took it from her, lifting it easily. "Where do you want it?" he said.

"Out by the fire pit," she said. "We're cremating them. I considered burial, but I don't have a backhoe to dig the pit."

"There's one in the garage," he said, before he could catch himself.

"Like I know how to operate it," said Artemis. "I think this will be fine. Can you help me carry all this out there?" She motioned to the pile.

It took them a half dozen trips to carry the menagerie of heads outside. When they returned, Buzz pointed at the Cross and One.

"What are you going to do with that?" he asked.

"Now that's a hard question," said Artemis. "I don't really know."

"Can I have it?" he asked, hesitantly.

"Does Zeus mess around?" she said.

"Uhm," he replied, thinking of Chrys's story about Peg and Zeus. "I don't know him."

"It's just a joke," she laughed. "Of course. Take it. I'm glad to find someone who wants it. I have no desire to desecrate it. A Christian, are you?"

"Yes, ma'am. I certainly am." Buzz stood tall, full of pride until the tiniest drop of doubt soaked into his brain." Aren't you?"

"No, I'm one of those pagan babies they used to tell you about in vacation Bible school, but, please don't try to convert me."

It seemed to him that his dreams ought to make a big old slurping sound as they went down the toilet. He stood very still for a moment, just feeling the fresh wound bleeding. He picked up the big cross and began dragging it toward the door.

"Do you want any help?" she asked.

"No," he said, in a despairing tone.

"Suit yourself," she said, and heading toward the kitchen. "Don't scratch the floor."

Buzz found an old bedspread behind his seat. He carefully wrapped the cross in it and laid it in the bed of his truck. He was too heartsick to go back in the house, so he decided to walk around the property. Whitey had been worried about the statue. Maybe he could find it and take it back to the old man. They might trade him for some work and he could make a present of it. He needed to do something to restore his sense of order.

The cold slipped through his shirt and chilled him to his bones. The moon was sidling upward, slipping in and out of dark clouds blown across a blue black sky. His mood was darker than the shadows between the tall trees. He would never find his Lady Diana. He knew that now. He would spend the rest of his life selling tires and hanging out with angry old men. In another ten or fifteen years he would be like Hank and Ace, ugly, sullen and mean. His Daddy would die and leave him sorry land that only grew debts and taxes. He'd end up living in the ramshackle house alone, cleaning Granddaddy's guns, eating soup out of cans and fixing holes in the old roof. He would never have a son of his own to leave the worthless place to. He could sell it, if anyone would buy it. He thought of his mother, standing at the ironing board in her underwear and wondered if she ever thought about him. Maybe she was dead. He hadn't heard from her in years. A tight knot was forming around his heart and tears were threatening. He wanted to hide somewhere. He ran for the shed and let himself in with a key that he himself had hidden beneath a rock years ago.

When he closed the door, his eyes were able to register nothing. Black shades blocked the last twinges of twilight that might have come in through the windows. He fumbled along the wall and located a switch. The room appeared untouched since his last visit. There was a thick layer of dust over everything. He touched a panel on the wall and it swung open to reveal a set of controls identical to those in the kitchen pantry. He stared at them for a while, but turned nothing on. The idea of turning them on made him a bit queasy, remembering the days when Whitey would put him on guard duty for months. Before he had gotten to be part of the leadership team, he had logged in thousands of hours during the long nights, staring at the little screens.

In those days, he'd watched the older men going into the meeting hall or strategizing around the kitchen table. He eavesdropped while they soaked in the hot tub, or lounged around at the picnic area with their wives and kids. It seemed like a very long time ago. In an old brown corduroy armchair with a deep butt impression in the threadbare seat, he had dreamt about the day when he would become an officer in the Cross and One. With a deep sigh, he turned on the rickety floor lamp and switched off the overhead light. The building was old, a small stone structure built by Elwood J. White. Across the tin ceiling ran conduit to carry wires. Electricity had been added when the structure was converted to the surveillance center by Whitey. He had also added heat and a lock on the door. The strangest thing about the "shed," as it was called, was that it concealed the entrance to a tunnel. Hidden at the back of the closet was a small door that opened onto some narrow, rickety steps. Elwood dug the tunnel himself to provide an escape hatch if he ever needed it. Buzz had never been down there, but he heard that it was a kind of emergency bunker, with a generator, cots, lanterns, water and provisions. They called it the Armageddon Tunnel. It came out near the trail where he had walked with Artemis. The thought of that morning brought a fresh pang of mortification. He turned slowly around. It was just another reminder of silly fantasies he'd once had about his future. He closed up the surveillance panel and leaned down to click off the lamp. Locking the door, he replaced the hidden key and jogged toward the house.

A black Jaguar pulled up at the gate, the headlight casting shadows of the running Ws across the road. The driver entered the code and slide past the gate as it opened. Buzz stood staring at the retreating car, at the sticker on the bumper that was identical to the one on Artemis's car. He tried to think what it could possibly mean, since his first assumption had been so inaccurate. He was beginning to wonder if he wasn't wrong about everything.

Just as he was about to head back to the house, he caught a glimpse of headlights coming down the road from the highway. They turned into the woods and disappeared. Buzz slipped through the gate just before it closed and ran. He kept to the road as long as he could, fearful of tripping in the darkness. Then he slipped quietly into the forest at about the place where he thought the lights had turned in. He didn't have to go far. Ace was leaning up against his Silverado, smoking, one boot propped on the door. Hank stood near him, his hands in his pockets and a grimy cowboy hat perched on his head.

"Well, look what the Boy Scouts left behind," said Ace. "What the hell you doing here, boy?"

Buzz said, "Following orders. What are you two doing here?"

"You won't believe it," said Hank. "Ace and me followed that lawyer bitch after she left work and this is where she ended up."

"Maybe she's just doing some legal work. Handling the sale or something," said Buzz."

"Maybe," said Hank. "Something interesting might be going on in there. Something Whitey would like to know about. I say we go on in and see what we can find out. Maybe that Meskin woman is in there—the one that stole our ranch."

"She's not here, Hank. In fact, there's nothing going on in there that would be of any interest to you, or Whitey, or anyone else. A bunch of women are cooking supper. That's it. There is one thing that I thought was funny, though. You remember that girl we saw at McDonald's, the one with the license plate that said PUNKIN?"

Hank tried to stifle a laugh and ended up choking. Ace was suddenly quite alert.

"What's the matter with you?" said Buzz to Hank.

Hank grinned. "Well, I never told you fellas, but I had me a good time pulling some Halloween pranks on that little gal."

"Are you the one that sliced her tires?" asked Buzz.

"Maybe," he said, grinning.

"That was an idiotic thing to do, you peckerhead," said Buzz.

Hank answered him with a gloating smile. "I hear you got her fixed up again. Is her car up at the house?"

"Wait a second," said Ace. "Is this the Lopez girl?"

Buzz stared at Ace. "Yeah. Did Whitey tell you that? Mr. Worthington was interested in her, too. She's just a high school girl. I can't understand what's the big deal. It's quite a coincidence, finding her here."

"What's she doing?" Ace asked.

"She was setting the table when I saw her," said Buzz. "What do you care?"

"I just wondered," said Ace. "Is it a party or what?"

"It's six women having dinner together. There's going to be some kind of blessing of the house afterwards. Then they're going to burn Whitey's hunting trophies in the fire pit. They're giving them a funeral, or something."

Hank found this funny as well. "A funeral! For a dead antelope!" He snorted.

"Well, just for the head. We done ate the rest." Putting his hands on his knees, he bent over with hilarity. Finally, he straightened up, his chuckles trailing off. "Come on, Ace," he said. "It don't seem like there's much happening tonight. I don't know what that lawyer bitch is doing, but it probably ain't nothing. Take me back to Whitey's. I need to pick up my truck. It's Friday night and I'm going to see what I can pick up at the Lonesome Bear."

"Is she there, the one that sued us?" asked Ace.

"Maria? No. I think she's gone for good," said Buzz.

"That's one greasaria that won't be having anymore mud babies."

"What I can't figure out," said Buzz, "is why her baby died. We didn't do anything but blindfold her and scare her a little."

Hank gave Ace a knowing grin. "I reckon you never told him about your *private* moments alone with the Señora?"

"What is he talking about?" said Buzz. "Didn't you take her back to the parking lot after we left?"

Ace, ignored his question. "How much longer are you staying, Buzz?"

Buzz gave him an angry look, but answered, "I'm going home in a minute or two. Got to load up my tools first."

"And after that?" said Ace.

"After that, it's a microwave dinner and a diet root beer in front of the television."

"Well, you call in and report to Whitey. You hear me? Go on home and get some sleep. He's probably got some work he needs done tomorrow and it sounds like ole Hank here is going to be hung over."

"Probably so," said Hank, still in a state of amusement.

Buzz watched the taillights of the truck until they turned on to the highway. He didn't like the thought of either one of those two able to get to Artemis. He decided he would change the code before he left.

Letting himself back through the gate, he hoped no one was going to notice. He got back to the house and rang the bell. "God Bless America" tolled through the empty rooms. The front door opened and a scowly-faced Artemis looked out at him.

"Would you disconnect that damn thing before you leave? Can you install a plain 'ding dong'?"

"I'll be happy to replace it," he said. "I can't do it today, though. I'll have to buy a new doorbell."

"Buy whatever you need. Just get it to quit." She was in her socks, running pants and a red turtleneck. "Aren't you about finished? I thought you had gone."

"Yes, ma'am. I'm just loading my tools onto the truck. I thought I'd change the codes before I leave. You don't really know how many people have the old one. Would you choose a number for me to use? I need six digits."

"Sure," she said. "Use 10-31-44. That's Cate's birthday. We'll all be able to remember that."

Buzz said, "Who is Cate?"

"Cate is the matriarch of this family. She's the one doing all the preparations in the kitchen."

"This is a family?"

"Yes, what did you think it was?"

"Oh, I thought a corporation had bought this big compound. What are you going to use all this for?" He gestured toward the mountains.

Artemis gave him a little shrug and said, "For living." She pointed toward the kitchen. "Would you mind finishing up as quickly as you can? We're having a family get together tonight and it's getting late. Give me a call next week about the doorbell."

"Uh, ma'am?" He trotted along behind her, matching her brisk stride.

She stopped abruptly. "What? Are you wondering about getting paid? What do I owe you? I'll write you a check."

"No, I was wondering," he stammered. "That statue...?"

"The one out in the yard? What about it?"

"Would you consider trading me for it? I'll know that the work probably isn't equal to what it's worth, but..."

Artemis interrupted him. "There's an extra fifty bucks in it for you if you'll haul it off. It might be too heavy for that little truck of yours, though. You'll have to get something bigger, and bring someone to help you load it."

The kitchen was empty when they got there. Buzz caught a glimpse of a tray sitting on the counter. Cate's ritual tools were neatly laid out on it.

"Will two fifty cover your work to date?" Artemis asked, pulling her wallet out of a purse sitting on the floor. Buzz nodded, still a bit dumbstruck by her beauty. "Here you go," she said, handing him the check. "Can you let yourself out? I've got things I need to do. I'll tell everybody about the new code."

He watched her leave, then walked over to stare at Cate's tools. There was a straight wooden stick. Oak, he guessed, by the look of it. It was about as long as a woman's forearm and hand. An empty silver cup was engraved with what looked like the star of Texas, and a tiny silver bell stood beside it, the kind used to summon servants in PBS mysteries set in English castles. There was a small blue bowl of water and a matching one holding what looked like salt. He confirmed this by touching a grain to his tongue. Sitting on top was a single briquette of charcoal. A third bowl, even tinier, held herbs and slivers of wood. He lifted it to his nose and discovered that it smelled of rosemary, cedar and juniper. He detected a hint of cinnamon and cloves, but thought that it might be coming from the soup on the stove. All of this seemed exceedingly strange. Most surprising to him was a double-edged knife with a silver handle, encrusted with red stones. By running his finger lightly across the blade, he discovered that it was not sharp. On the counter sat a black soup pot. Three-legged and made of cast iron, he supposed it was used for cooking things over a fire. As far as the rest of the paraphernalia went, he could not imagine their use. Hearing voices in the hall, he slipped into the pantry and softly closed the door.

"I am, like, ecstatic that I have my own bathroom," said Chrys. "You can't imagine what a pain it is to share with PZ. He *never* puts the seat down. He leaves wet towels on the floor and his clothes smell like a sweaty horse most of the time." Chrys and Flora entered the kitchen, both in terrycloth bathrobes with towels wrapped around their heads. "I think Mattie and Artemis are still in the shower. Cate's already dressed and ready for the ritual. She's meditating, I imagine. You want something to drink?"

"Just water," said Flora. "I don't like to eat much before," she said. "I like being hungry for the feast. It makes everything taste better."

"I'm having some mint tea. I want to warm up my insides," said Chrys.

"Okay, that's fine," replied Flora. "Where's my Mama?"

"Probably with Cate. Isn't she usually?"

"Yeah, if she's not cooking. Looks like that's all done," Flora said, lifting the lid on the soup pot. A spicy steam filled her nose and she inhaled as deeply as she was able. "Mmmm. Punkin soup. My favorite. I hope she didn't use PZ's barfing pumpkin to make it."

Chrys laughed. "No. I think she uses a different kind than any of those we used on the illuminart. It's a small, sweet pumpkin. She gets them at the Farmer's Market."

The two girls chattered happily, fixing their tea and talking about the coming evening. Chrys grabbed two oatmeal cookies, but Flora stood firm in her resolve to fast until the evening meal was served.

"We've got to dry our hair," said Flora. "It's going to be chilly. I think I'll wear my jeans and sweater under my robe."

"I hate blowing my hair dry, but I look like a tumbleweed if I don't. I'm going to need one more cookie to keep up my strength," said Chrys.

"Cate wants us outside by seven-thirty, in time to sweep the area around the fire pit," said Flora.

"Then she'll create the circle," said Chrys.

"The fire pit is perfect," said Flora, and the two girls were gone.

When he heard their footsteps fade, Buzz relaxed a bit in the dark pantry. He was consumed with curiosity. What did she mean, "create the circle" and what was she saying about the fire pit? Why would girls wear bathrobes over their clothes? Debating what to do, he flipped on the switches that illuminated the video monitors. He couldn't see much at the moment, but there was a good chance he'd be able to observe something if he waited long enough. He turned up the audio and adjusted the focus on the camera at the deserted fire pit. In the darkness, he could barely make out an unlit stack of firewood, carefully arranged around the kindling that would make it easy to ignite. He zoomed in and out until he was satisfied that he would be able to view the entire circle. Too bad, he thought, that I only installed one camera there. Two or even three would have been better. Several cardboard boxes of files were sitting on the floor of the pantry, labeled "A's research." He stacked one on top of the other until he had made a comfortable stool for himself. Leaning his back against the wall, he settled in to watch the show.

Cate's gossamer cape blew behind her outstretched arms, like the wings of a giant silver moth. She lifted her face to the moon. Strands of hair whipped about her face and a lunar reflection illuminated her eyes. She inhaled deeply, paused, and exhaled. Closing her eyes helped her to focus on the air flowing in and through her, dispelling the residue of a busy day. As she prepared herself for her role as priestess, she concentrated on releasing fears, anxieties, doubts and resentments that might impair her abilities. She conjured a mental image of herself as a gleaming silver vessel, clean and empty. She was ready to meet her gods.

Luna approached her from behind and, wrapping a grey wool shawl around Cate's shoulders, she said, "It's cold. I built a fire in the pit. Come and warm yourself."

They walked down the hill toward the blaze. The area was recessed into the ground. Two sets of four steps descended to a limestone walk. In the middle was a circular hole where the fire leapt up from dry pine logs. Rock benches curved around the walls. The fire pit had been built in the twenties as a setting for male bonding, a site for smoking, drinking, and telling whoppers. In the storytime world of the fire pit, the fish are always wily and weighty. Dangerous prey always end up dead. Women swoon when confronted with the enormity of masculine superiority. Theirs were stories of order maintained in a world ruled by men. The participants had fully expected that life would go on in this manner indefinitely. On this night, Cate had something else in mind.

Flora came out of the house, wearing a long black robe and carrying a new broom. She removed the cellophane wrapper, wadded and tossed it into the fire. With a smile for her mother, she began a wordless sweeping, pushing dust and fallen leaves into the flames.

When the area was spotless, she stopped, leaning on her broom and looking to her mother for instructions.

Luna watched her daughter with pleasure, the girl's body glowing in the firelight, her black hair as shiny as polished onyx. She said, "Go get the others, *hija bella*. We are ready to begin."

Flora ran to the house. The robe flapped behind, her running shoes and blue jeans incongruous beneath the voluminous garment. She returned, followed by the other women. Mattie wore her black velvet cape over dark slacks and a turtleneck. A topaz pendant hung around her neck. Artemis, walking beside her, wore a grey velvet cape that stopped at the knees, with matching slacks and a sweater. Her pendant was an emerald, and the same stones glittered in her ears. She and her cousin strode purposefully toward the fire, intention in their gazes and strength in their spines. Bringing up the rear was Chrys, wrapped in a plain black cape identical to Flora's. She walked more slowly than the others, careful not to tip the tray she carried with Cate's ritual tools. Each entered the stone circle in silence.

Down the steps came Luna, carrying a wooden altar, which she placed on the south side of the circle, facing the fire. Cate discarded the shawl she had been clutching around her shoulders. She rose from her seat, took the tray from her granddaughter and carried it to the altar. Luna took it from her and held it as Cate assembled the altar.

On her left, at the top of the altar, she placed a silver candlestick and put a white candle in it. On the right side, she put a brass candlestick with a yellow candle. She arranged the bowls of water and salt, the cup and the bell. She wrapped her fingers around the athame and clipped it to a silver chain about her waist. The cauldron and wand went near the bottom. She nodded at Artemis and Mattie.

They disappeared into the darkness and returned, carrying the hunting trophies. After several trips, the benches around the limestone walls were lined with animal heads.

Firelight glittered in the glass eyes, giving them the appearance of life.

Flora emerged from the shadows holding a clear vase filled with bronze chrysanthemums and greenery. She placed this in the center of the altar and took a seat beside the head of a bison. She wrapped her arms around the animal and he seemed to enjoy the attention.

Cate smiled at her, then turned to her task. From her pocket she drew a knife with a mother of pearl handle. Holding it in both hands, she touched its tip to the water. "We ask of the Goddess a blessing upon this water." She touched the blade to the salt. "We ask of the God a blessing upon this salt." Laying the knife on the altar, she took up her wand, and turned her face skyward, orienting herself toward the North Star. She walked around the fire until she reached the northernmost corner. Wand raised, she said, "I call upon the powers of the North, realm of the earth. From the soil we come and to it we will return. Each day you provide us with food, just as you do for our fellow creatures and the plants that grow around us. The molecules of our ancestors are immortalized in the leaves of the trees, the flesh of the deer, the undulating grasses. Join with us in our mission tonight—a blessing of this soil and a renewal of its powers."

Cate moved clockwise. "I call upon the powers of the East, the realm of air. We share the realm of air with plants and animals, each drawing in and letting go. Molecules of oxygen make our blood red just as they did for every creature who has lived. Inspire us, spirit of the East. "

She followed the perimeter of the circle until she reached the southern corner. "I call upon the powers of the South, realm of fire. Fire transforms the food we eat into energy and power. Burn in our hearts and minds that we may be filled with compassion and a zeal for living in spirit. Illuminate, that we may see into the dark shadows and resurrect that which has been buried, ostracized or demonized, both within ourselves and in our world. Purify our desires so that we may bring love. Light the flame of transformation."

Finally, she stood before the steps that marked the western corner. "I call upon the powers of the West, realm of water. Our bodies are comprised primarily of water. Cleanse us of hatred and fear, for they pollute the heart and the soul. Wash away resentment, anger and the desire to harm, for we are all part of a great whole. When we harm another, we harm ourselves. Dissolve within us the illusion of separation. Quench the thirst that has made a desert here." Cate completed her trip around the circle, stopping at the altar, where she gently laid her wand.

She pulled a box of matches from her pocket and lit the white candle. "I call upon the Great Mother, Goddess of all that is. I open myself to your power that the work we do here tonight may serve the highest good." The flame leapt up. Cate's rubies gleamed in the light, her pentacle glittering. With a second match, she lit the yellow candle. "I call upon the Great Father, God of all that is. I open myself to your power that the work we do here tonight may serve the highest good." She set a piece of charcoal in the bowl of salt.

Atop it she put the incense, touched a match to it and blew to encourage the smoldering. "It is our way to speak of the divine as the Goddess and the God. However, we know that divine powers reveal themselves in many forms and are called by many names. We honor all manifestations of the Deity, blessing all divine forms. We bless those who worship differently. May those who have been here before us come to see that all are one in the divine scheme. May nothing enter here but love. May nothing leave here but love. I declare this circle sacred and complete." She tossed the spent matches into the fire and took a seat.

Hand in hand, Chrys and Flora stood. Flora said, "It was our idea that we hold a ceremony for the animals tonight, so I guess Chrys and I will begin. I have chosen brother bison as my companion." She struggled with the huge head, staggering under the weight. "I thank you, brother bison, for the gift of your life. May the element of fire release you and send you on to your next journey. Blessed be." She managed to throw the burdensome trophy into the flaming pit.

"I have chosen brother elk," said Chrys, behind a mask of antlers. "I call upon the element of fire to release you. Blessed be."

One by one, each of the women chose an animal to feed the flame. The old trophies burned quickly. An acrid stench of singed hair stinging their nostrils, the women watched flesh and wood turn to ash and smoke curl upward toward the moon.

"Where are the antlers?" whispered Mattie.

"I don't know. I put them out with the trash and they were stolen. I guess somebody wanted them." Artemis removed her cape and folded it up. "I figured it was okay. They lose them every year."

"I didn't know that. How do you know that?"

Artemis just rolled her eyes. "I know stuff like that."

"We're in the middle of a ritual here," admonished Cate.

Artemis folded her legs up with her feet tucked under her thighs and clamped her mouth shut.

Cate spoke. "At this time of year, we think of those who have gone before us. Artemis, Atticus and I begin a new cycle in our lives. The earth begins a new cycle in her own. On this night, we focus on the inhabitants of this beautiful piece of land where my children have become the temporary caretakers. Through the sacrifice of the animals, we acknowledge their many gifts, releasing the power inherent in the images in thanks giving." She lifted the vase of flowers skyward. "We recognize also the gifts of the land, the beauty and nourishment that rises from the soil." She pulled the bouquet from the vase and tossed it into the fire. "We make this sacrifice as a sign of gratitude." Cate set the vase aside and raised her arms skyward. "I call upon the spirits of those who have occupied this place before us, plant and animal, including human beings. Close your eyes, my dear ones, and see who visits you."

They sat for a minute or two in silence. "I am seeing elk, deer, rabbits, mice, snakes, so many kinds of wildlife that I can't name them all. There are thousands and thousands of them. Oh, yeah, birds, too," said Chrys.

"I see a field of wildflowers, pine trees and spruce, aspen, grasses, moss, all kinds of plants in all seasons," said Flora.

"I am seeing the men in white robes and heads covered in hoods. They are on horseback, carrying torches and riding hard," said Cate.

"A beautiful Native American woman stands before me," said Luna. "She has her daughter by the hand, a girl who looks like she is about four or five."

Mattie spoke. "I see a woman in a gingham dress, driving a wagon. It seems to me that she is a widow. There are two children, a boy and a girl, sitting beside her on the wooden seat. She has a look of determination on her face as she urges the horses on."

Artemis rocked her body gently. Rather than closing her eyes, she stared into the firelight, entranced. "I'm seeing the people in that statue, only they are alive. Elwood J. White was a strong man with wide shoulders and muscular forearms. His wife is a mousy little thing, trailing along behind him with a baby on her hip and another little kid hanging on to her skirt. He is yelling at her about something. I remember three kids in the statue. Wait. Maybe she's pregnant here. Holy smoke. He just smacked her across the face. Why that old bas...."

"Artemis!" Cate rebuked her.

"I'll try. I'll send him love, even if he is an old *buzzard.*"

"In the name of the Goddess, we bless *all* who have gone before us. We are one in the great chain of being."

"I don't want to be one with Elwood J. White," muttered Artemis.

"Whether you want to be or not, you are. Examine your heart, Artemis, for traces of the same kind of fear and alienation that made him behave the way he did. The absence of love is fear. We all experience both."

"Yeah, but I don't make the same kind of behavioral choices he did."

"You don't have to like him to send him love," said Chrys.

Artemis furrowed her brow at the girl, but gave her a wink. Chrys smiled at her.

Cate shushed them and continued. "Bless those that are in despair. May they find joy. Bless those who feel alone. May they be reunited. Bless those who are in distress or dis-ease. May they be healed. Bless the hatred that finds haven in our hearts and the hearts of others. May it be transformed to love. May we live our lives and do our work in harmony with our own purpose and all that is."

Cate retraced her steps, North to East to South to West, raising her wand. "We are earth, air, fire and water. We are nourishment and matter. We are spirit and mind, inspiration and divination. We are passion, strength, and transformation. We are emotion, beauty, healing and love. With these powers we declare this land to be sacred, our lives to be purposeful and the world to be one."

The six women stood, holding hands. They raised their arms to the sky and spoke in unison. "And so it is."

"We thank the God and Goddess for their presence and their power and invite them to be with us all the days of our lives. We call our energy back into our bodies, with gratitude and joy." She took the knife and pierced the invisible sphere. Luna dismantled the altar, quenching the candles with wet fingertips. Chrys poured the water on the ground, and consigned the incense to the fire.

"That was a powerful circle tonight," said Chrys. "I'm all sweaty. Can we get in the hot tube, A?"

"I don't see why not," said Artemis.

One stifled sob escaped from Buzz. He stared into the video monitors, letting tears run down his cheeks. He watched Chrys and Flora gleefully pull off their clothing. They carefully folded their black robes, discarded their running shoes and socks, wadded their jeans and sweaters. Flora unhooked a red lace bra and dropped it on one of the stone benches. She stepped out of the matching thong, threw it on the heap of clothing. Silhouetted against the flames, her lithe body stretched upward as she raised her arms over her head and stretched. Buzz let out a groan. The slim, prepubescent figure of Chrys appeared beside her, grabbed her hand and began to tug her toward the pool.

"Come on, Flora. I'm getting goose-bumps standing out here," said Chrys.

He heard the voice of Artemis. "I'm going to let the dogs out," she said. "Then I'll join you."

Buzz moaned again, and momentarily squeezed his eyes shut. His heart beating fast in his chest, he found the monitor that covered the pool area and zoomed in on the hot tub. Chrys and Flora were stepping down into the bubbles. A swirl of steam rose around their bodies. He turned off the audio feed from the fire pit, and activated the microphones at the pool. He zoomed in on Flora's beautiful cara-mel colored breasts, bobbing in the water, her nipples peaking through the mist. She leaned her head back against the edge and groaned in pleasure. Buzz did too.

A woman's foot and ankle appeared beside Flora's head. He zoomed out to get the full view. This was no girl. Mattie was voluptuous and curvaceous, full-breasted, with wide inviting hips and luxuriant pubic hair. Placing one hand on the top of Flora's head to balance herself, she descended into the frothing water. Cate's body was still lean, but her breasts drooped and she had a slight belly pouch. Luna was brown and round, with breasts like cantaloupes and plump buttocks. Buzz held his breath, waiting to see if Artemis would appear. He stared at all those breasts, different shapes, colors and sizes. He had never touched a breast before, never even seen one except in magazines, on television, or in the movies. He wondered if he had ever touched his mother's breasts. He doubted it. He couldn't even imagine such a thing. Nevertheless, this feast of femininity filled him with longing, deeper and sadder than the usual loneliness he walked around in. He was breathing faster now, and he felt an erection straining at his jeans. Then he saw her, just her feet and calves.

The muscles were taut, like a runner. Her toe-nails were unpolished, unlike the girls' whose pinkies gleamed like fresh cherries.

He had his hand poised to change the angle of the camera so he could zoom in on the goddess Diana, when a flicker of movement on another screen caught his eye. There appeared to be someone in the shed. He saw the monitors come on, one by one, a hand moving along the switches. Buzz turned down the sound of the happy, bubbling women and selected the audio feed from the shed. He heard only the slightest rustle of movement. Then, on his own screen, he saw the intruder flip the switch for the hot tub camera.

"Sweet Jesus!" came the voice from the shed. The monitors cast enough light for Buzz to make out the figure moving to the dilapidated old chair. The rickety floor lamp came on, shining directly on a pair of pointed toe cowboy boots. Elaborately stitched into the leather was the sign of the Cross and One.

"Sweet Jesus!" murmured Buzz.

✷ ✷ ✷

Delighted to be released, the greyhounds raced about the lawn in ecstasy. Artemis marveled at their speed and grace, the delight they took in their own bodies. She stood naked, beside the tub full of celebratory women, watching her exuberant dogs, thinking that life can be truly grand.

Mattie said, "Get in, Cuz. I have some amazing news."

"You're as bossy as Cate," said Artemis.

"I am not," said Mattie.

"Neither of you have reached my bossiness proficiency. You haven't the maturity," said Cate.

"Mattie is getting there," said Artemis. She stepped down into the water, sliding under until the water touched her chin. "What's the big news?"

"The biggest news is that Maria wants to send Flora to college," said Mattie.

Flora sat up straight, creating a splash of waves. "What! What did you say?"

"I spoke with Maria yesterday. She and I are working on creating a scholarship for Mexican-American women. She wants you to be the first recipient."

"*Mi Madre!* How much is the scholarship? Is it for a specific school, or can I choose?" The girl's dark eyes sparkled. "I can't believe this. I'm going to call her tonight. She is the most wonderful aunt in the world. Oh, Mattie, how can I thank you both?"

"Could she, like, go to Stanford, Mom?" said Chrys, a smile of self-satisfaction on her face.

"She can go wherever she likes," said Mattie. "Well, wherever she is admitted. So you better start thinking about those applications, Flora. I understand they're a real hassle."

Flora spoke to her own mother. "Did you know about this?"

"I knew that Maria was considering it. She and I spoke on the phone last night. She loves you very much. Still, it is very generous of her," said Luna.

"I hope she has kids of her own some day," said Flora.

"The doctors don't hold out much hope for that," said Luna.

"Not all children come to you that way," said Cate. "Look how many I have and I was pregnant only once."

"Which produced the superior one, of course," said Mattie.

"Not necessarily," said Cate. "Chrys is the best cook, the best at decorating…."

"…the best at dioramas, pumpkin carving and oatmeal cookies," said Mattie.

"Funny, Mom," said Chrys. "My diorama was fine. It was just Bozo Breath who didn't do anything…."

"I know, honey. I'm just teasing you. Your grandmother thinks you're her best kid. The fact that I am your mother is irrelevant."

"Chrys is tied for first place with Candle." Cate grinned at Mattie, who glared back. "Come on, witch baby. This is all just teasing. You know that I love each of you with every ounce of my being. There is no hierarchy to unconditional love. I think now is the time to talk about the will."

"What will?" said Chrys. "Who died? Nobody we know, I hope."

"Punk Kincaid is dead," said Mattie.

"Good," said Luna.

"There's a will," said Mattie.

✫ ✫ ✫

"They know about the will," said Ace. "I just heard them talking about it." He sat slumped in the corduroy chair, his boots on the ottoman, speaking into his cell phone. "They're all here. The Lopez girl, her Mama, and that bitch lawyer, along with the witch that Buzz has got the hots for and her crazy Mother. I'm watching them float around in Whitey's hot tub, naked as the day they come into this world. And Ms. Lawyer Lady just said something about Punk Kincaid's will."

Ace listened. "Okay. I understand. I'll handle it." The voice on the other line rattled more instructions. "Won't nobody know I's ever here. I'll leave the same way I come in, through the Armageddon Tunnel."

Buzz only heard Ace's side of the conversation, but he could imagine who was on the other end of the line. He knew of only one person that was interested in Punk Kincaid.

CHAPTER 33

The Silver Bow

Mattie recounted her research about Paul N. Kincaid and his companies. Moon Doggie and Streak came sauntering over to the tub. With an exhausted sigh, they plopped down near Artemis, tongues hanging out of their happy faces.

"Where is Lightning?" she asked them. They didn't answer. "If there's a way to escape this fortress, I'm sure that rascal will find it. She reminds me more and more of PZ."

"So, that's all I know," said Mattie. "There's a possibility that Flora might inherit something from her grandfather. However, there's been a lot of controversy over the terms of the will and it is a complicated estate. I wouldn't count on anything, if I were you."

"I don't want any of the old man's money," said Luna, bitterly. "Paulo hated him. I can't think that anything good could come of this."

"Perhaps," said Cate, "this is the time to stop hating. That's one good thing that might come of it."

Luna sighed. "I never met the man, but I used to get furious when Paulo would tell me about his childhood. Particularly the stories about his mother and how his father treated her."

"Actually, it isn't your decision to make. Flora is the one that is involved. I just wanted to tell you what I found out. Tonight is not the time to decide and we don't have all the information. I'll call his attorneys on Monday," said Mattie.

Flora was as white as a golden-colored girl can be. "I don't have any idea what to say, or do. First I find out that my *Tia Maria* is going to send me to college. Then I hear that my grandfather, who never heard of me and was cruel to my father, might or might not have left me some money. I don't know what to think, or feel, or want." She pulled her straight black hair up off her neck, holding it on top of her head. "I am boiling in here. I have to get out and cool off."

Steam rose from her body as she climbed out of the water. She walked into the darkness, trailing clouds of mist. She turned her back to them. With outstretched arms, her beautiful body stood silhouetted in the moonlight.

"Leave her alone," said Cate. "I think I'll get out and get supper on the table. I'll holler when it's ready."

"I'll help," said Artemis. "I think I'm pickled."

"Help would be nice, dear. You know you're my favorite," said Cate. The women laughed.

Artemis climbed out, and wrapped a big fluffy towel around her breasts. "Come on, girls. Where's your bad little sister?" Just at that moment, Artemis caught sight of a blur of white in the woods. She tucked the towel edges together under her arms. "I'll be there in just a minute, Cate. I'm going to get Lightning."

The two greyhounds trotted beside her as she walked briskly toward the shadowy pines. She crossed the lawn, staring into the forest for another flash of her wayward puppy. He bare feet were growing icy and she danced in pain when she stepped on a pinecone. Peering into the shadows, she debated whether to go back and get dressed or just try to lure the wayward hound back home. She thought she saw movement, but instinct stopped her before she called out. It was not her dog she saw. Instead she caught a glimpse of Flora, being dragged into the shadows by a man with a knife at her throat.

Artemis put two fingers in her mouth and let out a piercing whistle. Ace froze. He caught sight of Artemis and muttered a curse. She met his eye with a fierce look, and he returned it with one of pure hatred. She dropped the towel she was clutching around her body. Ace was so taken by surprise that he loosened his grip on Flora, who twisted away. He grabbed her arm, twisted it behind her back and yanked her tight against himself.

Gris Lightning came flying out of the blackness. She headed straight for her mistress, but when she caught sight of Flora, she could not resist the temptation to greet her with doggy kisses. Lightning flung herself at the naked girl and her abductor. Ace went down, slicing Flora's arm as the knife slid across. She was, however, momentarily free and she ran like a fawn. Ace fought off the dog, whose instincts told her this was no friend. Lightning leapt back when Ace lunged at her with the knife. He tried to grab her, but the dog was too quick. In a flash, she was after Flora and out of his reach. Ace pursued the girl. He was only yards behind her. She was running barefoot and it was rough going over the stones and pinecones. He grabbed for her hair. Her head snapped back and she went down.

Artemis heard a shot. Ace fell, his hands still clutching Flora's hair. She screamed and yanked herself away.

Beside the empty swimming pool, stood the lonely figure of a young man, his Granddaddy's rifle at his shoulder.

CHAPTER 34

Las Sombras
A week later

"He read somewhere that a cat always lands on his feet," said Mattie. "So he put one in the dryer. Left the door open but taped down the button, and turned it on. He wanted to see if the cat would keep landing on its feet."

"What happened?" asked Luna.

"Where did he get a cat?" asked Cate.

"The cat belongs to one of his friends. We were keeping it over the weekend. She threw up all over the inside of the dryer. That's what happened." Mattie folded her arms, looking disgusted.

"I cleaned it up," said PZ. He was across the room, standing in front of Cate's big fireplace.

"Then Artemis disinfected it with bleach," said Mattie. "We haven't even moved in yet and PZ got cat puke all over the inside of the dryer."

"There's another laundry room in the bunkhouse. I may have to use that one. The idea of putting my underwear in that dryer gives me the willies." Artemis dunked a cookie in her coffee.

The family was gathered around Cate's table, having just finished one of her glorious meals. A basket of pinecones and gourds sat in the center of the table, flanked by two bronze candlesticks. Amber candles burned low, dripping wax on the wood. The carcass of a chicken sat on the kitchen counter, along with bowls holding leftover carrots and peas, mashed potatoes, green beans, and a fruit salad. They lingered over coffee and fresh chocolate chip cookies.

"Okay, Mattie. Tell us what's happening with Buzz," said Artemis.

"Gods, do I hate dealing with the police. I think he's going to be okay. I found him a good lawyer."

"Why aren't you representing him?" asked Chrys. "You're the best."

"That wouldn't be ethical, honey," said Mattie. "In the first place, I'm too involved in the case. In the second place, I was a witness."

"Oh. I guess I'm a witness too," said Chrys. "Can I testify in court?"

"I hope not," said Mattie.

All six dogs were snoozing on the floor near PZ, who was using the remote to turn the fireplace on, off, on, off, on, off.

"Stop that, PZ," said Cate. "Take the dogs out."

On, off. On, off.

"PZ. Do you wish to continue breathing?" said Artemis.

"Huh?" he replied.

"Your grandmother said to take the dogs outside, and quit playing with that fire." Artemis gave him a look rivaling any of Mattie's glares.

"Okay, okay," he said, giving it one last on, off. He picked up Candle by the scruff of the neck and placed the dog around his shoulders. Lightning, thinking she would enjoy riding up there too, tried to climb up on him. He grabbed his jacket off the floor, gave a whistle, and headed for the back door, with the dogs in tow. The door slammed behind him.

"So, catch me up," said Atticus. "Did you find out who assaulted Maria?"

"Yes," said Mattie. "It was Ace. Joseph Worthington hired him."

"Wait a minute," said Atticus. "Back up. Why did Worthington want Ace to go after Maria?"

"By the terms of Punk's will, Worthington would inherit everything if there were no heirs. With Paulo dead, Worthington figured that John was the only thing standing between him and millions. He talked Punk into letting him come out here to look for investment opportunities. Supposedly he was looking for a good site to build an office park. In reality, he was planning on getting rid of John."

"How was he going to do that?" asked Atticus.

"I don't know exactly, but it had something to do with the Whites. He joined the

Cross and One and started buttering up old man White. Whatever it was he had planned, the Whites were going to take the blame for it. He's the one that got them all riled up about marriages between so-called white people and Latin Americans. Then John died in a forest fire. Worthington thought he was home free until he saw Maria on television, pregnant."

"Which is why the Whites started harassing her," said Cate.

"And why he hired Ace to make sure she never delivered," Mattie said. "The baby was dead. The Whites took the blame. Nobody knew that Worthington was involved except Ace, who wasn't going to blab. Everything seemed fine until he found out about Flora."

"So, he contacted Ace again," said Artemis. She put her bare feet on the seat of her chair and rested her chin on her knees. "This reminds me of the resolution scenes in an old Perry Mason. I feel like Della Street."

"Della was a hell of a lot more supportive than you are," said Mattie.

"And subservient," said Atticus.

"I guess that makes you Paul Drake," said Artemis. "And subservience isn't even remotely possible."

The back door opened admitting a rush of cold night air. Luna and Flora entered, bundled in coats, scarves, and gloves.

"Any food left?" asked Flora.

"If it isn't the heiress," said Artemis. "Come over here and tell us what you are going to do with your vast empire."

"Let the child get some food, A. She looks frozen," said Cate. "There's plenty for both of you, but you might want to warm some of it up." She pulled out a chair and laid her hand gently on the girl's shoulder. "How's your arm, sweetheart?"

"It's better. The stitches come out at the end of the week. I'm going to have quite a battle scar," Flora said.

"Sit down, dear," said Luna. "I'll fix us both a plate."

"Did you tell them, Uncle At?" Flora draped her coat on the back of the chair and dropped into the seat, her cheeks still red from the cold air.

"Flora, if I'm going to work for you, I would rather you call me Atticus."

"Okay. When I'm old enough to be your boss, I'll call you Atticus. But since you are basically taking care of me, I think Uncle At will do for the time being." She leaned over, threw her arms around him and gave him a big kiss. He blushed.

"What's all this?" said Artemis. "What are you two talking about?"

"Atticus is the new CEO of PNK, Inc.," said Mattie.

"And Mattie is going to manage the foundation. At least until we can find someone else," added Atticus.

"That's fantastic, Uncle At," said Chrys.

"You're the one to blame for her calling me that, Chrysaor Madisdater."

"Pro-bab-ly," she said, in a sing-song voice. "Uncle Atticus Leighson."

"What will Sun Systems do without you?" asked Artemis. "Eclipse?"

"Do you have to move?" said Cate. Her eyebrows were lowered in a frown.

"No," he said. "The job consists primarily of managing investments. There are four employees in Charleston. I'll give them the option of moving here or taking a nice severance package. That is, if it's okay with my boss."

Flora giggled, her mouth full of chicken. "Mmmm," she muttered, before shoveling in a forkful of mashed potatoes.

"I'm thinking of hiring Buzz to help me set up the computer systems. What they are using now is archaic. I think old Punk might not have been all that computer literate. Buzz is really very knowledgeable. He's the one that designed all the security for Whitewater Ranch, and he did all the computer work for the Cross and One. I don't think his former employer is much of a reference, but I think he deserves a break after saving Flora."

"Maybe, if he gets away from the Whites, he'll give up that silly nonsense about the Cross and One," said Cate. "He needs to be around some nicer people."

"Cate will be feeding him before he's worked there a week," said Artemis.

"Pro-bab-ly," said Cate. "Everyone deserves a bit of nurturing now and then. I don't think he's gotten much in his life. There are cookies in a tin on the counter, Luna. These heathens ate a whole plateful, but I hid some for the two of you. Would you like milk, honey?" Cate picked up the empty plate and rose to go to the sink.

Artemis, Atticus and Mattie seemed to find this funny.

"Maybe you could fix a picnic basket to take down to the jail, Ma," said Mattie. "A thermos of coffee, ham sandwiches, a loaf of pumpkin bread."

"You hush," said Luna, taking Cate's seat and setting down her own plate. "All three of you would have starved if she hadn't been feeding you all these years."

"That reminds me," said Flora. "Speaking of pumpkin bread. How about a new logo for PNK? I was thinking of something like the illuminart. Cate's design of the tree on the pumpkin was really nice."

PZ came in just in time to hear this last remark. "The barfing pumpkin would be better," he said. "Logos are supposed to catch the eye."

"Eeyew," said Chrys. "You're gross. Flora, are you going to buy a new car? What kind are you going to get?"

"Oh, no. I don't want a new car. But I am getting the seats reupholstered. In orange. Then I'll really have the perfect Latina punkin coach. *Cinder-ella es muey alegre.*

"Where are the dogs, PZ?" asked Mattie.

"Outside," he answered. "Except for Candle." He pulled the pup out of his jacket and set her on the floor, where she promptly piddled.

"Clean that up," said Artemis, Atticus, Chrys and Mattie.

"What?" said PZ. One glance from his mother made him reconsider. He went to get a paper towel. "She said it was too cold to pee outside."

"Well, go outside and bring in the rest of them," said Mattie. "Do you have homework?"

"A little, maybe," said PZ, tucking Candle back inside his jacket and heading for the door. The family waited for his usual slam, and they weren't disappointed.

Artemis ran her fingers through her hair and stretched. "There's only one thing that really bothers me," she said.

"What's that?" asked Mattie.

"That I still have that damn statue of Elwood J. White sitting in my yard. Buzz was going to haul it off for me, but he now he won't be able to—at least not for a while. Since I gave it to him, I can't very well bury it. Even though there's a backhoe in the garage, just like he said."

"Well, Cuz. You owe me one."

"More than one, Mattie. But how has my vast debt to you increased?" said Artemis.

"Because," said Mattie. "Ling arranged for the statue to be delivered to old man White this afternoon."

"No kidding."

"She talked to Buzz and he said that's what he wanted it for, to give to the old man. She says Buzz feels sorry for him. Can't say I do, but Buzz has a softer heart than I.

Anyway, the geezer was all choked up when they put it in his back yard."

"I hope he kept on choking," said Artemis.

"Now, A. He's a deluded old man who has lost everything. Be gracious in victory," said Cate.

Artemis and Mattie exchanged glances and burst into laughter. "And they say witches are wicked! Okay. We'll bless the old buzzard and let it go. Balance has been restored."

"If he comes around the Silver Bow, or approaches Flora again, I won't let it go," said Atticus.

"Nor will I," said Mattie, Artemis, Chrys and Cate in unison. Luna and Flora looked at each other and shook their heads. Flora called their speaking in unison the "Witches' Chorus." It always amazed her.

CHAPTER 35

Whitey

The backyard at Whitey's house was stripped of grass where Zach and Micah had beaten a path pacing alongside the cyclone fence. They had dug two body size holes next to the house where they lay panting after a barking furor with the neighbor's cat.

Elwood J. White stood in the middle of the yard, his Cross and One lifted skyward, connecting to that Great White Father in the sky. Whitey, from the warmth of his little den, stared out at the snow as it settled on his postage stamp yard. He watched the flakes land on the face of his grandfather, the slumped shoulders of his grandmother and her children. He stuck his finger into an old-fashioned glass and twirled the bourbon around with the ice cubes. *It's hard to hold the faith,* he thought, in a kind of half prayer, half musing. He set the glass down and closed his eyes. Bowing his head, he began his conversation with his God. *I know you are testing me*, he prayed. *Seems like everything is gone. My ranch, my family, my flock. My most trusted lieutenants have betrayed me. Turns out Ace has been working for that sorry sumbitch Worthington all the time. Not that I trusted that wily bastard. I was suspicious of him all along, but I never thought I would see the day that Ace turned his back on me.*

Whitey paused for a sip of bourbon and returned to his prayer. *Hank's locked up in the nuthouse. Actually, just between you and me, I've known every since I caught him setting the cat on fire, that the boy wasn't right. I just thought that…. Well, it's a hard thing for a man of the cloth to admit that his own son is so…twisted. You know, his Mama 'bout wore out her knees praying for him. Nearly killed her when she found him humping that pig. I never could figure out how he got that thing tied up…. Well. Seems like you would have answered my prayers for the boy, even if you didn't pay no mind to hers.*

Talking about sons. Now Buzz. There was a boy I treated like he was my own. How did he repay me? By shooting my first lieutenant and climb-

ing in bed with Satan's whores. Guess I'm not the first one to have a disciple betray me. Buzz is my own personal Judas.

A rage swelled up in him. He eyes flew open and the color rose in his face. He clamped his jaw hard, staring out at the bronze statue of his grandmother kneeling obediently before her husband and master.

"God Damn Whore!" The words exploded from him. "How could the bitch leave me now!" God Damn all women! May they all burn in Hell!" He reached for the 8 × 10 glossy photo of his family—he in his white suit and Cross and One tie, Hank at ten grinning in his matching outfit. His two daughters had a kind of scared, shriveled look, kind of hanging back, hiding behind their Ma. Their Mama, standing there pretending to be the perfect wife, when all the time she was Lilith, an evil descendent of Eve, corrupt, sinful, perfidious. He picked up the gaudy gold frame and hurled it across the room, where it shattered.

Tears were running over his red cheeks and snot dribbled from his nose. He took a belt of bourbon, and wiped his face on his sleeve, struggling to regain composure.

He spoke in his preacher voice, raising his arms skyward. "I *know* you are testing me, Lord. I *know* that these hardships are just part of your plan to make me stronger. I *know*, for *I and the Father are One!!*" He lowered his arms and seemed to crumple. "But I could sure use a sign," he whispered. "Give me a sign, Father."

The snow just kept falling silently on the dingy dirt patch of a yard. He sat motionless, waiting, listening alertly. Nothing came. With a sigh, he stood, deciding to try his Bible. After all, it's the word of God.

Propped up against the wall, beside his desk, was a parcel wrapped in brown paper. It was thin, but large, about three feet by four feet. He looked at it, puzzled. A pink post-it stuck to the corner, in his wife's handwriting—*This was going to be your birthday present, but since I don't plan to stick around, I'm giving it to you now. Sure as hell no one else would want it.*

He surprised himself by being reluctant to open it. Carefully he peeled of the masking tape that held the paper together. First he saw the edges of a frame—wide, gilt, elaborately carved. He peeled the wrapping away to reveal a large chart, hand calligraphied in an ornate design. In each corner was the symbol of the Cross and One ascending from flames and at the top was a title, drawn in gold with vividly colored letters. He struggled to remember the term for such letters but an image of a medieval monk laboring over a sacred manuscript came to mind. *Illuminations*. He remembered, as he read, *The White Family Tree*.

He felt a rush of pride. He straightened his spine and set his jaw. This is your sign, he thought. Remember what kind of stock you come from. No matter what trials and tribulations life threw at them, throughout the ages the White men have prevailed. As would he.

He strode into the garage to fetch a hammer and a picture hook. With purposeful strokes he drove the nail into the wall in his den and hung the genealogy chart. He poured himself a fresh slug of whiskey and settled back on the sofa to scrutinize each and every detail. There he was, at the bottom of the page, paired with the woman he now thought of as his first wife. His son and two daughters dangled below him. He followed his royal line back in time. His own father was there, along with his mother, who he felt spent each day in heaven watching over her beloved son. There was Elwood J. White, practically glowing on the page. Whitey didn't know much about the family before Elwood J. He read each name carefully, imagining them as distinguished men with faithful, obedient wives. Stern, pioneer stock, he supposed. He came to Elwood's grandparents and there he stopped. One name leapt out from the page. He read it over and over, hoping that somehow he had misread it. Delores Ortez y Alvarez.

CHAPTER 36

Las Sombras

Atticus poured the last of the wine into his glass and gave it a swirl to admire "the legs." He always enjoyed pointing out the presence, or absence, of "legs" on wine. Artemis gave him an inaudible warning lest he be tempted to bring the subject up once again.

Luna brought the coffee pot to the table and waved it in the air by way of offering a re-fill. She set it down on the table and paused a moment, struggling to find her words. "Flora and I appreciate the help you have given us. Mostly, however, we thank you for treating us like family."

"We thank you for being a part of our family," said Cate.

"There's one thing I want to do before you all leave tonight," said Luna. She reached into her pocket and pulled out her cards. "A reading for Artemis. I never got around to it after the Samhain party."

"Ah, my dear Luna. I am too weary for the Celtic Cross this evening," said Artemis. "Let's just pull three cards—the maiden, mother and the crone of the coming year."

Luna shuffled three times. Artemis cut and pulled three cards. The first was the Hermit. The second was the Wheel of Fortune. The third was the Queen of Swords.

"The Hermit. This describes where you are now, in the early part of your yearly cycle. This is a time of introspection and solitude. You may be beginning a personal quest or just in need of solitude. Whichever, it is appropriate for the dark time of the year."

"Considering that Perry Mason is moving in, along with Hermione Granger and Dennis the Menace, a period of solitude sounds good to me. I'm working on a new book," said Artemis.

"Something is going to change, however," said Luna. "The Wheel of Fortune means that you will reach a turning point in your destiny. There will be a surprising turn of events that will transform you, expand your view of the world and change your course. It should be exciting, even if it is challenging."

"I haven't gotten over the last round," said Artemis.

"The Queen of Swords," continued Luna. "This is a woman who calls a spade a spade. She reminds me of that saying that the Texans use. 'I know when somebody is pissing on my boots and calling it rain.' The Queen of Swords approaches life with a sense of humor and a lot of wisdom. She knows that most things aren't as important as some would think. She tells it like it is because she's been around long enough to know. Her motto is 'Blessed are they who can laugh at themselves, for they shall never cease to be amazed.' She's direct, honest and astute."

"Sounds more like Cate than it does like me," said Artemis. "Maybe it's the wise woman I'm supposed to become, in twenty-five years or so."

Cate was staring into the candlelight.

"What's up with you, Mom?" asked Mattie.

"'O Winter! ruler of the inverted year,'" said Cate. "'I crown thee king of intimate delights,/Fireside enjoyments, home-born happiness,/And all the comforts that the lowly roof/Of undisturb'd Retirement, and the hours /Of long uninterrupted evening, know.'" She smiled at her family. "William Cowper. Time to start planning for the Winter Solstice."

THE END

7:25
gate 21

Made in the USA
Lexington, KY
25 March 2013